THE LAST OF THE SMOKING BARTENDERS

A NEW PULP PRESS BOOK

First New Pulp Press Printing, October 2013

This book is a work of fiction. Names, characters, places, and incidents either are the products of the author's imagination or are used fictitiously, and any resemblance to actual events or persons, living or dead, is entirely coincidental.

ISBN-13: 978-0-9855786-8-8

ISBN-10: 0-9855786-8-8

Printed in the United States of America

Visit us on the web at www.newpulppress.com

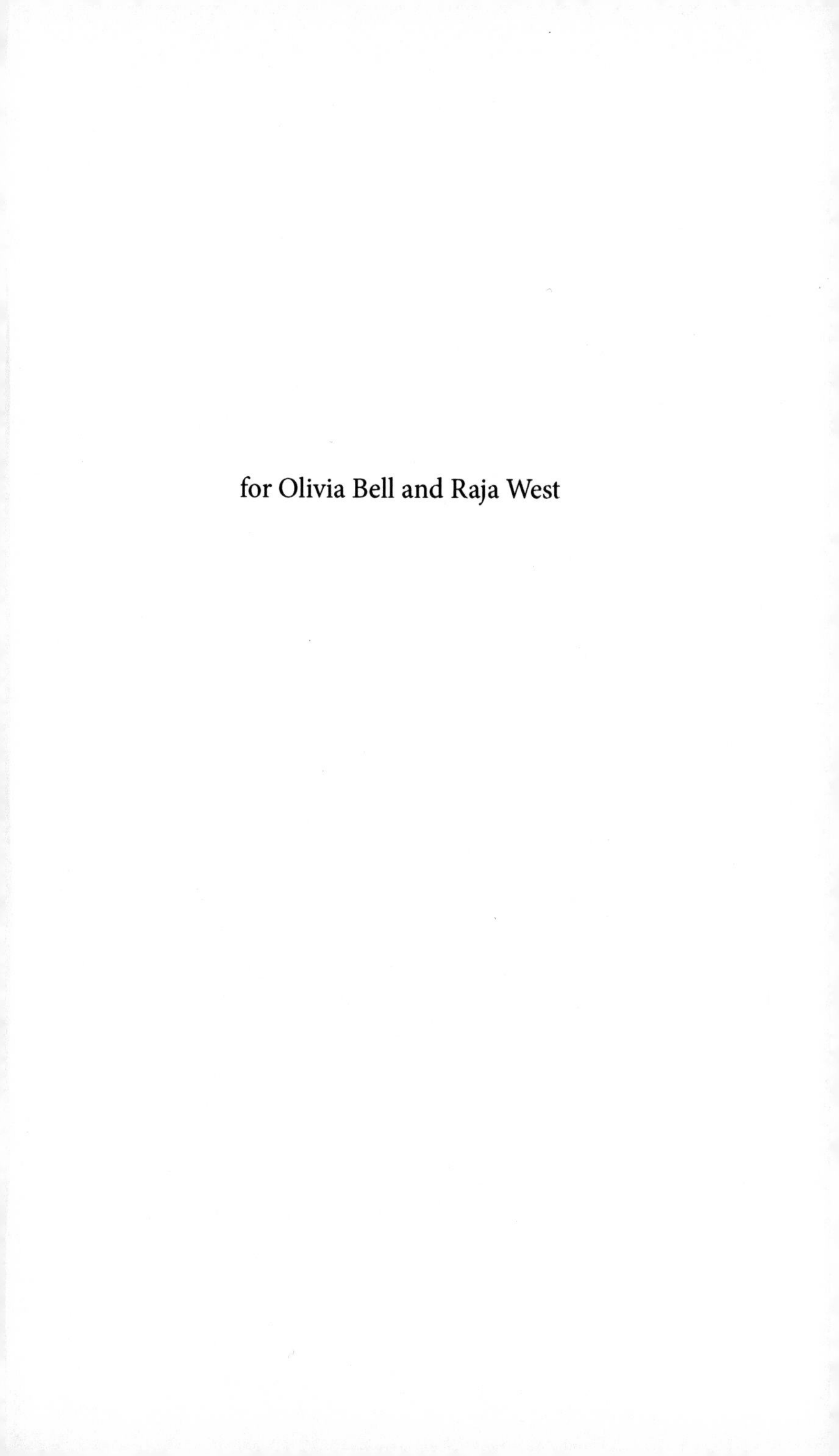

for Olivia Bell and Raja West

Praise for
The Last of the Smoking Bartenders

"A zany, violent road trip through madness and paranoia. The Southwest as seen through the haze of a meth pipe while you cruise on a ninety-proof buzz. Visceral and intense."
—Mario Acevedo, author of *The Nymphos of Rocky Flats*

"*The Last of the Smoking Bartenders* is hilarious and intense, a book that nailed my feet to the floor, grounding me to my favorite reading chair for two days and ruining all my plans. I love it when that happens."
—Matthew McBride, author of *Frank Sinatra in a Blender*

"A heated adrenaline ride of pulp and madness, if you have a taste for the harsh, the downtrodden and the psychotic, C.J. Howell brings something fresh and entertaining to this landscape of storytelling, while flipping it on its ear. If not too bad for you!"
—Frank Bill, author of *Crimes in Southern Indiana*

"*The Last of the Smoking Bartenders* is a druggy road trip across a burned out southwestern landscape that's both bizarrely off-kilter and strangely recognizable. With gallows humor and a keen eye for American absurdity, C.J. Howell has fashioned an apocalyptic epic that takes place in the here and now of our darkest national fears and neuroses."
—Jake Hinkson, author of *Hell on Church Street*

THE LAST OF THE SMOKING BARTENDERS

C.J. Howell

Chapter 1

I-70 West outside of Green River, Utah. Under the overpass it really wasn't bad, almost cool in the shade. But it was 110 degrees in sun. And sun was everywhere. If Tom sat very still he didn't sweat. But he would if he had to start moving, and move he must.

Five hours. Five hours crouched against the concrete hull of the overpass and no rides. Tom stood and stretched. A classic white VW bus approached westbound, slowed slightly, and continued past. Tom watched the bus plow onward into the desert. When the engine's whine finally merged with the cicadas, Tom spat once and sat back down. Even fucking hippies don't pick people up anymore.

Now it was decision time. Four miles back to Green River. If he started walking now he'd make it fine. But if he stayed out here, low on water, he might get too weak to make it all the way back to town. Best not to take chances in the desert.

Tom reluctantly put on his dark wool overcoat. He simply didn't have room for it in his pack, and he needed it. It got cold in the desert at night.

He started out into the sun. His backpack, an Eastman day pack, was small but heavy, due mostly to the sack of coins at the bottom.

The overpass may have been a bad call. Four miles back to town, the way he'd come. He shouldn't have been surprised that the arc of the on-ramp was a good half-mile by itself. He'd been doing this long enough, and the distances that seem inconsequential in a car were always deceptively large on foot. But no one was picking him up in town, and once he'd started toward the interstate there was no choice but to keep going to the overpass. The only shade out here was man-made.

Sweat began to trickle. The heavy lump of change in the backpack bounced off his tailbone as he walked. He followed his feet one step in front of the other over the sand on the shoulder of the interstate. As he reached the on-ramp he noticed a car slowing as it approached. He could tell right away it was a state trooper. Tom simply stopped and waited. There was no place to run or hide.

The trooper rolled up to him and stopped. Tom took off his backpack and coat. He knew the coat made him look like a bum. You are a bum. He could smell his body odor rush out from the confines of the coat.

You trying to get a ride?

Yes sir.

Tom smiled. He liked talking to fellow law enforcement, although he wasn't stupid enough to tell this or any other lawman that they were on the same side.

The trooper opened the passenger door.

Get in, I got the air on.

Tom got in, placed his pack and coat on his lap, and let the cool blast from the dashboard vent wash over him.

You know you can't hitchhike on the interstate.

Tom nodded.

I'll take you to the greyhound station in town. You got money for a bus ticket?

Sure. Tom smiled again.

You don't look like it.

Tom nodded in agreement.

The trooper put the car in gear and wheeled it back onto the on-ramp with one hand. As the engine revved up, the blast from the air conditioner intensified. Tom enjoyed the sensation of motion, even if it was short lived. He eyed the console computer, the scanner, the radio. If he had that kind of equipment, any equipment, he wouldn't be so desperate. Those he chased had everything. He supposed that's why he couldn't have anything. Traveling this way was the one way he wouldn't be tracked. But money, Jesus, to travel without paper money was really pushing the point of diminishing returns. He'd devoted years to being under the radar, any radar, but what good was it if he never prevented an attack, if he got everywhere late?

Green River was awash in dust and sand. The wind picked up outside the car. They passed a few houses abandoned decades ago, tumbleweeds bunched up against a low barbed wire fence, a new Shell station and food mart with a fairly brisk traffic of motorists fueling for either the fifty mile stretch to Grand Junction, Colorado, or the ninety mile stretch to Price, Utah, a few more abandoned houses and a few more occupied but in various stages of disrepair, and then Main Street with three blocks of the original 1890's buildings, most storefronts vacant.

The trooper pulled in front of a small stone building with a Greyhound poster in the window that no one would have seen unless they were looking for it.

Eastbound comes at eight. Westbound comes at eleven.

Thank you, sir, God bless.

Yeah. You get on that bus you hear?

Tom opened the squad car door and felt a blast of heat.

Listen, I can take you to the shelter in Grand Junction. No shelter out here.

Mighty kind of you, sir. But I'm moving on.

All the same, I'm letting you know up front I'm gonna tell

the Emery County Sheriff you're here. If he finds you hanging around long enough he'll put you in.

I understand.

Tom tipped the brim of his frayed Red Sox cap, almost a salute. He sat his pack under the Greyhound sign and watched the trooper wheel the cruiser back around and head back down Main Street toward the interstate.

Tom had almost forty dollars in change, but he wasn't about to waste it on a bus ticket. He removed a pack of GPCs from his inside coat pocket. Inside were three full cigarettes and half a dozen butts. He gently pulled one of the full cigarettes out, lit it, and took a big drag. He decided to wait until night. He sat on the sidewalk, legs stretched out, and watched the sky orange and then fade to purple.

His sweat had cooled and dried, and he contemplated putting the coat back on. But he'd combed his hair and brushed off and he felt, at night at least, he was passable.

There was more traffic than Tom would have thought. More than in most little towns he'd been in. A car passed every so often, driving slow, with music seeping from the interior.

The sound of glass smashing, probably a bottle breaking, caught him by surprise. He was jumpy from habit, not because he thought there was much to fear in this town, other than the elements and the police, of course. A figure emerged from one of the few side streets and ambled toward him on the other side of the street. The figure weaved a bit, not quite a stumble, swinging something big in one hand. When the man, it was obviously a man, drew parallel to Tom, he stopped and stared straight at him.

Hey, the man called out and started crossing the street. Tom could see now the man wasn't stumbling but limping due to a large cast over his right foot with a peg to keep the cast off the ground.

Tom, alarmed now, pressed his back against the stone building and drew in his knees. He reached for his pack.

Hey buddy don't worry you wanna drink?

The man extended what had looked like a club but now Tom recognized as a two litter plastic bottle of Coke.

Tom didn't move.

Nice night huh? Slept out here many a night.

The man was young, mid-twenties, soft eyes and full beard blending into his long hair. He had a toothy smile, although one front tooth was bent back toward his throat. The bottle still extended straight out at ninety-degrees.

Tom took the bottle, two-thirds full, awkward, almost heavy in his hand. There was no cap on it. He took a swig of warm cola, sharp with what was probably Old Crow. He coughed, tasting fire in his breath. The man was clearly a vagrant. It was a wonder he hadn't been picked up. Maybe it wasn't so bad here, the Sheriff had better things to do.

Thanks. I'm not sleeping outside.

Oh, me neither if that's what you're thinking. Got a room above the tavern. Work there too.

The man, Lorne was his name, sat right down on the sidewalk. He took back the bottle and drained a good third of it in heavy gulps.

Good to sit down.

They passed the bottle back and forth. Tom was feeling good in spite of himself. It wasn't that he disapproved of drinking, but he needed to be focused now. He knew he was in dangerous land, and the least of his worries was that he had no transportation and it was ninety miles to the next town. He knew it was going to be a tough stretch, but the desert was proving a problem. Yet two conversations in one day had Tom feeling pretty good. There were weeks when that wouldn't happen. And now the drink.

The stars came out shimmering like tinsel, dancing and

spinning small circles inside the dead black sky. The bottle turned mostly to backwash, but they drained it anyway. Lorne was gregarious, talking constantly, swinging his large chipmunk arms for emphasis. Lorne had driven out west from Florida—swamp Florida, not beach Florida—with a buddy four or five years ago. He lost the buddy along the way, some town in Oklahoma, or was it in the Texas panhandle? No, if it was Texas he was sure he wouldn't have made it out either. Who could know? It was an endless string of towns all the same, a silo next to the rail yard on one side of highway, a bar on the other, a few rows of white painted houses and then another stretch of dirt to the next town. He'd run out of money in a little town in Colorado and was literally on his last bourbon and Coke in the corner bar when he met a chick. She was a raft guide, hundreds of them were in town for the summer season, camping by the Arkansas River, making forty dollars a day. They camped and she lent him the money for the one-week guide certification course, and he took a boat down once or twice a week. Something happened with the girl, or maybe the town, and now he was in Green River, Utah, the last place to pull the boats out of the river for the companies that float the Green River. Green River is the end of the road for the Green River! Lorne interjected into the conversation at least a half a dozen times.

He tapped the cast over his right foot. It looked like it had gotten wet and was unraveling.

Can't guide with this thing, but I got lucky with the tavern, clean the floors and the bathrooms at four every morning, whatever else needs to be done. Got a room there too.

Tom nodded, he had been thinking about the room. Lorne had mentioned that a half a dozen times too. Lorne wasn't the type to deny a stranger a little spot of floor.

Let's go to the tavern, Lorne said, crushing the empty two-liter Coke bottle.

The tavern was on the corner two blocks up. A neon sign hung over the door that read, Tavern. Stenciled in gold paint on the door was 'welcome to the Tavern—live music since 1902.'

Lorne grabbed the door. It jingled when it opened. Tom felt his pulse rise. It wasn't often he went into public places full of civilians. Inside it was more crowded than he would have thought. A barrel-chested doorman nearly blocked the entire entrance. Tom was sure this was a mistake. He wouldn't have been surprised if the Emery County Sheriff was drinking here, this being the only bar in town.

Hey brother! Lorne screamed to the bouncer.

Lorne was effervescent, hands everywhere. The bouncer reluctantly high-fived him. He eyeballed Tom closely, but let him pass, shaking his head and glancing toward the bar, a silent nod to someone to keep an eye on them. Inside it was warm, as if the bar was lit by candle light. Rows of bottles behind a long oak bar reflected the green and red neon beer signs along the walls. Tom was relieved to be let in, but self-conscious. Around him were red sun burnt faces, tourists fresh from their rafting trips down the Green River, unshowered and happy to be back in civilization replete with chicken wings and beer. With any luck, he would just be considered local color.

Why's it so crowded?

Friday night, Lorne said, grinning.

This was new information to Tom. Lorne pulled his long hair back beneath a dingy white baseball cap and headed to the bar. Tom was grateful there was an empty table against a wall with two folding chairs. The bartender, a big breasted woman probably younger than she looked, greeted Lorne with a hug. She poured him a shot and one for herself. They clinked glasses and tapped them to the bar in unison before downing their shots. She poured a pitcher of Pabst Blue Ribbon and pulled out two icy mugs from the dented beer cooler. Lorne grabbed them and spun to see where he'd left Tom.

Lorne, stay away from the customers now, she yelled with no effort to keep her voice low.

Lorne returned with the pitcher and two frosty mugs. Tom reached for his bag of change to make his contribution, but Lorne put up his hand and shook his head no. Tom was mesmerized by the heavy bar mugs, so cold that an icy film formed over the top of the beer. The beer was delicious. They clinked glasses.

Here's to beer.

Lorne drained his beer, foam streamed from the corners of his mouth and clung to his beard. A band began playing from a low stage at the back of the bar. The sound was deafening.

These guys rock, come through every summer.

The three piece jam band started into a cover of Tombstone Blues.

The sun's not yellow—it's chicken! Lorne yelled giving the thumbs up, and he was up off his chair and pushing toward the front of the stage. The foot with the cast on it wobbled under his weight.

Tom clutched his beer in both hands, watching the ice melt. He took a short drink, and then a long one. It felt good to be in civilization. A makeshift dance floor had formed, a ring of onlookers with four or five couples dancing in the center, and Lorne of course. Tom tapped his finger on his glass to the beat. The wind picked up outside, and a tumbleweed pressed up against the window and then rolled passed. Tom filled his mug, less frosty now, from the pitcher and sipped it down. When his mug was empty again he waited for Lorne, not wanting to take more than his share of the pitcher. But Lorne appeared to be talking to an actual girl, one apparently too inebriated to notice Lorne's funk. She was in her early twenties, blonde hair pulled back, solid Midwestern arms and thick legs. Tom figured she was one of the rafting guides, probably didn't shower much herself. Tom poured the rest of the pitcher into his mug. He sipped the last beer as slowly as he could, but eventually it was empty and he felt immediately vulnerable for no longer being a paying customer. He thought he saw the bartender glance his way and shake her head. Lorne was dancing with the girl, or at least dancing next to her.

Lorne, I told you to stay away from the customers! the bartender yelled over the wailing guitar. Lorne spun around on his cast and shot the bartender a look, almost knocking the girl down in the process. She punched his round chest playfully but signaled with her hand that she was sitting down. Lorne kept dancing.

The empty pitcher stared at Tom. Eventually the doorman took the empty pitcher back to the bar to be washed. The table was as empty as the desert outside. Tom began to sweat. He had no idea what to do with his hands with nothing to hold onto. They felt awkward on top of the table, but he felt too shifty if they were under the table. Lorne was right in front of the stage, eyes closed, playing air guitar. He almost looked like he was in the band.

Eyes were on Tom, he was sure. The pressure proved too much. Tom stealthily dug into his backpack, and without exposing his bag of change removed sixteen quarters. He made his way to the bar, no one particularly getting out of his way. The bartender crossed her arms and waited.

Excuse me, Tom whispered, raising a finger.

Can I get you something? she said, shaking her head.

Pitcher? Tom tried to smile.

Of? The crossing and recrossing of arms.

Whatever's cheapest. Tom shrugged, smile gone.

She poured a pitcher of Pabst.

Three-fifty.

Tom counted out fourteen quarters. He took the pitcher and placed two quarters on the bar for a tip. She made no move to pick them up.

Tom drank the pitcher slowly, but not so slowly he couldn't enjoy it. The band moved into an acoustic set, a soulful string of bluegrass and old coal miner folk songs. Couples took a seat to get a breather, with mugs of beer and rounds of shots. The room was dark and warm. Lorne returned but wasn't saying much. He leaned way back in his chair, his beer resting on his belly. He sang along with the band he'd seen many times, turning to Tom when he knew a lyric. 'Eat, when I'm hungry…Let me drink, when I'm dry…Two dollars, when I'm hard up…Religion, when I die.'

A large group of red-faced tourists headed for the door. The doorman told them to drive safe.

So what are you doing anyway? Lorne said, as if noticing Tom for the first time.

Tom took a second.

Heading west.

Lorne held his glass out for a toast, 'living the dream,' Lorne grinned the bent tooth at him. Tom knew he should measure his words, but he was drunk now, feeling the music deep inside like he hadn't in years.

I'm on a mission. Trying to stop…something.

Your ex take your kids or something?

Tom caught himself.

Something like that.

I know, I got a son out there somewhere, damn woman will never let me see…not like I should…like I am now… you know. Lorne held out his arms, as if he was inviting examination.

Tom nodded. Yeah, you know, sometimes you just… Tom ran out of words. Yeah, I'm heading west.

The band finished their last set. Lorne banged his hands

together and then put two fingers in his mouth and let out a shrill whistle. Tom politely clapped.

The bartender called last call.

Last call, the doorman bellowed. People perked up their heads, and the few remaining couples got up to leave. A table of locals slammed their beers.

Lorne suddenly sprung into action.

Last call! he yelled with his hands cupped at the sides of his beard. He walked up and down the bar yelling in peoples' faces 'Last call, get the fuck out!' Tom cringed, but remarkably, the bar staff didn't kick Lorne out; this appeared to be part of his job. In fact, when the Budweiser clock above the bar was nearly at two, the doorman joined Lorne in screaming, 'get the fuck out!' The locals filtered out the door. A few sunburnt rafters looked annoyed but complied with the order.

Tom went into invisible mode, and it worked, nobody saw him. When all the customers were out, the bartender, the doorman, and Lorne worked feverishly for about half an hour, locking the doors, wiping down the tables, pulling the mats, picking up the glasses and ashtrays and washing them and putting them away, putting up the barstools. And then the three each opened a bottle of Bass and took a shot of Jamison while the bartender counted the money and changed out the tips.

Lorne motioned Tom over to the bar.

Lucia, give him a beer will you?

She rolled her eyes.

He can have a draft. What do you want? She stared at Tom.

Whatever's chea—

Yeah, yeah whatever's cheapest. Have a real beer. She poured a pint of Newcastle Brown from the tap and slid it across the bar to Tom. The doorman put music on the jukebox. The bartender used the remote to put the volume down.

The beer had bite and Tom savored the taste. The bartender,

doorman, and Lorne were laughing about the girl Lorne was dancing with earlier. They all lit cigarettes. Tom lit one of the butts from his nearly empty pack of GPCs.

So Lorne, is the homeless guy crashing with you?

Lorne looked at Lucia. She turned to Tom. Well, you are a bum aren't you? Tom froze, and then shrugged, speechless.

Lorne laid big hand on Tom's shoulder, almost knocking over the doorman's beer. Hey, he's going to see his kids.

The bartender laughed. Tom, still speechless, did not correct Lorne.

He's on a mission, head'n west. Isn't that right, Tom? Lorne held up his bottle. Tom, a beat slow, raised his glass and tapped Lorne's bottle in salute.

Tom's on a mission, the bartender said to the doorman. To Tom's mission, she said in a hushed tone, emphasizing the 'Tom' a little too sharply. The doorman joined in the clinking of glasses.

Let's go west, Lorne spat. Get on the highway, drive through the desert, it'll be epic!

Sounds like a great plan, Lorne, the bartender deadpanned.

Lorne demanded a round of shots. The bartender told them this was the last one. Lorne was reaching a crescendo, dancing to the jukebox with unwanted energy.

No, no it's early! Let's hit the road, keep the night going.

Lorne slammed down his empty beer bottle.

Lucia, let me get a six pack, here's five for the till.

Are you serious Lorne? If you're leaving you're taking the homeless guy with you.

Lorne grabbed Tom by the elbow and they stumbled out the door of the Tavern. Outside, the night was very different. Tom squinted into total darkness punctuated by two overhead streetlights. When his eyes adjusted he saw an empty dust swept street.

Come on, let's blow this dump, Lorne shouted.

Lorne used Tom as a crutch, trying to keep his weight off his cast foot. They bumbled forward and immediately tumbled off the curb and fell onto the street. Tom put his hand out to brace the fall. He scraped his palm but couldn't feel it. Lorne bust out laughing, said, Didn't see that coming! Tom didn't find it funny at all. The street was quiet, but that didn't mean an Emery County Sheriff's Deputy couldn't roll past at any moment, or worse. Rule Number One—remain undetected. How would they look face first on the street in front of a bar at 3 a.m.? Tom pulled up Lorne. Getting off the street was imperative. But there was no place to hide in this town. He held onto Lorne's arm and, like a divining rod, or fingers on a ouija board, Lorne weaved his way into an alley behind the Tavern where an old Chevy Malibu was parked under a gnarled and bare crabapple tree.

Lorne didn't want to drive with the cast on his foot so he tossed Tom the keys. Tom hesitated, he couldn't remember the last time he drove, but he didn't hesitate for long, he had to make ground. The Malibu rumbled to life filling the alley with noise and smoke. Headlights illuminated the century old brick wall of the Tavern. Fortunately, the Malibu was simple to drive, automatic transmission, basically a big go-cart. Tom put it in drive, tapped the gas, and the Malibu lurched forward. The tires spun, and dust billowed around the wheel-wells and funneled through the windows. The Malibu screeched onto Main Street. Lorne howled into the night. Tom's heart beat fast. He was drunk, noticeably, and of course, he carried no identification. He had long ago sanded off his fingerprints so a police stop of any kind would not only mean jail, but probably a psych eval.

Tom gained control of the V8 under the hood and slowed to 25 mph. The Malibu was the only car on the road. To Tom's disbelief no one followed them out of town. They cleared Main Street. The four miles to the interstate crept by. Still no headlights behind them. The narrow on-ramp opened onto the wide interstate. Tom nudged the car up to cruising speed. Lorne turned on the radio and caught a classic rock station out of Grand Junction. He slammed his beer and stuck his head out the window, the night air blasting back his long hair and beard.

What made the interstate fast also made it dangerous; there were no exits, no traffic, nowhere to hide. But the sensation of movement and control, after so many days of walking and waiting, was exhilarating.

Ten miles outside of town they were in total darkness, desert in every direction. It was then that Tom noticed the stars, even through the clouded windshield. Millions of stars. For an instant Tom smiled. He felt free. But in the next instant the stars transformed into a memory. A map taped up on a wall in a room in S.E. Washington, D.C. full of different colored pins, too many to count. Water stains on the ceiling, coffee stains on the floor, the pins doing a poor job of visually describing the Network.

They had begun with reconnaissance, then infiltration, then the chase. Re-con had been fruitless. The Network was impenetrable. In fact, they were quickly the ones being re-conned. The Network had every gadget that they had, and the Network had the advantage, they knew who was in the Network, and Tom did not. And the Feds stood out in southeast D.C. They were going in the wrong direction, losing ground.

So they went from high-tech to low-tech. Infiltration. They had slightly more success. Tom went off the grid. Everything erased. Records purged, photographs burnt, deleted, and scrubbed from every server. Tom didn't exist. It was with Tom that they had their first penetration of the Network. He became roommates with an operative. Before he came home from his six dollar an hour job washing dishes to find that his roommate had cleared out, along with all traces of the Network, he learned that the next big attack was out west, the Hoover Dam, Tom was sure.

Then the chase. Tom traveling the only way he could, any way he could, off the grid. It was the only way. That was two years ago. Any time he passed a news stand he was sure he was going to see some grisly headline. He couldn't believe it hadn't happened yet, but it would be any day now, of that he was sure. Millions would die.

He gunned the Malibu up to 90 mph.

That's it brother! Lorne yelled and tossed his beer can out the window. It bounced on the road behind them.

The sky lavendered. A band of red on the horizon appeared in the rear view mirror. They pulled over to take a leak. Anxious moments for Tom. Lorne was oblivious, relaxed. But not a single vehicle passed them.

Eighty miles passed. Eighty more under his belt. More than he had covered in a single day in a while. He had traveled in fits and starts ever since D.C. Good ground some days, and then bogged down for weeks. The last layover had been a three week stint in county jail in Grand Junction. But now he was moving, and with no time to waste, he would have to do things he had never done before.

They lost all the radio stations on the dial except for a crackly AM preacher. Lorne talked non-stop to fill the void. He finished the six pack, the words flying out of him, some stories, some parts of stories, mostly stream of consciousness commentary on everything, nothing, life held together by strains of thought, or maybe just coincidence. He kept talking because he chose not to stop and he knew Tom was listening. He didn't know if Tom cared, but he was listening. And the desert morning was beautiful. The air was fresh before the heat of the day. He breathed it in. Bald mountains of sand and rock cast yellow and orange in the sunrise blurred together out the passenger side window. Lorne was on an adventure. They were heading to Vegas. He hadn't informed Tom, but Las Vegas was the logical destination for a road trip. He'd forgotten all about finding Tom's kids and rescuing them from his old lady. He was road tripping to Vegas with a buddy. The new friend's name slipped Lorne's mind at the moment, but it didn't matter. He felt good. That was all that mattered.

The Malibu rumbled along, bouncing comfortably on a loose suspension down the blacktop. The morning chill burned off as the sun cleared the eastern mountains. By mid-morning it was nearing one hundred degrees.

We passed Price yet?

About an hour ago.

Still on the interstate?

Yeah.

We're out of beer.

Tom was starving. He was mostly sober, but he hadn't eaten in almost 24 hours, and a combination of stomach acid and hunger burned in his gut. They pulled off the interstate at a truck stop. When the car came to a complete stop at a gas pump, Tom kept his hands on the wheel and stayed silent. He didn't want to broach the subject of money. Lorne pulled at his beard. His face was numb.

With the car finally stopped the heat poured in. Lorne had the spins, but he was optimistic that he could stave off getting sick and hungover if he kept going.

Put twenty in the tank. I'll be back. You need anything?

Tom mulled it over.

Can of beans?

Lorne laughed.

Can o' beans it is.

Lorne opened the door and fell out of the car. Tom watched him stagger to the truck stop Food Mart. Tom wheeled the Malibu to a pump and carefully filled the tank with regular until the meter hit twenty dollars. A little over six gallons. Tom knew it wouldn't get them far, but all he could do was worry about it later. The service station was busy. It made Tom uncomfortable. Crowds of people always made Tom uncomfortable. But what made Tom really uneasy was a State Trooper parked around the side of the Food Mart. It was parked behind a row of cars, most folks probably wouldn't have even noticed it, but Tom had honed a sense for these things, for spotting danger. It was all around him.

As inconspicuously as he could he returned to the driver's seat. The Food Mart was a wall of windows facing the pumps. He could see the trooper buying coffee inside. He could also see Lorne studying the beer cooler, oblivious. For a split second Tom thought of taking off with the Malibu. Then he saw Lorne at the counter, pointing toward the Malibu, paying for gas and buying a bottle from a shelf behind the counter. It seemed to be taking too long, some kind of commotion inside. The trooper was four or five customers behind Lorne in line. Yes, if Lorne got into it with the trooper he would take his chances in the Malibu. But then Lorne fumbled with the glass door, nearly knocked over a trash can, and lugged a weighted down plastic bag to the car.

Got beer! he said too loudly. Natural Ice, six percent alcohol instead of the usual four, and cheaper! Couple pints of Old Crow too. He had forgotten the beans.

Nice, Tom said as cheerfully as he could. He saw the trooper glance their way when he exited the Food Mart.

Tom eased the Malibu back onto the interstate. He kept it exactly at the speed limit, an even seventy-five. Lorne took a sip from one of the pints of Old Crow. He started a story. Tom wasn't listening. Traffic was brisk on the interstate, mostly SUVs and tractor-trailers, but he worried that the trooper was there, lurking four of five cars behind. Soon Lorne was quiet; he appeared to be dozing.

Tom glanced in the rear view mirror, and his blood ran cold. The trooper was right behind them. The intimidating black and white pattern, tinted windows, and unmistakable grill, equipped with a cattle guard bumper that looked more like a black painted steel battering ram. Tom didn't dare wake up Lorne. Lorne was unpredictable. The less movement the better.

Tom kept at seventy-five. Five minutes past. Ten minutes. The trooper was equidistant behind. He didn't even bother rehearsing his lines. Booze all over the car, no license, no insurance, no fingerprints, there was no talking his way out, not like that had ever worked. And time was short.

An exit approached. State highway 616 to wherever. Tom angled the Malibu onto the off-ramp. Long moments passed. The trooper stayed on the interstate, missing the exit. Stateys don't like to leave the interstate. Or maybe the Statey had some place to go. Tom exhaled. Momentary relief, but he couldn't be sure that it wasn't some ploy, or that he hadn't radioed some other cop to track him.

The exit circled to an overpass where on the other side of the interstate heading south there was an abandoned filling station and an Indian curio shop. He drove another ten miles, constantly checking the rear view mirror, before his breathing returned to normal. It was a simple thing, not getting pulled over, but he let out a mighty sigh of relief.

He was spent. Exhausted, he pulled the car over onto the shoulder next to a filled in fire pit full of rusted beer cans and trash. Dust billowed when the wheels finally came to a stop. He didn't like stopping on the side of the road, where any cop that rolled by would find them suspicious, or at least question them to see if they were broken down or needed help. But he needed to rest.

With the car stopped he could hear a fierce wind blow unimpeded over the desert. Dust blew across the highway.

He hadn't slept in days. He was hungry but had no food. He took the open pint of Old Crow out of Lorne's sleeping hand and got out of the Malibu. His joints groaned. He stretched his legs and looked around. One end of the flat valley stopped at a mesa, stratified red, orange, and yellow, not far off. In another direction, pillars of rock rose out of the sand in the distance. Tom guessed he was looking at Capitol Reef fifty miles away, although it easily could have been a hundred. The eerie formation shown purple against a light blue sky. He looked both ways and took a slug of the whiskey. Jesus, what the fuck had brought him here.

He walked up a small embankment and looked down on a valley of cactus. He looked back and saw the Malibu, obscured in waves of heat from the white orb burning above. A dot weakly anchored to a desiccated land. A low buzzing settled between his ears. His own thoughts echoed back at him as if he were being spoken to. How strange to see so much vast expanse stretch away from him as if he could see the very curvature of the Earth. And yet, still within sight, the interstate in the distance with eighteen wheelers keeping schedule, the flow of commerce. He looked at his hand, leathered and rutted, sunburn upon sunburn. He bent down and touched the sand. It was hot.

And then for the second time today a chill went up his spine and he broke out in a cold sweat in the hundred and ten degree heat. His gaze focused on an unnatural object. An antenna, hidden among the cactus. He capped the Old Crow, shook his head, squinted and looked hard, but it was still there. The Network. He scrambled down the embankment, drawn toward it. He ran reckless, frantic, dodging cactus and yucca. There was no road or trail leading toward the antenna. They were covering their tracks. This wasn't meant to be found. Thorns lodged in his boots and thistles stuck to his old corduroys as he raced toward the object. As he approached he saw a low square chain link fence around an antenna and a transformer sunken into the earth. There were no signs or markings of any kind. It had to be one of their uplinks. They had their own grid. No high-tension lines or utility poles. Everything underground or linked to satellite. This was how they kept one step ahead. He ripped off a piece of cloth from his undershirt and stuffed it in the bottle of Old Crow. Then he took the lighter he kept in his pack of GPC's, lit the cloth, and tossed the bottle at the transformer.

When Lorne woke up, the first thing he noticed was that his head pounded and his neck was stiff from sleeping upright in the passenger seat. The second thing he noticed was that the car stank. A film coated the upholstery, humid and fecund. The third thing he noticed was a scraggly, unkempt man running toward the car. The last thing he noticed, before everything else became unimportant, was a loud pop pop pop BANG, and the sight of a transformer exploding into flame not more than a hundred feet away.

Tom skidded around the grill of the Malibu, flung open the door, and threw himself into the driver's seat.

Jesus…the fuck you do?

Tom turned the key, still in the ignition, and floored it. The Malibu fishtailed violently and screeched onto the road, leaving a chunk of tire tread and a plume of burning rubber.

You really are fucking crazy!

No, Tom said matter of factly, regaining control of the Malibu and then accelerating as fast as it would go. You are fucking crazy.

Chapter 2

The Malibu barreled down the two lane state highway. They were heading due south. A column of black smoke shot toward the sky behind them.

Motherfucker you fucking did it now, we're both going to jail. Man, do I always get fucked…Stupid, stupid, stupid! Lorne banged the side of his head with the palm of his hand.

It had to be done.

The fuck are you talking about?

Long story.

Oh we'll have a lot of time to talk about it in County.

We're cool.

But Tom had no idea if they were cool. Sweat streamed down his forehead. The sun burned above. The horizon shimmered with waves of heat. The Malibu topped a hundred and ten, taking up both lanes, straddling the yellow center line. No sound of sirens in the distance yet, not that they could have heard over the sound of the engine and the rush of wind through the open windows. No sign of police, but the problem with being on the run through the desert was the great distances. They couldn't outrun a radio. What would they find at the first town down the line? Tom was determined not to find out. Five minutes and ten miles later Tom spotted an intersection approaching at light speed. He pumped the brakes and the Malibu weaved from side to side. U-joints buckling, Tom made a hard right onto a narrow county road heading west. The Malibu drifted wide and took out a reflector on the shoulder before straightening and accelerating back to speed. Maybe it would buy them a few minutes.

Lorne's stringy hair was in his hands. He opened the remaining pint of Old Crow and drank half in series of gulps. He fingered the coin pocket of his jeans and popped something in his mouth.

The county road rose and fell over a series of dunes. The engine revved and the tach redlined as they crested the dunes and the wheels momentarily lost contact with the faded pavement. But Tom kept it on the road. The Malibu careening forward, the square chrome grill battering the breeze at a cool hundred miles per hour. The road wound behind a rocky outcropping and cut between sandstone boulders dotted with scrub brush. At least they were out of the line of sight of the highway and the burning transformer, which by now resembled a giant roman candle. Tom still didn't feel safe. But he hadn't felt safe in years.

Ahead there was a long white line that ran perpendicular, an intersecting dirt road stretching into infinity. Tom blew by it, not wanting a dust trail for someone to follow. Tom was thinking clearly, crystal clear, and fast, like right before he blew the transformer, but controlled, adrenaline cutting through the hunger and alcohol and sweat and filth that perpetually enveloped him.

Lorne finished the Old Crow and tossed the bottle out the window. He moved straight into the twelve of Natty Ice, a froth of foam, beer, and whiskey soaked his beard. He cranked the radio so it could be heard over the roar of the speeding Malibu.

Jesus, you're crazy! he yelled and then gave one of his patented whooping yee-haws, drunk again. It was a good sign, Tom calculated, lessened the chances of Lorne turning him in, or attacking him, or leaving him out here to die. Not that

Tom was going to take a chance of any of that happening by slowing down. Lorne was powerless as long as Tom kept the Malibu over a hundred mph.

Minutes were crucial. Put as much distance between them and the fire as possible, as unpredictably as possible, then try and blend, as unlikely a proposition as that seemed.

A vehicle approached from the west, coming the opposite direction, a dot on the horizon. Tom backed off the accelerator just enough to keep the Malibu in the right lane. A red pickup blew by going almost as fast as they were.

Damn, people drive fast out here, huh?

Not much to run into, Tom said pushing it to a hundred and twenty.

I like the way you think.

The road narrowed and the shoulder disappeared completely. The sides of the road were eroded by weather and neglect. Tom went back to straddling the center line. Hit the wrong chunk of broken asphalt on the edge and they'd barrel roll into obliteration.

A battered brown sign indicating a town and a distance flew by too fast to read. Lorne downed another beer—if Natty Ice could be called beer. Tom figured it was probably more precisely categorized as malt liquor and then quickly chastised himself for any wasted thought when the fate of the nation hung in the balance, not to mention Lorne and his lives, or at the very least, the possibility of lengthy prison terms. Lorne began cackling merrily. He actually seemed to be enjoying himself.

A few structures appeared on one side of the road. Tom didn't slow down. From their distance he couldn't tell if they were inhabited. He recognized a windmill and some fences, a few wooden outbuildings. As he sailed past he still couldn't discern if they were in use or not.

Thirty miles later a paved road branched to the left. He

slammed the breaks and skidded past it, coming to a stop a few hundred feet later. Smoke streamed from the tires and the smell of burning break pads penetrated the moldy interior.

Jesus, ease up on my ride, man.

Tom wondered if Lorne could have already forgotten, if he appreciated the gravity of the situation. Tom spun the Malibu back around and headed south on State Route 312A.

He gunned the Malibu back up to speed but within two miles the road began to deteriorate. First cracks in the pavement with weeds filling the gaps, and then potholes rapidly increasing in size and depth. The road rose gradually as mountains on either side shot up around them. The road was maroon in color as if the dust from the rising sandstone cliffs had integrated into the asphalt over time.

The six gallons of gas they'd bought was already dwindling, but at this point, problems had to be prioritized. Still, with the road worsening, Tom backed way off the gas, dodging potholes and conserving speed when he could. He guessed the V-8 Malibu got less than ten miles per gallon doing over a hundred. Lorne started singing along with an old Dylan tape he put in the deck. Eyes watery he leaned way out the window.

The colors, the colors, he whispered to himself.

Tom slowed to under twenty miles an hour on hairpin turns. For an hour they ground up a mountain pass, gaining almost a mile in altitude. At the summit the afternoon heat was more diffuse with the sun already close to its hiding place behind the mesas. Cloud veins and contrails tinged with orange stretched to the white horizon. Through thin air the sky gave away traces of purple lurking a few hours in the future. A wind battered sign announced the summit of Barton Pass. A smaller sign read: Bartonville 5 miles. Sure enough, the road wound down tight switchbacks to a town wedged in between canyon walls. Tom put it in neutral to save gas and coasted the switchbacks until the brakes got too hot, and then he put it in first gear until they reached the bottom of the canyon where a small stream carrying mine tailings, shining acrylic blues and yellows, and metallurgic greens and silvers, ran over smooth rock to an unseen outlet. Up the canyon walls rocks balanced precariously, as if they could fall at any moment. There were no trees of any kind.

The road began to climb again through a notch in the canyon cut by weather and dynamite and then followed the stream to a town. Tom realized the town looked much larger from the summit because one side was a huge mine running up the side of the mountain. The main facility looked like a giant rusted castle made of sheet metal rising ten stories above the town, with spires of corrugated tin and rickety towers supported by a matrix of wooden beams. The mine was terraced on several levels cut directly into the mountain, walled in by a chain-link fence topped with barbed wire. The actual town was a strip of houses and businesses along the road surrounded by the mine. As they entered the town they drove under a series of covered conveyor belts that ran ore from the mine to transport facilities on the other side of the road.

Tom pulled the Malibu up to a gas pump at a roadhouse directly underneath a mechanized chute carrying ore over the road and through the town to a small rail yard.

We need gas.

Lorne swung his head around in a loop that swiveled on his collar bone. His eyes tilted up, pupils clear, but dilated to the whites. He exhaled deeply.

Here.

Lorne flipped through his wallet and held out a twenty.

Tom hesitated.

No, I can't take that.

Don't be a fuckhead.

No, I mean, I can't take the bill…you pay.

Lorne held up hands incredulously. What are we six years old? Lorne shrugged his shoulders and pushed his way out of the Malibu.

I'll meet you inside, Tom apologized. I need to eat something.

Tom desperately needed to eat something. He felt light-headed. His breath was short. His limbs felt limp. He fumbled with the gas pump. Dust blew over the curb and across the two-pump lot and gathered alongside the white aluminum siding of the roadhouse. A sign reading 'BAR' in black stenciled letters banged against the aluminum siding with the rhythm of the wind. Tom put twenty in the tank and then parked the car, reversing into a space alongside the roadhouse so the Malibu faced out toward the road. Cool air funneled down the shear canyon walls, devoid of any vegetation.

A bell jingled overhead as Tom pulled open the door to the roadhouse. Inside, it felt like a doublewide. He had to bend his head to get beyond the screen door. To the right were two rows of snack foods, bags of chips, and peanuts, salted and honeyed, and assorted cured meats, jerkyed and dry rubbed. To the left, past the register and a stand of knickknacks, key chains, and shot glasses, was Lorne at the bar with a pitcher of beer in front him. A thirty- or forty-something blonde sat on the beer cooler and eyed the corner television. Two old-timers were anchored at the far end of the bar.

I'll get the tab. Tom pulled up a barstool. I'm gonna get a burger.

Tom was thinking about the emergency cans in his backpack stashed in the backseat of the Malibu. But he needed a meal, and Lorne on his side.

You want a burger?

Tom ordered two burgers and fries from the bartender. Lorne cocked his head at a severe angle and looked at Tom through clumps of hair.

Two things. First, I got the gas and I'll get the tab. Money's only good if you spend it. Second, you gotta keep driving. I ate some acid right after you torched that transformer and it's starting to kick in.

The words seemed to come out of Lorne's mouth, orbit Tom's head for a few rotations, and then ricochet around the room. Tom froze. Lorne had just connected them to the recent arson in front of at least three witnesses. Yet the witnesses didn't seem to hear. Like a good shoplifter who steals so openly that bystanders don't register it as a theft. Lorne had also announced to the bar that he was tripping, which had not generated interest either. Lorne did seem weirder than usual.

Put this in the jukebox, will you? Lorne extended a five. His hand shook. Five bucks seemed like a ridiculous amount to spend on a few songs.

You put it in, music's your thing.

Okay. Unsteady, Lorne negotiated the barstools to the jukebox, holding onto tables to take the weight off the cast foot.

The burgers arrived and the smell about made Tom weep. He bit into his burger like a bite of soft-serve on a hot day. The juices, a scalding mix of blood and grease, exploded in his mouth. He felt as if he were eating strength itself. When the burger was gone he ate the pickle and the garnish. He dumped ketchup on his plate and methodically ate his fries, spooning the ketchup, until his plate was clean. He poured himself a beer from the pitcher and drank it in heavy gulps. Life breathed back into him. He ordered another pitcher and drank deeply. He felt good. On a full stomach he could think again.

The first song from Lorne's set came on, an old Hank

Williams tune. Tom figured they were about seventy-five miles and a few right angle turns from the fire. Maybe across county lines if they were lucky. Tom planned to keep going south. If they got to Arizona they might be all right. Lorne picked at his burger, more interested in his fingers than his food. Maybe no one was after them at all. Tom was having difficulty telling what was real anymore.

What do they mine here? Lorne asked the barmaid as she topped off his glass.

Nothing since Phelps Dodge shut her down five years back. Used to be the biggest copper mine in the state.

The old-timers at the end of the bar perked up at talk of the mine.

They still pulling some outta that mountain, piped in a tiny old man in a fleece-lined windbreaker, an old crumpled miner behind a beer mug.

Most folks left in town just work as security guards for the mine, or do maintenance, skeleton crew, the barmaid continued.

Copper? Lorne said. They should mine gold instead. More money in gold, Lorne nodded to no one in particular. They ignored his comment.

I see 'em sometimes. They come with a small crew, sometimes, deep in the mountain, pulling rock out of there.

They ain't mining up there anymore, Emmit.

Tom's mind started up again. What were they doing up there? The Network would have many uses for a clandestine mine. One out of the way, fenced off, one everyone thought was closed. No. Tom fought it. Not his problem, not here, not now.

Well, they doing something up there, geological surveys or something at least.

I'm sure they're doing all kinds of shit, but scaling back up again ain't one of 'em.

Didn't say it was. Emmit made a motion with his hand like he was brushing her off.

Tom wondered what was going on in that mine. The old-timer and the barmaid argued half-heartedly, an old argument, one they'd had before. Lorne chimed in with non-sequiturs but they didn't seem to mind. In fact, they liked Lorne. He laughed at everything they said, fully engaged, drinking and dancing haphazardly on his peg leg. You're all right son, they told him.

On the third pitcher, Tom lost the strength of a full stomach and felt the bluntness of beer. The mine was on his mind. Even if the Network wasn't here, and he was now beginning to believe they were, these people should be set free. A dying town with a couple dozen people left, chained to the corpse of the mine, too scared to leave. They'd be better off if the mine was truly gone forever, burned to the ground. But that wasn't really his fight...wasn't really real...wasn't real.

He turned to Lorne. You know I took this music class in college...I was a chemistry major so I took the easiest classes I could find for my non-science classes. I could have been a music minor even though I never played an instrument and can't sing a note. So this music class, was an ethnomusicology class really, was basically about how you can't study music, or anything else, without understanding that you are part of the equation. There were only two of us in this class, me and a young woman who had grotesquely large breasts. I don't mean in an attractive way, it was like a deformity, triple E or some size that's off the chart. Seriously, she probably had to have her bras special made, like she had a whole other person growing horizontally out of her chest. We'd have class outside sometimes, since it was just the two of us and the professor, and when she'd sit cross legged her breasts would actually rest on the ground. And she wasn't fat, but not pretty. All we did in this class was read one book, Hermeneutics: The Art of Understanding. The art of understanding. I like that, you know, like understanding was an art. All we'd do is read the book out loud. It was this dense, post-modern, deconstructionist linguistic theory. Really hard to understand. We only got through a page or two a day. And the whole point of the book was that you can't study anything without affecting the thing you study. So me, this girl, and the professor, this middle-aged Jewish woman who had lived with Rastafarians on some Caribbean Island and taught classes on reggae and blues, would struggle through this linguistic theory, and here was this perfect example of hermeneutics, this girl, who went through life with this obscene physical oddity, these cartoonishly huge breasts, like a sideshow attraction, and how that must color everything she understands about the world. The art of understanding was understanding that who you are affects how you understand something. I think, of late, I've completely forgotten that lesson.

You create your own reality?

I'm afraid so.

Cool. Hey listen, you wanna go check out that mine?

Yeah.

Chapter 3

Hailey's Sunday was ruined. Special Agent Hailey Garrett, Federal Bureau of Investigation, part time, switched on her scanner and knew Sunday was ruined. The fire at the mine made it a federal matter, but it was the fire at the power substation thirty miles south of Price that worried her. Two fires within twelve hours in that sparse country was quite a coincidence. And Hailey had been in law enforcement long enough not to believe in coincidence.

She put on her morning pot of coffee. In the time it took to brew she did the math and knew it didn't add up. As far as motive, there were plenty of reasons to torch the mine, insurance money, revenge of a laid off miner, even hiding environmental waste or impeding an investigation were possibilities. But none of those reasons would explain the power station. That left vandalism, which she was sure would eventually become the operating theory of the Sheriff's Department. But it didn't seem likely to Hailey. The delinquents and losers prone to that kind of behavior around here were holed up in trailers or basements doing meth. They spent their time doing meth or getting meth. A completely random act of vandalism simply wouldn't occur to them. Their crimes would be for some sort of pecuniary gain, no matter how small or temporary. That left teenagers. The 'those darn kids' explanation, as Hailey thought of it. But she kept track of the local high school kids, at least the ones who drove (particularly the attractive football players, of which there were exactly three: Ray Thompson, Matthew Baker, and Ryan Harris) and she couldn't see any of them committing the crime. Most of the kids were Mormons, and as a general rule, Mormon kids did not rebel. The few who did, rebelled in one of three predictable ways: 1) dressed inappropriately and listened to inappropriate music (or refused to listen to the right music, K-DOG 101 FM Country) 2) gave or received handjobs in parked cars or 3) left town. As far as anyone who fell through the cracks, well, they were tweakers and spent their time doing, buying, or making meth.

The coffee maker made sucking sounds and then beeped three times. Hailey poured her first cup of coffee. She knew this case didn't track, and it would bother her. Maybe the two fires weren't related, or maybe some random kids from Colorado on a road trip went on an arson spree. But now she wanted to know. She was curious, and Saint George was slow. Special Agent Hailey Garrett, Federal Bureau of Investigation, part time, let her Sunday be ruined by choice. She was, after all, part time.

Hailey was the sole agent in the FBI's Saint George, Utah office, an office that existed more figuratively than literally, consisting almost entirely of Hailey's laptop that occupied her kitchen table. Agent Garrett had a special arrangement with the FBI on account of her plastic hip that never quite became a proper part of her body and caused her to limp slightly as well as no small amount of pain. Normally, Hailey would have had to ride a desk in Salt Lake City until her twenty years were up and she could retire with her pension at eighty percent pay. But her hip was a special circumstance she owed to a single car accident late one night four years ago. The driver was the Section Chief for the Western Division. He walked away without a scratch. So with a kiss on the forehead, Hailey kept her credentials, her gun, and her pay, and got to work one case at a time, when she felt like it, from her house in Saint George.

Hailey was thirty-one, but she felt no different then she did at twenty-one, except she had the hips of an old woman. Her friends, who she kept in touch with via email chains and still spoke to on the phone every few months, implored her to leave Saint George. There were no eligible men to speak of. She wasn't even from Utah. Wasn't Mormon. She was still a young woman. But the truth was that she liked it here. She liked the wide open spaces, the long drives she was forced to take to get anywhere, the anonymous privacy of being an outsider in a tight community, even if she knew most folks in town. She liked the house she'd bought three years ago for $89,000. She'd be living in a studio apartment in any city in America for that price. And there was the dog to think about, some kind of weird desert dog. The dog liked the house too. At a hundred and ten pounds, Hailey didn't think the dog would do well in the city, he needed room to run, and Hailey got instantly melancholy when she thought about taking the dog out of the desert. And she liked the job. Poking her nose into the little dramas that came across the scanner. At thirty-one she had found freedom, even if her friends thought she was hiding out.

Sun streamed through the east facing kitchen windows. Hailey switched off the scanner. The dog watched Hailey. Hailey watched the dog. The dog had one brown eye and one blue eye. The dog looked at her sideways, suspiciously, the blue eye on Hailey.

Hailey finished her coffee. Her Sunday plan had been to drive the three and half hours to the Ak-Chin resort and casino on the reservation just across the Arizona border and spend the next two days alternating between the spa and the blackjack table, sipping Coronas and taking advantage of the

$29.99 mid-week rate. But she could put that off a few days. Arson at a federally regulated mine and another fire destroying utility infrastructure was worth looking into.

The truth of the matter was that there really wasn't that much to interest a Fed out here. There wasn't much point to setting up taskforces and bringing down interstate meth rings. The meth heads would get themselves arrested or dead faster than the Feds could set a trap to catch them. You didn't need to track them, conduct electronic surveillance, or infiltrate the organization, just walk down the street and you could pick them out on sight, rail thin and pockmarked and scabbed, twitching and restless. They'd get themselves locked up before the Feds could get a wire up. Take down a meth lab and four more spring up. Better to just sit back and watch them self-destruct. So two utilities attacked…could utilities be the link? No, that was stupid, might as well be random. No radical environmentalist or Islamic extremist would target a defunct mine…but even if it was random, it was new.

Hailey got up. The dog got up. She thought about the cane but she left it. She could walk, just with a hitch. She moved toward the door. The dog whined with anticipation, spun a marionette dance, and crouched as if to pounce.

I'll be back. You stay be good.

The dog's head lowered. He knew he was to stay.

Hailey locked the door, the handle to the screen door wedged in her bad hip. She freed herself from the screen door and dug for her car keys. Outside it was bright. Not a sound on the street. The sunlight cast a halo around her dark gray unmarked Chevy Capris. She put on mirrored sunglasses. The daily Percocets made everything look overexposed. She ambled to the car. Inside it was hot. She saw the curtain part in the kitchen window, and the dog pressed its face to the glass. She turned the ignition. Too hot to take the dog.

And she was having a bad hip day. She watched the dog and popped another Percocet.

She backed the unmarked cruiser onto the street. To anyone who cared, the Capris was easily recognizable as a cruiser, red and blue lights still visible through the tinted rear window, two black antennas, one short one long. Inside, it felt hermetically sealed. Dashboard vents blew stale cold air at full power.

She put it in drive. The car rocked slightly and uttered a low groan when she took her foot off the brake. She crept to a stop sign, spent an interminable amount of time deciding which way to go, thinking about nothing, and made a right onto Grant Avenue.

The scanner crackled a low murmur. Even with the sunglasses and the tinted windows it was bright, and she squinted behind smartly cropped blonde bangs.

The streets were wide. Saint George, at least as it was today, was shaped in the mold of the suburban west even though there was no metropolis to be a suburb of: low density, streets far wider than could be for any useful purpose, developers using cheap land and ample living space as a hook rather than quality. Grant Avenue ran through a commercial district, six lanes across and three businesses to a block.

She wheeled the Capris at a casual thirty miles per hour. The light traffic passed her going fifty, at least the ones who didn't notice the tell tale signs of a cop, the ones who wouldn't need to know, with nothing to hide. Only criminals drove the speed limit.

Right as she had forgotten what she was looking for she saw it, a yellow sign on the right past the Tractor Supply and Feed Store that read Patio Pancake. She signaled and came to a near complete stop before turning onto the gravel parking lot. She found a spot at the far end of a row of pickups.

Inside it was busy. The woman behind the register smiled

hello and nodded, clearly miffed that she could never remember Hailey's name no matter how made times she came into the Patio Pancake. She showed her to a table by the window facing the road. Most tables were full with ranchers or families with prodigious young rolling over themselves and circling the tables. She received passive looks, displaying neither recognition or non-recognition. Part of the scenery but not the community.

A new girl served her. Kimberley something, Echols maybe, she thought, remembering her yearbook picture and visualizing the name that went with it, junior at the high school. She thought she had dated the starting nose guard, she knew this from the nose guard, not the girl.

She ordered coffee, bacon, and eggs over easy. She stared out the window and sipped her coffee. Grant Avenue looked like a highway running through town. Then she unfolded her map and spread it across the table. She looked again at the location of the two fires. Not that far apart as the crow flies, but a substantial distance on the grid of roads out that way. She ate her breakfast, moving the plate around the different sections of map.

The bill was $4.79. She left a ten. She drove back to her house. The dog welcomed her return with a series of high howls. She pet him until he calmed down, lying on his back while she stroked his chest, her other arm lolling in his mouth, his sharp teeth gently probing her hand, his fangs bared and lips pulled back in a loving scowl, a vicious killer with the soul of a lonely child.

She took his harness from the closet, and he sprang to his feet and danced in excitement all over again. She had to fight to get him in the harness. He wanted to go with her, wherever she was going, but he was a nervous creature, the world was wrought with danger.

She got him harnessed and leashed, and wrangled him to

her Toyota 4-Runner—the cruiser she needed to keep clean of the dog hair that coated the 4-Runner's upholstery. The dog circled clumsily in the back seat, tangled in his leash, and collapsed mightily behind the driver's seat, his head wedged in between Hailey's elbow and the door.

She wheeled out of town driving even slower now that the dog was with her. With the air at full blast, the heat quickly became tolerable. She found the on-ramp to I-15 and gently eased onto the wide expanse in front of her. She caught the NPR station for a good stretch of Wait Wait… Don't Tell Me until it was inaudible above the static and she switched to an AM sports talk station out of Salt Lake recapping the latest incarnation of the Utah Jazz. The dog perched his head on her left shoulder and drooled on her sleeve.

She took the exit on to 616 and was surprised at the desolation of the road. Truly a road to nowhere. Ahead there were distant mesas, a barren mountain range to the southwest. She would have driven past the crime scene except for a Statey parked on the side of the road. The 4-Runner bounced as she turned onto a dirt pull off. The dog grew restless. A cloud of dust billowed over the hood. The dog jumped into the front seat and tried to bully his way out of the truck. His claws dug at her thigh and scratched her arm.

Settle the fuck down, she hissed to no effect.

The Statey got out of his car and leaned on the door. Too hot to leave the dog in the car. She cracked the door open and the dog vaulted into her chest. She pushed him back until she could get a hold of his leash and then opened the door wide so he could get free of the interior. He lunged forward but she was ready, bracing the leash against her good hip.

The cop came over waving his arms in grand gesture.

Ma'am, ma'am…

The dog started one way and then the other, sniffing the air in excitement and confusion, stopping to inhale the ancient burial ground of some rodent or other desert dweller and then bounding to the next smell.

You can't be here, this is a crime scene.

She fumbled through her purse for her creds. The dog saw the man for the first time and immediately stopped, sensing a threat. He backed up into Hailey's legs. Standing at attention, the dog's back was even with Hailey's waist. She muttered underneath her breath, still fighting with her purse. The dog let out a low growl and a three-inch band of coarse hair running the length of his spine stood straight on end in a bristling mohawk.

Ma'am, control your animal. You are interfering with police business.

Federal ag — She coughed, her throat swollen by the heat and the painkillers. She realized she hadn't spoken to anyone but the dog in a while.

Federal agent.

She pulled the badge from her purse. The dog backed up until his butt was pinned against her thighs. He bared his teeth in a snarl.

The cop squinted at her creds.

Agent, can you control that thing?

Unfucking believable. She'd killed a man. This yokel had probably never drawn his gun except to scare truck stop hookers into giving him free head.

Come on boy.

She snapped his leash and dragged him past the cop and toward the tracks left by the fire trucks. She struggled up a low dune following the ruts in the sand and veering when the dog's nostrils demanded. When she looked back, the cop was leaning against his cruiser, staring at her ass. She made it to the top of the dune and saw the fire blackened remains of a series of transformers. The sand was scorched in a starburst pattern from the epicenter of an explosion. The scene was crisscrossed with tire tracks and footprints, like the earth had been tilled.

She didn't know what she expected to find, but she found it always helped to look. What struck her this time was the incredible randomness. From behind the dune the road wasn't visible. Nothing but desert for 360 degrees. Blue sky scraped with high clouds until the horizon. Vandals she thought. No motive.

She watched the wind form zigzags in the sand for a while, and then she trudged onward, her arm flinging with the gyrations of the leash, until she saw something she recognized. A plastic cap, new, not yet disintegrated by the elements. She had seen it many times before. Old Crow. The cheapest brown liquor at the liquor store. Two dollars and ten cents at any Loaf & Jug. Half the price of a half pint of Jim Beam or any respectable whisky. She picked it up.

As she put the cap in her pant pocket, something caught the dog's attention and he bolted exactly when she held the leash loosely by her pinky. The handle to the leash snapped free. The dog immediately raced up the dune. Panic hit Hailey in the throat. She started after the dog. It moved like a predator on the savannah, back low to the ground, hind legs coming in front of front legs, like a greyhound or a Cheetah, covering ten feet each bound. The dog disappeared over the dune in the direction of the highway and that asshole trooper. A terrible image flashed across her mind's screen. She went to all fours and fought her way up the dune.

At the top, out of breath, she rose to her feet. Below, the dog was circling the 4-Runner. The cruiser was gone. No traffic on 616 in either direction. She sighed with relief and hacked up sand she had inhaled. The dog stood up with its paws on the window of the driver's side door. Finally free, and the only place the dog wanted to go was home. He looked back at her and wagged his substantial tail.

When she reached the truck and let the dog in she found it odd that the trooper was gone. She flipped on her police radio and found out why. There was news from the mine fire. A body had been found. The case was now being treated as a homicide.

Chapter 4

The Malibu was out of gas or broken. Either way, it wouldn't start. Tom pushed open the heavy door. It creaked with rust and wear. Tom got out slowly and stretched. He lifted his pack from the passenger seat, cinched up his wool coat, and started to walk.

The dirt road had hit a stretch of loamy sand in which the Malibu had come to rest. There were a few houses around, marked by flood lights or telephone poles. The sky was an inky black, just before dawn. The coldest part of the night. Tom's joints were stiff. He could see his breath. The road was dark. As the sky gently lightened he could see that the sand was red, surrounding him in a contourless sea.

The road was marked by a low barbed wire fence buttressed by wind blown sand drifts. Tom walked, sand filling the cuffs of his trousers. He was fully awake now. The crisp air taking away the dull beer ache. Tom felt good being alone again. Mobile as only a man on foot could be. Hard to save the country spending half his waking hours in bars. As dawn broke, Tom could see the road he was on, washboard track for as far as the eye could see. No houses now, just occasional jeep trails leading deeper into the desert. He picked up his pace. The road would lead somewhere.

The sky briefly turned orange and the sand yellowed. Tom became aware of birds chattering in whistles and phrases of song. A desert mouse scooted across the ruts in front of him, its footprints disappearing behind it.

As the morning chill melted away, Tom felt his skin tingle and hum, and eventually sweat. His breathing became easy, the air suddenly rich and humid. His muscles relaxed, the tension releasing in his neck. It was no longer painful to swivel his head, and he looked from side to side in wide sweeping arches. He noticed lizards scamper between rocks, and birds hop from cactus to cactus. There were flashes of movement everywhere. Yucca fronds and clumps of tall grasses and bottle-bush waved with the wind.

There was a road sign in the distance. The sun was well on its path by the time he reached the sign. A small tin plaque on a wooden post read Navaho 63. He was hot now. The wool coat his cross to bear. He listened but the birdsong was gone now. Too hot already he guessed.

He heard the whine of an engine. It stood out immediately from the faint insectual buzz that always seemed to keep Tom company. There was nothing ahead. He looked behind him and waited until his saw a faint dust cloud following the road. He briefly thought about hiding. But he could die in the desert before reaching a town and fresh water. He also quickly realized that the approaching vehicle was too big and moving too slowly to be police. It took another twenty minutes for the truck to pass him on the road. An old Ford dually eased to a halt. Tom waved to the cab and scaled the wooden cargo crate framing the bed of the truck. He joined six or seven men in the back. Three of the men appeared to be asleep with their backs against the rear window of the cab. The rest stood, leaning against the wooden planks, watching the horizon. They held on tightly as the truck lurched into gear and rumbled forward down the road.

Hours later the truck bounced once and then the ride evened on a stretch of pavement leading to a town. The truck ground to a dusty stop in front of a general store. The men climbed out of the back of the truck, handing their small backpacks and parcels to each other. They stretched and shuffled to the cab of the truck where they each handed the driver a dollar. Tom withdrew four quarters from his pocket but the driver held up his hand, took a look at him, and waved him away.

The General Store was a long white washed one-story adobe with wooden beams notched beneath the ceiling that extended out to also support a covered awning that stretched the length of the building. A group of Indians crowded against the wall in the shade. Three women sat on a bench next to the door, a cluster of children at their feet.

Tom wheeled about like a sailor returned to dry land. The people stared. The sky was blue. A brilliant blue cast against the white building and the red sand. The street was virtually empty, other than the truck he'd rode in on, which soon executed a three point turn and went back from whence it came. Across the street from the store was a small post office, a fenced red brick branch of Arizona Power and Light, and a pawn shop with a sign over the roof that said simply, 'Guns.' But that side of the street was deserted. All the people were in the shade of the General Store's portico, watching Tom.

One of the women sitting on a bench beside the door said something in what must have been Navajo, and the row of people against the wall erupted in laughter. A pink and green shawl wrapped around her shoulders, covering a white embroidered blouse. She motioned her hand at him, palm forward, fingers coming down in a digging motion bending at the wrist. Tom first thought that she was shooing him away. Not an altogether unexpected reaction. Small towns discouraged new vagrant arrivals, content with the ones they already had. But she seemed to be smiling, her maw a black hole, toothless save for two oddly placed teeth set in her lower jaw. But she was smiling, dimples even, and insistent. Tom realized she meant to call him over with her hand gesture. He wiped his brow and cautiously approached the General Store, stooping under the awning to get in the shade. An old man squatting on his haunches against the wall said something and received another round of laughter. The woman's colorful shawl extended all the way down to cover a woven basket at her feet. She lifted the ends of the shawl to reveal a mound of warm frybread.

One dollar. She held up a solitary finger.

Tom paid her in nickels and dimes, and she handed him four large pieces of frybread wrapped in napkins. Tom sat crosslegged against the wall and ate a piece. He pressed his back against the cool adobe. It soothed the knots and dissipated the heat radiating off of him. The woman took a piece of frybread from her basket and ate it slowly. They ate in silence.

Chapter 5

Hailey was good looking. She knew she was good looking because people told her so. They told her so a lot. She knew she wasn't stunning, but then again, stunning was good looking with a three beer buzz.

She sat at the corner of the black lacquer bar at the Barking Spider, a slender hand toying with a vodka tonic. She should have driven up to Bartonville to interview witnesses, but the episode with the dog had rattled her. It upset her how much she needed the dog, and how fragile he was, even though he could have ripped her throat out in one swift motion, if he so chose. So instead of doing her job, however she decided to define it, she'd driven straight home and deposited the dog inside to both their great relief.

The Barking Spider was in a nondescript strip mall a few miles from her house down Old 63. Next to a music shop and a karate studio you wouldn't have known it was a bar except for the neon Coors sign behind a black window. It was dark inside, lit by the glow of three televisions and two rectangular lights suspended above two pool tables.

She came here often, although no one seemed to recognize her. The bartender did of course, but he never spent much time trying to engage her. She spoke little enough to indicate she didn't want to talk, but just enough to not seem too weird. He figured she just liked to drink, just came here to drink, which was true. Or maybe it wasn't. After her third vodka tonic she looked around at the few customers, even though she didn't need to. She knew without lifting her head that there were six men in the bar—two a few stools apart on either side of the register, two at a corner table next to the black window with a view of the parking lot, one working the Golden Tee machine, and one staring at the jukebox. She could tell you their approximate ages, height and weight, and income bracket. But she looked around anyway. She didn't need to come here, she could easily drink at home. It wasn't what the bartender guessed, that she drank in the middle of the day because she had kids at home or was playing hooky from work. So why did she come here?

The man who was at the jukebox took the seat next to her. She scolded herself. Funny how one lapse in concentration somehow made her approachable. Sympathy for the Devil launched out of the jukebox.

Buy you a drink?

No thanks.

A shot then? Come on, do a shot with me.

She knew the man, had talked to him a few times. He was in his mid-fifties, white curly hair mushroomed off his head. She knew he was a drywall contractor, not that he did any of the drywalling, had Mexicans for that. She also knew he cheated on his taxes, but that never really changed her opinion of anyone. He was friendly, always friendly.

Make it something easy.

Purple Hooter, no wait, Kamikazes then.

She nodded.

The bartender poured vodka, triple sec, and sour in a metal mixer, clamped on a pint glass and shook once, and then poured out two shots and one for himself. It wasn't often the blonde, he didn't even know her name, was being social.

The contractor had a wide frame, broad shoulders, a square block head, and a gulf-filling twinkle in his eye. Not fat, but thick as a tackling dummy. Jeans, Old Spice, and a blue denim shirt. He leaned in close when he talked, bourbon on his breath. There seemed to be no space at all. She clinked shot glasses with the man and drank the tart shot with one gulp. The bartender waved his glass in their general direction. The man squared up and smiled.

What's your name sweetie?

She nodded to herself, pretending like she was struggling to swallow.

What's yours? Larry McCabe she thought to herself.

Larry McCabe. Pleased to make your acquaintance.

Well Larry, thanks for the shot. She patted the cuff of his denim shirt and grabbed her keys and sunglasses off the bar.

Why you gotta rush off? You gotta man at home?

Oh yeah, I got a fat hairy man at home.

She flipped open her phone and showed him the picture on the screen. It was a dog, asleep on the couch, head propped up and eyes just barely closed like a sleeping seal.

Aw that's a good looking boy, what kind is he?

She set her purse back on the bar.

I have no idea. I've asked three different vets and gotten three different answers.

Fucking vets will tell you anything.

Tell me about it. Really, he's got about six different dogs in him.

His mama got around.

Oh, she was a total whore. Must have been queen of the dog park.

Best not to tell the boy.

I would never! He's just a little boy!

Hey lemme see that again.

She handed him the phone.

You know why they can never tell you what he is?

Why?

That's dog's got coyote in him.

And suddenly it made so much sense. The weird blue eye. The crazy fight or flight mohawk and curled lip snarl. Feral aggression just below the domesticated veneer, predatory, all claws and teeth. The way other dogs and people avoided him.

Really, coyote, you think?

Sure, well, a Cahouly dog anyway.

She repeated the words, Cahouly dog.

He made off with any chickens? Livestock?

No, he's very well mannered, and cleanly.

You've tamed the beast then, good maternal instincts.

Yeah right.

Good breeding stock.

She laughed and looked up at him, blonde bangs in her eyes. She didn't mean to give him that look.

This is mine.

He took a photo out of his wallet of a pretty girl and little black dog.

My daughter. Sent her to school up in Colorado, at the university, she does nothing but snowboard, ride she says, five years now, she picked this little guy up and she can't even care for him properly, new apartment doesn't take dogs or some shit, pissed all over her place anyway, so he's staying with dad now till she gets things sorted out.

Hailey looked at the picture again. Chow mix, black tongue hanging out.

Well, at least she's enjoying life. Smarter than the two of us.

No, she's a good girl. I'm proud of her. She's my whole life. I've bonded with the little guy now anyway, I'd hate to give him up.

The remaining men in the bar had coalesced around a game on the TV above the other end of the bar, and the bartender, who'd been washing glasses and listening to Hailey and Larry's conversation and was beginning to feel slightly embarrassed for doing so, drifted away to join them. The warm yellow-orange glow of the bar now seemed debilitating, dark. She tried to find the door with her eyes. All she saw was Larry's wide frame.

Yeah well, I should get back and feed the dog.

I'll bet he's fine, probably feeds himself anyway. You find a lot of missing cat flyers in your neighborhood?

No, really, can I have my phone back? Larry still had her phone strangled in his hand, flipped open to the picture of the sleeping dog. He looked at it, paused, held it in two fingers and dangled it in front of her. She reached for it but he pulled it back, grinning.

He winked at her.

She stared back at him.

Fine, no need to be a bitch.

She snatched the phone from his right hand, but as she did he grabbed her left wrist and pinned it to the bar.

I'm just messing with you—don't go now.

She froze for an instant, mouth slightly agape, blood draining from her face. Her wrist was locked to the bar. He stared down at her, blue eyes crystalline as November sky.

Hey Larry, what's going on? The bartender took two steps toward the back of the bar.

Are we talking to you?

The bartender was silent.

Mind your own fucking business.

Hailey felt paralyzed, drawn within herself, her will just out of reach. She looked down at herself as if outer body, looking from a thousand feet in the air at the barroom below, an exit, blocked by Larry, pinned in at the back corner of the bar, trapped in a five-foot corridor between the bar and low wall separating the pool tables. She picked up her purse with her right hand and moved to get off the stool, but Larry held her left wrist firm.

Let me go…I have to go.

Her voice was small, without wind.

Larry looked down at the hand, as big and round as the end of a dumbbell. He spread his fingers and released her wrist.

She gathered her things and hurried out of the bar. As she pulled the door open, a blast of cold air hit her, and a whistling gust whipped her hair from one side to the other. Outside it was night, the same color as the darkened windows had been inside the bar, a clear desert night. They were all clear desert nights. She struggled across the parking lot, slammed the door of the 4-runner shut behind her, and studied the rear view mirror for any sign of someone coming out of the bar after her. But there was no one.

Chapter 6

Lorne first became conscious of a repetitive scratching noise, the dull dragging sound of something scraping against metal and glass. He then became aware of pain in his knees and back, aching muscles screaming to be stretched. His foot throbbed. He tried straightening his legs, but they were jammed. Consciousness quickly bubbled up to the surface and he tried opening his eyes and found only one lid would function. He panicked, bolted himself upright, ripping his face free from the vinyl seat cover to which it was stuck.

The Malibu. He was in the back seat of the Malibu. Tom was gone. A foot and a half of bent metal molding that had popped out of place rubbed back and forth against the side of the car, making that scratching noise that permeated his sleep. He could tell it was morning by the quality of the light. Beyond that he knew nothing.

He wedged himself into the front seat, found the door handle with his pinkie finger, and tumbled onto the road. He found himself elbow deep in loamy red sand. The sand had been blown into a drift as high as the rear wheel well. Two deep ruts in the sand trailed the Malibu to its inexplicable resting place. They were at an intersection of sorts, between what looked like a foot path and a bend in the road. There was a house a hundred yards behind, and two randomly placed off the road ahead. Other than that there was just empty desert and the road stretching to oblivion.

He stood up, stretched, scratched his ass, looked around in all directions, and hacked up a wad of phlegm.

Fuck me, he said aloud.

The Malibu looked half-submerged. Every wisp of wind washed more grainlets of sand higher against the sinking frame. He knew it wouldn't start, but he had to try. Fortunately, the keys were in the ignition. The engine rolled over once, a slow grind like hand cranking a jammed pencil sharpener, then nothing.

He scanned the interior of the car. No water. He felt through the trash on the floor. No food. He found a beer at the bottom of a cardboard twelve pack. It felt hot to the touch. He got out of the car and cracked it open, white foam spewing from the lid. Even piss warm it tasted good. Lorne was grateful.

He looked out at the open range. It might have appeared that he was contemplating his options, but in reality he just stared blankly at the expanse. He finished the beer, crumpled the can, and tossed it in the backseat. He tried not to litter when out in nature. He dove again into the trash on the floor hoping to find another beer. When he picked his head up he was startled to see a figure through the windshield. He extracted himself from the Malibu ass-first, revealing half of his pasty white buttocks. He pulled himself upright and straightened his pants. An Indian boy of sixteen or seventeen stood a few yards away, examining him.

You lost?

Uh, yeah…I'm lost.

Where you trying to go?

Uh, Well…I don't know where I am so I don't know where I'm going.

The boy thought about that for a time. He was not a bad looking boy, thin with a long face, long black hair pulled back in a ponytail.

Car trouble?

Lorne, hand on his hips, kicked the dirt.

Yeah…yup, car won't start.

Looks stuck too, the boy said.

I 'spect so.

They stood silent for a while, the boy studying the car, and then Lorne.

You looking to buy something?

Lorne cocked his head. He took a step back. A slight smile out of the corner of his mouth.

Well, what do you got?

You want green?

Lorne thought about that. He still had a few joints stashed somewhere, a couple in the car and one or two in the various inside pockets and folds of his army surplus utility pants and jean jacket. He knew what he really wanted.

Can you get white?

The boy spoke slowly, eyes on Lorne, nodding his head to an imperceptible rhythm.

No coke…we got glass. You go fast?

Glass will work.

The boy squinted into the sun. He looked Lorne up and down.

You got money?

Shit yeah, Lorne said, hands on his hips, sweating and panting now, pawing his foot at the dirt like a talking horse playing tic-tac-toe. Lorne handed the boy a twenty-dollar bill. The boy took it slowly. He watched Lorne for a long while, making no motion to leave.

Aren't you afraid to come to the res?

Lorne started to laugh and then thought better of it.

No, why…should I be?

The boy shrugged.

Most people are afraid to come to the res.

Lorne chuckled, thinking now that this was getting a little

too weird. The self-preservation instinct, generally ignored, making a feeble motion to be heard.

I don't want any trouble.

The boy stared at him, uncomprehending. Black eyes, opaque, giving away nothing.

No trouble, he said finally.

Wait here.

The boy turned around and walked up the road, his high-tops kicking up a cloud of red dust. At the bend in the road he didn't turn but rather kept going straight, hopping over a low ditch to one of the three lone houses. The houses sat askew, neither lined up with each other nor the road, as if laid out on the streets of a town that no longer existed. They looked government issue, one-story square blocks long ago painted tan with brown doors and window shutters.

Lorne stretched, spun a slow circle, and pondered his luck, already feeling a little speedy, pulse rising, feet tapping. The boy was gone for a time. No noise or movement came from the house. Lorne began to wonder if he'd been had. But where would the boy go? Could he slip out the back of the house and disappear with his twenty? There was nothing around for a hundred miles. Had he imagined the boy? Was he imagining everything? He thought then of the burning transformer, and about what had happened at the mine. But he quickly blocked it out. That was all Tom's fault anyway. He seemed far away now. Maybe it never happened.

He heard a low distant rumble. A large flat bed truck with dual rear wheels came up the road behind him. He stepped into the ditch at the side of road. The truck carefully edged past the Malibu. A half dozen men were in the back. He held up a hand in greeting. A half dozen dark heads turned to watch him. He briefly wondered if he should hitch a ride. Rides seemed few and far between out here. But the boy had his money, and the promise of something he couldn't leave behind. The truck slowed down and then kept going when Lorne made no move to run after it. And then the door to the house opened and the boy reappeared, evenly covering the ground toward him in his steady gait. And then Lorne only thought about one thing.

Here.

The boy placed a tiny heat sealed baggy in Lorne's hand. Lorne looked at it, an eighth inch of white crystal flakes at the bottom of the bag. He closed his hand tight around it. The boy turned to go.

Hey, where can I go...you know...to do this?

The boy shrugged.

And a little help here'd be nice. Lorne held his arms out and gestured to the desert. I mean where the fuck are we?

The boy turned back around to face him. He squinted and studied him some more, internally debating without moving a muscle.

You got any more money?

Yeah, Lorne puffed up defensively, testing out a hint of anger. The boy was impassive, unflinching. He saw things for what they were.

Okay. Come on.

They walked to the house the boy had gone into. Lorne was anxious to get out of the sun. He followed awkwardly, scooting ahead and then following behind, not able to match the boy's even pace, at one point getting his feet tangled with the boy's sneakers. The boy approached the house without a sound. He cracked the door open and poked his head in.

Hey, this guy needs a place to be. Says he has money.

Lorne didn't hear if there was a response. They stepped inside. The door swung shut with a slap. Inside it was dark, sheets put up over all the windows, and hot. Lorne blinked feverishly, eyes slow to adjust to the darkness. The only light came from an old television. He could make out two forms on a couch and hear the clicking of buttons on video game controllers. On the screen the Arizona Cardinals were beating the Dallas Cowboys in a game of Madden.

He's lost or something. He's not a cop.

Be the sorriest looking cop I've ever seen, said a voice from the corner, female. Lorne could make out a large woman by the glow of the television, maybe three hundred pounds with a swatch of bleached hair coming over her eyes and Indian braids in the back.

That's Pam, the boy said, she likes to bust balls.

Bust yours if you had any, Junior. One of the dark forms on the couch leaned forward and gave Pam a pound, touching fists.

Yeah, when are those things going to drop? A voice from the dark.

Never going to fill out your tighty-whiteys.

More pounds.

The other voice from the couch: You can have a seat if you want. Junior, give him a pipe.

The boy, unfazed by the ridicule, opened a metal folding chair, the kind that used to be common in institutional auditoriums and cafeterias, and set it next to the couch facing the television. Then he went into the kitchen, possibly the only other room in the house, and returned with a plastic cup of water and a glass pipe.

Good to drink water. People always forget when they smoke.

Lorne eased himself onto the chair, worried it might buckle under his weight, and drank the water.

Thanks....and thanks you guys. I'm kind of stuck you know?

No one responded. His eyes still hadn't adjusted. He could just see forms, big forms. The boy had retreated to a beanbag in the corner. Fuck it, he thought, and sprinkled a pinch of white crystals into the pipe. The pipe had a thin short stem of spun glass and a round bowl the size of a chestnut. He held his lighter to the bottom of the bowl. The glass that had looked clear except for a yellow tinge of resin spiraled blue and black when put to the flame. One, two, he thought, and then, one, two again. He gently rocked the bowl from side to side, making sure the flame tasted every curve. A beautiful little convection oven warming up, one, two, and the chamber began to fill with smoke. He pulled softly and then covered the bowl with the flat side of the lighter. One, two again, and he exhaled smoke, white as Christmas morning, into the hot, damp room, and watched it settle in a wavy layer just below the crushed drywall ceiling.

Yeah, he said, yeah.

Pam laughed. The others said nothing.

Lorne felt good, a bubble of goodness welling up from his insides around his gut and groin and expanding outward until it reached the surface and strained and pulsed against his skin yearning to be free. Words came to him then, he couldn't control it, he had to speak, to be heard, to know these people, for them to understand him.

I've had a…I've had a crazy couple of days.

Nobody took the bait.

He took a deep breath. It felt wonderful. He was content. And then he wasn't. The bubble of goodness was poking through his skin like an alien baby, stretching it thin to where it would burst.

Do you know how I got here?

Summersaults? Pammy said. You look like it.

No man, this guy Tom, he was driving. Did you see Tom? He drove me here, he must of come this way.

No, the boy from the beanbag answered.

Went to bed and there was no car. Woke up this morning and the car was there with you sleeping in the back. I know a guy who's good at fixing cars, if you want.

Lorne knew he should keep control if he could, but suddenly the line separating people and things completely disappeared, as if everything just merged together, could merge together, and words poured out of him and flooded the room.

At first I thought Tom was this homeless guy. We were driving to Vegas you know, like on a road trip, but then he started setting shit on fire and I thought he was crazy, but he's actually some kind of agent deep undercover on a mission to stop this terrorist plot, they call them the Network, and they are everywhere, in our economy—

Your economy, Pammy interjected.

—in our technology, in our infrastructure, in our communications, so he had to go completely off the grid…see, I thought he was a bum because he's broke, but it turns out he can't handle paper money because the little metallic strip that's in all bills, the watermark, they can track that shit from satellites, that's how they made all the agents they sent in undercover before. Any credit card, check, wire, bill can all be traced and instantly GPS'd and then they'd be on him, so he only handles change, that's why I thought he was a bum, but if you think about it it's the perfect cover.

Bullshit, Pam coughed, lighting up her own pipe.

Wait, you're with some kind of Fed? The couch spoke and Lorne sensed eyes training on him.

No, no, it's not like that. He's single-minded, they're going blow up the Hoover Dam, that's all he's about. It's life or death. Millions of people.

Bullshit, Pam said again.

The boy pulled up his beanbag next to Lorne's chair.

I've read about this, the boy said. They put those strips in all the dollar bills a few years ago.

Some spare-changer says he's out to save the world from some global conspiracy. Starts fires. That's textbook looney bin shit, Pammy said.

No, you don't understand, Lorne stammered, the line obliterated, all of them coming together in bonds so tangible he could almost see the wisps of thoughts connecting them. It all fitting into place.

I've seen it, in an abandoned mine, rows of computers and servers and all this high-tech shit. He was right. He torched the place and he was right. It all made sense.

Lord knows what makes sense to you. You been smoking too much glass, Pam said, passing the pipe to the couch.

No, you don't understand. The invisible bonds forming and unforming, Lorne almost desperate to complete the circle.

We killed a guy.

They were all listening to Lorne now.

Chapter 7

Memories are like any other thoughts except they might be real. In the telling of what happened at the mine Lorne knew that his perception of events may have been influenced by the acid, but he trusted that drugs affected only details, not the actual facts themselves. His life experience was entirely to the contrary. Nonetheless, this is what he believed.

The night was wild and windswept. The Merle Haggard from the jukebox was instantly extinguished by the door slamming shut, blown hard against its wooden frame by the swirling canyon winds. It was dark, the only light from a few distant and unearthly floodlights and the yellowed sepia of the barroom that seemed pinched off, dimmed and useless, swallowed by the night outside.

The mine loomed across the street. The two men followed a chain link fence so tall that at its top it curved out over the street, Lorne feeling the oxidized metal scrape against his fingertips imparting a dry metallic powder. After a time Tom eyed some irregularity in the fence that Lorne couldn't see. To Lorne the fence looked like it was melded into the road, like the road was really a tube, a massive particle collider in which they were two atoms waiting to be smashed. But Tom had adeptly spotted a bulge in the fence where the chain link mesh was slightly curled up and loose from the ground. He lifted up the flap and told Lorne to hold it up a few inches while he slid underneath, and then he held the buckling fold for Lorne to do the same.

The far end of the canyon lit up. Tom's first thought was that they'd triggered a motion sensor, but he quickly saw that the illumination was from a set of headlights sidewinding the empty canyon road at a less than safe speed. His instinct was to remain perfectly still and play the odds that the vehicle would pass them without incident, but Lorne had already started on a dead run, bad foot and all, across a dirt pit and up a slag pile toward one of the mine's towers. Tom gave chase, hit the slag pile, and the two of them clawed their way over junk rock and tailings even as the car continued down canyon without slowing.

Lorne, on all fours, reached the top of the rock pile and crouched against the corrugated tin siding of a six-story tower. His hands were scraped bloody, but they didn't hurt. In fact, feeling the pulsing blood produced an exhilarating tingle. Tom reached him, jogged once around the tower and, not finding a door, immediately started climbing the riveted steel beams like scaffolding, wedging himself up the crisscrossed supports stacked in X shapes up one side of the tower. Lorne climbed after him, laughing gleefully, his hands knowing just where to go, not sure how he was doing it, like he was flying, his muscles working in rhythm with his fingertips, never looking down, fear replaced by the lightness of energy, until Tom had his hands gripping his back from above and was heaving him up onto a flat platform high in the sky.

Lorne stood atop the platform and marveled at where he was. He could make out the dark silhouettes of the mountains encircling the mine at eye level against the blackness of the night sky, decipherable only by the scattershot of stars that seemed to move and multiply the longer he stared. Below and across were the parapets and ramparts of the skeletal mine cast in sharp shadows by sporadic floodlights, and further below the shacks, outbuildings, trussed conveyor belts and idlers, pumps, hoses and dilapidated machinery left aging aside and among a waste pond and various waste puddles.

The platform, really the bratticed roof of the mine's tallest and most menacing structure, shook with the wind, which made the stars move more and the entire canyon rise and sink as if on surf. To Lorne's dilated pupils the stars left tracers that jogged with his vision like a neon spirograph on the sky's black canvas. Lorne continued to stand until he felt it unsafe and then crouched hoping his hands could find perch on the weather worn metal. Tom took no notice of their greater surroundings but instead was on his hands and knees feeling the surface with his fingertips. He found a hatch and traced the dirt and rust that grouted its square outline. A heavy padlock clamped over its steel latch. It only then occurred to Lorne that they had no way to get down other than the way they came up. So he was astonished to see Tom quickly pick the lock with what looked like a pair of tweezers he kept in his backpack. He lifted open the hatch and climbed down a metal ladder into a small room. Lorne noisily followed him down the ladder and started to say something but Tom shushed him, physically putting a hand over Lorne's mouth. Tom froze, listening intently. The wind outside intensified, and through a plexiglass window he could perceive the tower rocking by marking its movement relative to the silhouetted mountains. He felt a steady surge of air leaking from a ventilation duct and knew somewhere a giant fan must be drawing air from the tower into the mine, and then he heard it, the unmistakable hum of electricity. The mine was in operation.

In the corner of the room was a cage and a circuit breaker. Tom removed a rubber cover and pressed a green button on a panel next to the cage, and a set of thick cables creaked to life, slowly bringing up an elevator car. The lift felt rickety but had the imprimatur of industrial grade. They entered the cage and slid shut the rusted mesh gate which bounced back slightly on its rollers. Neither man spoke as they descended story after story, passed electrical equipment for the ventilation unit, a backup generator system with rows of hazmat suits, lamplit helmets and other heavy fire retardant emergency gear, and an administrative office with dusty file cabinets until they were subsurface and the car came to an abrupt stop in a room with gunite sprayed walls and florescent overhead lights, filed with banks of black and white monitors and chairs with wheels on their bases, all empty save for one. At the far end of the room, a man in a white shirt, black striped pants, and a jacket with some type of emblem on the breast and patch on the shoulder was watching a monitor and talking softly into a microphone.

The man heard the elevator car clank to a stop and looked up from what he was doing. Tom and Lorne didn't see the man until Tom had slid open the elevator door. Tom and Lorne stopped in their tracks. The man looked at them as if trying to compute something, to put together pieces of a puzzle. The men stared at each other not moving for some time. And then in a flash, with what must have been well-practiced speed, the man drew a .38 service revolver with one hand and a flashlight with the other and trained both on Tom and Lorne.

Don't move.

For a moment, neither man moved. Tom felt naked, totally unprepared for this moment that he'd been spent years striving for, suffering for. And then Lorne reacted wildly, irrationally, struck by the primal fear of having a gun pointed at him heightened by the acid and the panic of not knowing what was real. Lorne leapt over a chair and threw himself over a bank of monitors taking an angle toward the man with the gun. Surprised, the man spun to his feet and fired three shots in Lorne's direction, sparks showering off the walls, countering Lorne's advance by sidestepping to the center of the room, his back now toward Tom. Lorne slipped and fell, regained his feet and came straight at the man, flailing his fists. The man took a wide stance to steady himself and raised the gun to Lorne's chest in perfect firing position. Before he could pull the trigger, Tom grabbed a fire extinguisher that was mounted to the wall and brought it down squarely on the top of the man's head, caving in his skull.

Chapter 8

She awoke to the dog sitting upright in bed next to her with one paw on her chest. The phone was ringing.

Yeah.

Hailey?

This is Hailey, who is this?

Damn girl, you are really worrying me.

Jen…sweetheart…it's like…morning.

It's lunchtime on the east coast. Don't you have a job?

I hate you.

So…seriously, what the hell is going on?

What? I'm going to work.

So what do I care? Are you going to Stef's wedding or not? What do you do, anyway? Don't you have drug dealers to arrest? I feel a lot safer for my kids knowing you're thinking about getting to work at ten-thirty in the morning.

Jen, my job's not like that. I work nights, and weekends, I'm like, on call.

You can't not go to this wedding. It's in freaking Vegas. You can practically see it from wherever it is you are. Borrow Uncle Fester's horse and meet us there. I'm making you a hotel reservation, we're staying at the MGM Grand.

I can't just commit. You don't understand my job—what if there's a murder or something?

Hailey, I know you don't understand this concept, but the wedding is in three weeks. They have to have a headcount for the caterer. They pay money for everybody who comes. So send in your invitation and get shitfaced with your friends. The only people who love you. Don't be a crack. We miss you. Tell them you are taking vacation time and get your fat ass to Stef's wedding.

Vacation time, like I can just punch out. And what about my dog?

No one can replace you? People take vacations Hailey. I've got a sitter for a whole three days, so don't mess this up for me. And the dog? I can't believe that thing hasn't killed anybody yet. Fill the bathtub with water and leave a carcass in the backyard. The dog will be fine.

All right, look, I've got to arrest someone. I'll call you later.

Just be there bit—

Hailey hung up the phone. The dog rolled on his back and stuck his arms straight up in the air.

She fell back asleep.

Hailey awoke ten minutes later. Last night fell on her like a weight. She was pissed. She slammed her hands together in a sudden and loud clap.

Fuck.

The dog flipped over and slinked off the bed with his ears pinned back behind his head. She couldn't shake the image of Larry McCabe, the look in his eye, the pain in her wrist, and felt ashamed, embarrassed, and guilty at the same time, like she'd allowed it to happen, to make her feel that way. Only she was allowed to make herself feel this way. But most of all, she was pissed.

She jumped out of bed and ran to the shower, slamming doors behind her and cursing at the bathroom mirror.

Fifteen minutes later she wheeled the cruiser onto I-15 and gunned it up to 100 mph, her blonde ponytail dripping water down the back of her navy blue windbreaker. She drove deceptively fast as police do, never blowing by the few station wagons and SUVs on the interstate, but rather closing gaps quickly and then passing smoothly on the left an even twenty or thirty miles per hour faster than them after she was sure they weren't going to swerve into her lane.

She did this unconsciously, out of habit. When she turned onto UT 23 she really opened it up, feeling the engine vibrate and the wheels spin faster than friction, picturing that white curly hair, like a bleached cheese puff. Something had to change, she thought.

She made Bartonville in under an hour and a half. She hadn't been here since the mine shut down, and she was shocked by the desolation. The last time she had been here was more than four years ago on an investigation of an interstate meth ring she had suspected was run by white supremacists. The investigation ended when the principal rolled his F-150 off of Barton Pass and was Flight-for-Lifed to Paige, Arizona, and then ambulanced to Flagstaff where he spent the next week on life support in Flagstaff Medical Center before dying with a Coconino County Deputy outside the hospital room door, sticking the State of Utah with a forty-seven thousand dollar medical bill. She'd had enough to indict some of the crew on gun charges, but Western didn't want to spend the resources, and the Garfield County Sheriff declined to go further with it since gun charges without anything else were not popular and the Sheriff had won the last election by fewer than one hundred votes. Of course, there were fewer than two thousand registered voters in the county. Not that there was wide support for white supremacists, but they'd styled themselves as some sort of militia, and guns are guns.

Hailey hardly recognized the town now. Even the pawn shop was boarded up.

She followed the road to the end of town, the massive mine on her right, still smoldering. Fire crews in dayglow yellow were spraying white foam and mopping it up. She was surprised at the size of the fire. It had been huge. The buildings were ash and blackened metal. There were no trees of any kind in the narrow canyon cut, but if there had been they'd have been vaporized. The earth was scorched black, like the very rocks had burnt.

When she'd driven the length of the town, she turned around and drove back looking for a place to start. At the entrance to the canyon, she stopped at a bar that looked more like a mobile home. Not quite noon but the parking lot was crowded. Most of the vehicles had the signs of some variety of emergency responder, sirens or the appropriate decals, stickers, and plates.

She claimed a stool at the bar. The place was tiny. It seemed full even though there were maybe a dozen customers. A side room with curios and postcards was empty. The bartender was a middle-aged woman, white blonde hair and red skin, dangling a cigarette, too skinny.

Well, aren't you adorable? What'll you have, sweetie?

Hailey smiled, and even might have blushed at little in spite of herself.

Miller Lite, draft, please.

The barmaid poured a pint of yellow beer with a practiced hand.

What brings you here, darling? Come to see the fire?

Yeah, work.

You a reporter or something? You're a little late, they all been here.

No, I'm an agent with the FBI.

Hailey said it as if it were a question.

Really? You don't look like a cop.

Hailey smiled again. It was good to know. She couldn't tell anymore.

To tell you the truth, I don't feel like a cop.

That's probably for the best, dear.

Is it always so busy in here? I mean, this early?

Hell no. I've done more business in the last two days than in the last year. I'm sorry the mine's gone, but if I'd known that thing burning would be this good for business I'd a burned the thing down myself.

Did you? Hailey twisted the ends of her hair. The barmaid laughed.

My goodness, you are a cop aren't you?

Well, were you working the night it happened, see anything strange?

A group of firefighters huddled around a table by the window slammed their glasses down in unison and called for another round of shots.

Hold on.

While the barmaid left to serve them, Hailey gulped at her beer. The icy bubbles burned her throat. She'd had no pain pills yet today. The beer was cold and good. Actually refreshing, she thought, like in the commercials.

The barmaid returned shaking her head.

Assholes.

Hailey turned to look. Four of the five were staring at her. The fifth was kind of cute, she thought.

So were there any strangers in here that night, anything like that?

Well, there were two fellas come in here that night.

The barmaid leaned in conspiratorially and lowered her voice.

They were a little strange, I'd say.

Hailey leaned in to meet her midway over the bar.

Really, like how?

Well, first of all, they backed in, you know, like they do when they're gonna rob you and make a quick getaway.

Did you see what they were driving?

No, just the taillights. But probably something big and American. I even brought the revolver out from the back office and set it under the bar, just in case.

The barmaid winked at Hailey as she said this.

Hailey leaned in even closer.

But it was okay?

Oh, they were cool.

What made them strange?

Well, they were longhairs you know?

Like hippies?

Well, one of them was sort of like a hippy, but the other was more like…a vagrant…you know, like he smelled bad. I mean bad.

Do you think they did it? Why do you think so?

I didn't say they did it. But one of 'em was talking about the mine with some of the old-timers who drink here, getting them all riled up. Getting those old farts riled up is about all I need, you know what I mean?

Was it the stranger that brought it up?

What do you mean?

Did he start talking about the mine first or was it the old guy?

I don't know, they didn't seem to care until Emmit started yapping about the mine starting up again, how there were people down there working it. It's all bullshit. There was nobody working that mine.

Hailey thought about this, about the body.

So you don't think these guys planned it…if they did it. They didn't seem like radical environmentalists or something?

Hailey figured this was where Western Division would be going with the case. Blame the Animal Liberation Front or Earth First; the eco-terrorist angle would open the money spigots and bring the cameras. Two things that made prosecutors drool.

Honey, I don't think these guys could have spelled environmentalist. Not that kind of hippy, not the college kind. I mean, the one smelled bad…not like patchouli stink bad… like dumpster diving bad.

Hailey thought about the plastic cap from the bottle of Old Crow she'd found. She finished the rest of her beer.

I mean, the one had a cast on his foot, but it looked nasty, like it was coming off, like he'd jerryrigged it or something. Now, a college environmentalist hippy'd be on his Momma's insurance, don't you think? Wouldn't let it get like that.

Were you scared of them. Did they seem like criminals?

No. Like I said, the one with the peg leg was really nice, even got along with the crusty bastards that call this place home. Even left a good tip, and honey, that makes someone okay in my book. The other was quiet, kept to himself.

Did you tell this to any of the other cops that came in here?

Nope.

Why not?

They didn't ask. Only asked for drinks.

Hailey drank another beer and left a twenty on the bar. She nodded to the barmaid, busy closing out a tab, who gave her a salute in return and then laughed in a way that Hailey could only describe as a cackle. Hailey stole a quick glance at the cute firefighter who was pretending he didn't see her and then made her way out to the parking lot and her cruiser. As she swung her car around she could make out the faces of the firefighters through the window. She headed south through town again and up the canyon. She was pretty sure she knew who she was looking for. She was looking for a bum.

Chapter 9

Tom woke on the cold earthen floor of the old woman's kitchen in her mud brick adobe hut. He had gone to sleep wrapped in his wool coat, using his backpack as a pillow, but now he found himself covered in a thick woven blanket, coarse as horsehair, but warm. The old woman kneeled over a blackened billy can suspended on a spit over a small fire. The smoke from the fire crowded the ceiling and slowly escaped through a hole in the corner that acted as a chimney.

Ya at eeh abini, the woman said, which Tom guessed could only mean good morning, so he reciprocated with a nod and a smile. A rooster crowed loudly. The culprit stood at an open doorway to the outside. Beyond a dirt courtyard, clouds hung low in the sky, and a steady drizzle rolled across the valley. The bird cocked its ugly head at Tom and strutted into the room a few steps before the woman shoed it back outside by throwing a small rock at it. She looked at Tom and laughed. He laughed too.

Steam rose from the billy can. She wrapped her hand in a cloth and grabbed the lid of the billy can and lifted it off its hook over the fire. With a little grunt, she poured two ceramic bowls full of coffee. She motioned with her hand for him to come closer, and he slid across the floor to take one of the bowls in both hands. She reset the can on the hook. The fire was fed by only three sticks that came together in a small point of flame. She pushed the sticks toward the middle with her fingertips as the ends burned down. Tom was impressed that she could get such a large can of coffee to a near boil with only a few sticks. He held the bowl to his face and felt the steam clear his sinuses. He took a sip and grunted his appreciation.

After a while, she removed the steaming can from the fire and placed a circular piece of sheet metal across the spit. She put two pieces of flat bread on the sheet metal. She filled their bowls with the rest of the coffee from the can. When the bread was good and heated she licked her fingers and picked up the bread off of the glowing sheet metal and tossed them on her lap to cool for second. When the bread had cooled enough for Tom to handle, she gave him a piece. She ate the bread slowly, pinching off little pieces and dunking them in her coffee, staring out the open doorway at the morning gray beyond.

Cold, she said, making a shivering motion.

Cold, Tom agreed.

They watched the world outside framed in the doorway. The drizzle turned into a steady rain. Mud began to splash a few feet into the room. Tom took out his pack of GPCs and held it out to the woman. She took one of the longer butts and lit it with a stick from the fire. Tom took the stick and lit his smoke and then carefully placed the stick back in the ashes with the ember-end next to the burning ends of the other two sticks, and the fire came back to life. She smoked hers down the filter and then put it in the fire.

Eventually Tom rose and stretched. He shook out his coat and put it on. He made a little bow and put his hands together as if praying.

Thank you, he said. He offered her a dollar in nickels and dimes, but she waved him off. She gave him a toothless grin, the deep rutted lines in her face zigzagged upward.

Thank you.

• • •

Tom hitched up his pack and started down the dirt road back toward town. Although it was only drizzling, little tributaries of rainwater meandered down the road, bobbing around newly uncovered rocks and clumps of hearty ditchweed, eroding small canyons in the single lane track. The old woman's hovel was on a small rise stretching uphill from town. A patchwork of houses spotted the descent below, some whitewashed, but most were brown mud brick adobe or cinderblock. At the base of the rise, the road crossed a gully before a short jog up to Main Street. The gully was probably bone dry ninety-nine percent of the time, but today it was a muddy stream rolling across the road at an indeterminate depth. Fortunately, others had crossed already today and left a wooden plank spanning the gully a few inches above the waterline. Tom took a cautious step onto the plank and felt it rock with his weight. The pack made him top heavy, and halfway across he nearly pitched in steadying himself with his knees bent in a wide stance and arms outstretched. It struck him then, as it had many times before since setting out, how tenuous this all was, all of his belongings waterlogged, or worse, lost forever with one misstep; the pack, the ziplock of change, the emergency cans, a roll of the dice away from slipping into oblivion. He was always a roll of the dice away from ruin. He wondered what he would do then, when he had no food, no clothes, no loose change, when he literally had nothing. He thought all this as he calmly slide-stepped across the plank to the other side, and as he scampered up the short hill to the road it occurred to him that he'd probably have no alternative but to turn to crime.

After waiting only an hour or so at the General Store, he got a ride in the back of a pickup truck with six or seven other men heading to Chinle to work. The truck was a Toyota, low to the ground, with a plastic bedliner. The sides of the bed were slick with moisture, and Tom lost his grip and tumbled into the bed. The men gave a forgiving laugh and handed him his pack, which had rolled into the mud. Tom laughed with them, laughed at himself, with himself; he'd sacrificed pride a long time ago.

The engine started like a whisper, the low purring of a loving mum, a small pickup that could still carry a load. In these conditions the driver was not in a hurry. The forks and coiled springs groaned a little under the weight, but at twenty miles an hour no damage was being done; it could run forever. It felt good to be moving. Immediately out of town the dirt road became a minefield of potholes filled with rainwater. The truck snaked around them, veering from one side of the road to the other, trying to pick the clearest path and avoid bottoming out. The men were grateful. Each bump, misjudgment, or lapse in concentration letting the speed get too great sent the men in the bed crashing into each other and the ones sitting on the sides of the thin metal rail of the truck bed holding on for dear life. No one was in a hurry.

The desert was beautiful at twenty miles an hour, the air damp but fresh, thick with sage and yucca. Hardpan and arroyos turned soft under the rare but much needed desert rain. The rain picked up in earnest, and gusts of wind stung with surprising cold. Tom tilted his face up to the sky and felt the pure rain pelt his skin. He imagined the road filth draining from the hard creases and lines his face had formed over the past years. A poor man's shower, his matted hair so greasy the water clung rather than ran through. He knew it wouldn't do much for the smell, but it felt good.

The sky was a white-gray wall of rolling, swelling clouds. The mesas and mountains that marked the boundary of earth were invisible. The boxed-in effect confined the world, restraining it to the immediate consciousness. Jostling in the back of the Toyota with the ebb and flow of the road, Tom imagined a life raft adrift on the ocean. But this was the desert, and the desert commanded attention. All around the visible spectrum from the road until the gray reached the ground, life, long left dormant, emerged, hibernating for just such an occasion. Green sprigs next to columns of long yellow thistle grass. Over the splashing beneath the tires Tom could hear the cactus drinking.

After two hours of twenty mph and weaving around the worst of the potholes and rocks, they intersected a two-lane blacktop highway. The last twenty yards were the toughest for the little rear-wheel drive Toyota. The highway was built up with fill to elevate it off the desert floor for drainage and to thwart blowing sand drifts, and the rear wheels spun to crest the lip of the asphalt and skid a harsh right turn onto the highway.

The Toyota accelerated slowly, a fine mist spraying behind it. The men nodded to each other and started rearranging and gathering up their things. Most of the workers carried small day packs or plastic grocery bags with the day's belongings. A few minutes later they passed the telltale signs of a town—a gas station, a tractor supply, aluminum sided storage bins, rusty water tower, decaying fencework, and the odd yellow or brown leafed tree.

It was a gray town on a gray day. Tom felt a little pinch of apprehension in his gut as the truck slowed down, the uncertainty of a ride ending and having to get a new ride, decisions to make, life back in his control rather then the driver's. Buildings appeared on both sides of the road, low, one and two story, some boarded up with plywood windows. The truck stopped in a parking lot rutted with broken asphalt behind a hardware and feed store. The driver, a large Indian man, got out and stretched. The men each gave him two dollars. Tom gave the man eight quarters.

The men shuffled across the parking lot and huddled under

a corrugated tin awning next to the metal back door to the hardware store. Tom followed. He lit a half-smoked GPC.

What are you waiting for? Tom lobbed the question towards the center of the group.

Work. They send a van to take us to the mine.

Tom twitched. The mine? Isn't that in the other direction, north?

It's on the Hopi reservation. South of here.

What do you mine?

Coal. But we don't mine. We work the pipe, mix the coal with water. They ship it that way, across many miles, to the cities.

They were silent for a moment, listening to the rain.

You want work? We could ask.

Would they hire me? I mean for a few days?

The man who had been answering shrugged.

We're Navajo. If the Hopi hire us they would hire a white man.

The other men mumbled their agreement.

Tom nodded. He stood at the edge of the circle, not quite under the awning. He felt the rain at his back. He daydreamed for a while, thinking about a paycheck, a few days work, what he could do with a hundred dollars. He imagined a little white envelope with crisp twenties, so new they stuck together. But they'd all be embedded with electronic strips, like all the money nowadays. Even out here he'd be traced in under eight hours. In twelve he'd probably be dead. Anyway, he couldn't waste the time working. He was close. He had come this far. He had to keep moving. The change bag would either last, or it wouldn't.

He made a spontaneous gesture that was a mix of a Hindu Namaste, with hands clasped together as in prayer, and an old west salute.

Take care.

The men nodded and watched him walk into the rain.

He walked around the side of the building and set his pack next to a brown stucco wall under the overhang of the roof, just out of the rain. He dug deep into his pack and fished out a badly crumpled and creased army green plastic poncho. He put the pack back on and did his best to stretch the poncho over his body and the pack. He tucked his hair under the hood and walked to the road. He looked left and right. Smooth, wet, blacktop. He walked on the gravel shoulder through town. He passed a defunct Indian curio shop and Mexican restaurant with two pick-ups parked around the side. He held out his thumb as a few cars and an eighteen-wheeler passed, but he didn't turn to face them. Experience had taught him that no one picked people up in town. A half mile to the next string of businesses and then unevenly spaced streets leading to shuttered homes every quarter mile or so. It was at least three miles before he felt he was at the edge of town and stood toward traffic and stuck out his thumb.

The poncho was a good move. He was picked up by the first vehicle he faced down, a late model Range Rover. It wasn't lost on him that with the poncho on, he might not look like a bum. He could be anybody with the bad luck to have to hitchhike in the rain.

The passenger side window descended automatically and a friendly voice asked where he was going. Tom didn't know, because he didn't know exactly where he was, but he knew he was in Arizona, so rather than scare the man with something like, 'down the road,' he said 'Phoenix,' the only town he could think of in under a second.

Hop in.

He looked at the upholstered interior, clean, practically manicured. He could smell the freshness of the air inside, the new car smell of another class, another world that he dimly remembered.

Hold on, I don't want to mess up your car.

He pulled off the poncho and unstrapped the pack. He got in the front seat and awkwardly pushed his pack and poncho into the narrow back seat.

He shut the door.

Safe.

The car started to move.

Don't worry. Been camping for the last two weeks, gonna clean it out when I get home. The car didn't look like it. Tom felt like he'd been camping for two years, and there was no getting clean.

Paul.

Tom.

They shook hands. The truck bounced back onto the highway and accelerated. They cleared the last remnants of the town in less than a minute and headed out into the desert. Out of town they rounded a hill, the few trees faded to none and they settled on a flat plain stretching to sights unseen. Towns always seemed to be placed around some feature with a benefit, no matter how slight, a hill, a clump of trees, but the spaces in between were truly no man's land.

So where you been camping?

Chapter 10

Despite Lorne's obvious deficiencies, he was not an uncharismatic man. He was young, but he almost always got along with people with all manner of experience. To his credit, he never misused this ability.

About the time that Hailey was being harassed by Larry McCabe and made her escape from the Barking Spider, Lorne sunk into his chair, the small room in the small house somewhere in the wasteland smelling like burnt aluminum, his eyes as glassy as the stuffed elk's head hanging above the door at the Tavern, and he felt fear akin to the same fear Hailey was feeling, not fear exactly, but dread. The one who'd been sitting on the couch named Chevis was wheeling around the room with a .357 magnum. He stalked in circles with long strides stepping on the couch and then leaping back onto the floor talking with his hands and jabbing the revolver at whomever he was talking to like he was shanking them in the gut, sweat pulsing from his closely shaved head. At least the gun wasn't loaded, Lorne thought, or it hadn't been before; now there was no way to be sure.

They had all plateaued. They weren't going up anymore, but they were a long way from coming down. Lorne couldn't remember when he'd stopped talking about Tom and his mission and when the others had picked up the trails and woven them into a plan, a philosophy that became a plan. It was a plan that could only be hatched at four in the morning, that only was ever hatched at four in morning. They would go intercept Tom at the Hoover Dam. Help him defeat the terrorists, or at least witness the fiasco. It all made sense. And they had nothing better to do.

Lorne took another hit of meth off the pipe, and the feeling of dread passed. And then it came back. And then it was gone again.

We should to get his car running, Pam said, gesturing with her thumb at Lorne like she was hitchhiking.

That sounded good to Lorne.

We have an obligation to uphold…a duty…a tradition, Chevis said, spinning toward Lorne and pointing the .357 at his chest like he was working a Powerpoint presentation. Lorne stared directly into the barrel. It looked dark and wide. A bare light bulb reflected off of the silver chamber.

I know someone who's good with cars, the boy said.

It's probably just out of gas. Pammy rolled on her axis. Why else would they stop here?

Do you know why we Navajo are the first to sign up for the army and fight in all of the wars? Chevis shook the gun at Lorne like he was trying flick dogshit off his finger.

You're warriors, Lorne said, finding his grin, and then not sure if he was being respectful, tried his best to look stoic.

Bullshit. It's because we signed a treaty. The treaty says there will be peace between the Navajo nation and the United States of America and that either side will come to the defense of the other in war.

Jimmy, the Indian at the end of the couch who moved little except to touch knuckles with Pam and looked like he had never cut his hair, not once, croaked his only words of the evening.

That's why each tribe sends soldiers to the army. We are holding up our side of the bargain.

Right on brother, Lorne said, sliding away from the hot

glare of the revolver and pointing at Jimmy with both his hands, thumbs up and index fingers out, in the shape of pistols.

Jimmy smiled yellow teeth and pointed back at him, a little glistening trail of spittle winding its way through his scraggly goatee.

This shit's not funny.

Chevis pointed the .357 at the ceiling and pulled the trigger a half dozen times inducing a half dozen dry clicks. The gun wasn't loaded. Lorne had been right the first time.

We're gonna fuck those terrorists up.

Chevis was born Charles Wilson Begay, but for as long he could remember people called him Chevis. Also for as long as he could remember he knew why people called him Chevis—because his mother drank Chivas Regal whenever she could get someone to buy her a drink at JJ's Roadhouse on highway 160 a couple miles off the res and a couple more miles outside of Second Mesa. That way people could say, boy that woman really loves her Chevis in clear conscience, a Navajo sort of joke. Chevis knew his name was meant as joke, but he never tried to get people to call him anything else. He figured there were worse things to be named after.

He had many memories of JJ's Roadhouse from his youth, or at least of the backseat of his mother's Chevy Nova parked behind JJ's Roadhouse, which was his playpen for the long hours of the evenings and, more often that not, his bed. Whatever else that experience did, it fostered a love of cars, which lead to the seminal event of his life. When he was sixteen he stole a tourist's Ford Mustang left idling at the Second Mesa Gas and Gifts and was arrested twenty minutes and thirty miles down 160 West. He was unlucky in that he was pulled over a dozen miles off the res, so rather than being pulled over by Navajo Tribal Police and taken to Navajo Tribal Court where the incident may have been treated differently, he was arrested by a State Trooper and tried in Mohave County as an adult and sentenced to fifteen months in Florence State Penitentiary. It was the defining moment of his life because it meant two things. First, he couldn't get into the army, since even though the army had drastically relaxed their recruiting standards because of the shortage of troops needed for Iraq, they still weren't taking convicted felons, and second, in prison he learned how to make and use methamphetamine.

Upon his release he found he had sole ownership of his mother's small house and his little brother, whom he only called Junior. Unbeknownst to Chevis, he had spent the last three months of his sentence less than a hundred yards from his mother who had begun serving an eighteen year sentence at Florence for vehicular manslaughter. She had fallen asleep at the wheel after an evening drinking Chevis Regal at JJ's and hit a minivan head on, killing the other driver and two of the three children in the backseat.

Junior didn't have Chevis's childhood, mostly because of Jimmy and Pam. Instead of playing by himself in the back of the Chevy Nova, Junior walked the hills and explored the mesas and canyons with Jimmy, hunting rabbits, and whitetail deer if they were lucky, and looking for antlers or uniquely shaped pieces of wood to carve into bottle openers and other trinkets. They also looked for turquoise, topaz and obsidian to make jewelry, sometimes with cheap silver if they had enough money, otherwise with thirty-gauge copper wire. They also looked for peyote and mushrooms that grew briefly after the monsoon rains, if the rains came. Pot they had to buy or trade for.

Pammy worked as a cook at a Barbecue joint in Tuba City midweek, driving the two hundred miles round trip to come home on the weekends with bags of pulled pork, baked beans, and black-eyed peas with dirty rice. On weekends they ate and she smoked meth, or glass as it was called at present.

Meth didn't affect Junior as it did the others, it was just another way to find his center, calmed him, but without the hallucinations and perversions of reality that peyote and mushrooms caused. It made the others act like they were tripping when they weren't. Sometimes this amused the boy, but mostly he stayed out of the way, especially when they'd been up for several days on end.

When Chevis returned, he was happy to find the home occupied by Junior, Jimmy, and Pam. Of course he claimed the only bedroom in the house—after fifteen months in the joint, he deserved it. But he'd also grown accustomed to not being alone. He was hurt that his mother was not there, but the hurt was vastly overshadowed by the feeling of freedom and violence that surged through him upon his release from Florence. He had always been pretty good at school, Junior too, but the idea of a straight job was ridiculous now, even if there were any jobs to be had, which there weren't. There was only one thing to do, make meth, which could be made out of ingredients that were readily available: Sudafed, baking powder, liquid Drano, and rat poison. Prison had taught him one thing, he didn't owe anybody anything, and getting out of prison gave him the most incredible feeling of his life—that he could do anything. Anything.

We're gonna fuck those terrorists up.

Chevis was feeling the inner power that comes from prison and meth, and what he wanted at the moment was to be the soldier that the United States government wouldn't let him be. Prison gave him the strength. Meth made everything draw into this singular moment and make the present be the past and the future too.

Come on motherfuckers!

Everyone laughed.

Chevis had an evil grin. Lorne knew what it meant. He was feeling good now. Time to saddle up.

You want to hit the road? Pammy had bloody eyes. She shook her head like she was saying no but she was saying yes.

We need to get his car working, Junior said with a distant smile, nodding at Lorne.

Junior, go see what's wrong with it. Chevis gave the order like he was platoon commander.

The boy went out the front door, letting in the first rays of dawn.

We'll need money, Chevis said, holding the gun flat against the side of his face, as if the feel of cold steel helped him think.

How much money do you have?

Lorne flipped open his wallet.

Thirteen bucks.

That's it? I thought Junior said you had money? Where's Junior?

The boy was outside.

Well, I gave you my last two twenties for the shit, you know.

Chevis nodded his head vigorously and waived at him dismissively, already digesting and plotting.

Yeah, yeah, don't worry, we're good. But shit, it's not enough. How much shit you got?

Plenty, why?

Sell it.

Shit, Pammy jumped in, don't you think we would if we could? A few tweakers come by to score, but most of the people who are into it out here make their own. It's not rocket science. I mean we get by, but it's no empire.

I know a guy who'd buy. As usual Lorne's mouth got ahead of him. Another surge of dread hit Lorne, panic almost, but then it passed. He always heard the voice that warned him not to do things, and he almost always ignored it.

Chevis cocked a wry smile.

I knew you came here for a reason.

Lorne was thinking of Bullfrog Frank who ran a small bar

in Alpine, a good hundred and fifty miles to the south east, not far from the Arizona/New Mexico line.

The screen door slapped open and shut, and they all snapped their heads. The boy was back.

I think it's just out of gas. I'll go siphon some out of the weed whacker.

The gas powered weed whacker along with a saw and two pairs of work gloves had been Jimmy's idea to try and get some work clearing the brush and undergrowth around the tourist cabins and second homes in the mountains around Pinetop, where there was a casino and a ski area. People had to create fire-safe spaces around their homes to make them defensible against forest fires. If they didn't they would be the fire fighter's last priority, not worth the effort and resources. A huge fire had swept through the year before, burning over a million acres, and there was plenty of work. But when Pammy's car died so did the plan. No way to get there. The weed whacker primarily served as a fuel storage container; this was not the first time they'd siphoned gas from it, although Jimmy kept the brittle yellowed thistle stalks trimmed for twenty yards around the perimeter of the house so they'd be safe from brush fires, even if there wasn't enough desert grass here to spread a fire. Too much rock and sand.

Chevis sent Junior out to get the car started. When they heard the Chevy's big 350 roar to life they poured out of the little house, shielding their faces from the daylight and donning sunglasses. Chevis got behind the wheel. Lorne figured it was because of his foot, but Chevis hadn't asked. Pammy rode shotgun on account of her size. Lorne was relegated to the backseat in between skinny Jimmy and a skinnier Junior.

Chevis plowed through the wind blown sand bar that had built up around the Malibu over the last day and fishtailed down the dirt and gravel road. They had just enough gas to make it to the nearest town where they hit rain. They bought a five gallon red plastic container of gasoline from the General Store. There were no pumps in town. Chevis emptied the container into the tank, smoking a cigarette and thumping his hand on the roof of the Malibu to Snoop Dogg pumping from the dashboard tape deck—As the sun rotates and my game grows bigger, how many bitches want to fuck this nigga?

The road worsened outside of town, turning muddy and deeply pitted. Chevis scarcely lightened up on the pedal, the weight in the car helping to keep it on the road. Mud splattered the length of the car and completely covered the back window. The air inside the Malibu was thick with condensation broken only when Pammy cracked the window to vent the continual exhalations of white smoke.

When they reached State Route 160 they turned left and headed east. The were not far from where Chevis's life had taken its fateful turn in the stolen Mustang five years back, and not far from Tom, who was at this moment heading the opposite direction on 160 West.

The desert was gray and desolate, and in the cocoon of the car it made Lorne feel as if they were hidden somehow, even if in reality four Indians and Lorne passing a glass pipe in a rusted and mud sprayed Chevy Malibu was far from invisible. As they ate up miles on 160 East, the rain lightened and eventually stopped. They passed through Kayenta and Dinnetiotso without slowing down. The only landmark at Cow Springs was a gas station that had burnt down, blackened walls uneven, left to melt, a fire that had been allowed to burn itself out. A thirty foot blue and white sign read $1.17 a gallon. They turned south at Navajo Route 59 just short of the truck stop town of Mexican Water, which they rode to the intersection of State Route 191 at Many Farms. To the right mountains potted with red cliffs and stunted pinions, to the left an occasional trailer and hogan adrift on a sea of desert expanse. A half dozen cattle stood in a sliver of shade against a sandstone butte not more than fifty yards off the road. They cruised along at an even eighty, bouncing on the rolling gray asphalt with no centerline. A few miles before Many Farms, a black and white Arizona Department of Transportation road sign that would have read:

REDUCE
SPEED
AHEAD

had letters strategically blotted out with white paint so it read:

RED
PEE
AHEAD

Many Farms looked like a dozen reservation towns they had passed, with its government built houses with alternating blue, red, and green roofs laid out in a repeating pattern. No other buildings. A town with no stores. A suburb without shopping.

They turned right on State Route 191, and traffic slowed though Chinle, a clog of tractors and pickups in no hurry on the two lane double yellow-line. At Chinle they had to slow down as half a dozen cows crossed the road, or rather, began to cross and then stopped to stare at the cars, unattended, before meandering back to the shoulder to graze on the sprouts of snakeweed and brittlebush. The only traffic light in town, at the intersection on Navajo Route 64, was blinking yellow. Jimmy elbowed Lorne, who was in the middle backseat riding bitch.

Down that way's Canyon de Chelle.

Canyon de what?

Nevermind.

Seventy miles past Chinle the landscape transformed from

barren desert to grassy prairie leading to pine forests. Basalt, red mesas and jagged rock outcroppings were replaced by mountains steeped in evergreens arching to blue sky and fast moving white puffy clouds. They steadily gained elevation and rolled down the windows to take in the fresh air—at eight thousand feet it was cool and crisp. Junior smiled. Jimmy nodded in agreement.

The road cut into trees along the mountainsides following a river down below.

Chevis snuffed out another cigarette in the ashtray.

This guy's going to be there, right?

Should be.

He don't have a cell phone? You can't call him?

Hell, I don't have a cell phone.

Me neither.

They all laughed. It seemed funny at the time.

The woods thickened and the tops of the pines obscured the sun. The trees cast long thin shadows across the road that washed over the car at dizzying speed, creating a strobe light effect in the back of Lorne's dilated pupils that he found paralyzing. For a moment that lasted a lifetime, Lorne forgot where he was. And then the mountains parted, and the river widened into a long meadow that filled the valley. The road pulled away from the river and through the meadow to the town of Alpine. Alpine sat on the tip of the meadow in the crease of a new mountain range that guarded the border with New Mexico, at the intersection of 191 South and 180 East. A small collection of buildings along a single street, 180 East, which lead to New Mexico fifteen miles away. There were no stoplights, or sidewalks, or any indication that any one lived here except for jeep trails and wagon tracks that led to homes somewhere in the forest. They slowed down to take the turn onto 180 East. The meadow sloped downward all the way to the river, and 180 East was a steep rippled street, with a bar, two restaurants, a gas station, and a souvenir shop in lock step up the grade. They drove uphill through town and pulled onto the dirt shoulder.

A sign read:

Luna N.M. 30
Albuquerque 256

Well, where to?

Oh, it's back that way, a roadhouse off 191.

So why didn't you say something earlier?

I thought you'd want to see the town.

Shit.

All right, turn around. It's just down there. Let's get some beers.

Just past the intersection of 191 South and 180 East, a dirt road led down into the meadow and opened into a large dirt parking lot next to a pinewood box with a short chimney belching greasy smoke that must have been the place. Three pickups were parked randomly in the lot. Chevis pulled the Malibu up to a wooden fence in front of the building, the kind you tie your horse to. A Coors sign glowed red behind a half-pulled shade and a dark smoked window. A sign on the front door read 'NRA Parking Only.'

Chevis paused to read the sign on the door and gave Lorne a crooked look. The wooden door creaked open, and they filed inside. A half-dozen locals were perched at the wrap-around bar in the center of the room. They all turned to look at the newcomers. All conversation stopped. Two men in jeans and pressed checkered shirts and a woman with stringy white hair stopped drinking in mid-sip. The woman, grandmotherly, round puffy face behind thick glasses above a flowered blouse, jean jacket, and lime-green stretch pants, smiled ironically and slowly shook her head like now she'd seen everything. Two men with their backs to the door lowered the brims of their cowboy hats down over their eyes.

Bullfrog Frank was unmistakable. He stood behind the bar with thick arms crossed and a disbelieving grin on his face. He looked different to Lorne, worse than before, but instantly recognizable. What had started as a baseball-sized goiter on the right side of his neck had either evened out or spread across his entire neck, giving him a second, enormous chin that was best described as a bullfrog's. The name was not creative, but it was certainly descriptive. At least six foot two and 250 pounds, Bullfrog Frank leaned against the back of the bar, his huge chest and various necks settling in a loosely formed pile on top of unnaturally skinny legs in unnaturally skinny black jeans. The whole ensemble appeared to be held together by a giant oval silver belt buckle, as if without the tightly strung leather belt his torso would melt over his waist and run down to the wooden pine floor. Long thinning red hair was braided in a single ponytail that leaked from the back of a black Harley Davidson baseball cap. He smirked at them with cloudy blue eyes.

Hey, Lorne… He let the words surf on a plume of exhaled cigarette smoke. Who are your friends?

The old woman now positively beamed. She fingered a Marlboro Light One Hundred out of a crumpled pack on the bar with white painted plastic fingernails and tightened her grip on her beer mug and scooted up closer to the bar for a better view.

Lorne, Pammy, Chevis, Junior, and Jimmy spread out in the small barroom, edging around tables and looking for a place where they could gather.

How's everyone doing? Pammy announced, all three hundred pounds of her jiggling to Lynard Skynard emanating from a set of speakers just above the register.

The locals lingered their gaze and mumbled an 'okay' or a 'just fine' before turning back to their beers. The old woman said something to Frank that they didn't catch, but Frank didn't hear her; he was smiling ruefully as Lorne jitterbugged up to the bar.

Frank, good to see ya.

Lorne extended his hand. Frank slowly grabbed Lorne's hand, squeezed noticeably, and pulled him toward him until he was halfway across the bar so they were face to face.

Didn't think I'd see you again. What are you doing here? Frank twisted his face and got even closer.

Business, Lorne croaked, his hand starting to throb.

Paying me back what you owe?

Lorne's damaged mind turned this over and came to a startling realization. He did owe Frank money. He knew there was a reason he hadn't been to Alpine in a while.

Better.

Better than paying me back?

Better than money.

Frank relaxed his grip, and Lorne hunched down over a barstool.

Okay, Lorne. You can live a little longer.

Lorne belly-laughed, slapping his knee, overdoing it, and looked over his shoulder.

Frank stared at him with dead eyes.

Hey, can we get a couple of pitchers of beer over here? Chevis said.

Frank stiffened his neck, smoothing the folds of his chins into one gigantic bulbous sheath of flesh.

No minors in the bar, Chief.

I'll wait in the car, Junior said.

Chief? Chevis repeated, squaring up.

Pammy squinted distastefully.

The old woman let out an audible 'Ha.'

Lorne, why don't you and the tribe go wait at my place, Frank said, never taking his eyes off Chevis.

Help yourselves to the beer in the fridge.

Okay, Frank. Come on guys, Lorne said, overanxious to get out before someone did something stupid.

They shuffled out of the bar making an inordinate amount of noise moving chairs out of the way, boots on the hardwood floor.

Y'all come back now, someone said as they were halfway out the door, followed by laughter.

They got in the car.

Rednecks.

Yup.

You got a purty mouth.

Squeal like a pig boy, Lorne joined in, and they all slapped hands and hooted and hollered as Chevis floored it, and the Malibu tore out of the parking lot leaving behind a hail of dirt and stones and a plume of dust that billowed over the shotgun shack and filled the valley.

Lorne guided them a few miles down 191 South to a narrow jeep trail that lead to a doublewide trailer deep in the woods. They unpiled from the car to the smell of dew and pine trees. The woods were quiet except for the sound of a generator running in a small pre-fab shed next to a rusted propane tank. A crow cawed from nearby. They stood and stretched.

Should we go in?

Frank said to.

Lorne tried the door expecting it to be locked, but it wasn't. The door was light, and he pulled too hard. Like all trailer doors, it bent flimsily; he didn't know why this one would be any different. They wiped their feet on the Astroturf doormat and went inside. The trailer was cluttered and dark, lit by a television and a florescent light in the kitchen. It was so dark that they had found the fridge and passed around beers before they noticed the girl stretched out on a couch, maybe sixteen, bare legs, boy shorts and a wife-beater tank top, her head resting on her elbow, watching them with faint amusement.

Can I help you?

Spread out around the island of the couch were piles of fashion magazines, video game disks for the X-Box, potato chip wrappers, used Kleenex, and empty diet Pepsi cans.

Bullfrog Frank, I mean, Frank…told us to wait here for him.

Said we could drink his beer, Chevis said, holding an open beer.

By all means. Mi casa es su casa.

Chestnut bangs falling just above green eyes. Lorne stared open-mouthed.

I'm Ashley. She shook Lorne's hand, then Chevis's, then Jimmy's, and finally Junior's.

Well, aren't you a treat. Pammy cooed and brought her hands up to her cheek like she was ogling a newborn baby. Are you the Keeper of the Glass in this shithole?

Why, you got any? Ashley arched an eyebrow with practiced expertise.

Well, why else would we be here sweetie? Pammy passed her the glass bowl. Ashley took a hit, held it in, exhaled deeply and searched for her pack of Newports resting on a Us Weekly magazine with Jessica Alba on the cover. She lit a smoke and ashed into an overflowing ceramic ashtray clearly made by a child.

You're Lorne aren't you?

How'd you know?

Well, you're the only white dude here.

Gotcha.

He's going to kill you, you know.

Lorne took a hit off the pipe and just shook his head as if he hadn't heard a thing. The others looked at each other.

We got business.

You look like quite the accomplished businessman.

What, are you and Frank together or something?

Oh yeah, we're a happy couple, she deadpanned.

What's on TV? Junior said.

Nothing, static, sometimes git the Tucson channels, but that's it.

Junior sat on the floor next to the couch in front of the TV and took off his sneakers, revealing the holes in his socks.

Salud.

Lorne held up his can of beer. The others shuffled over and touched their beer cans to his.

Hey, Ashley said, gimme a beer. I want in.

Chevis, who was closest to the fridge, handed her a beer. She got up on her knees on a brown plaid couch cushion and pushed her can into all of theirs.

Cheers.

Lorne bent over to take a look at her ass perched up on heels of her feet. She shot him a look which shook her hair into her eyes. Lorne didn't know if she meant it or not.

Chevis rambled into the kitchen, opining fake oak cabinets and letting them slam shut.

You got any food?

The girl appeared to be watching her fingers closely.

There's venison in the ice box. Frank got a deer last season, but it's frozen solid. Want me to take some steaks out to thaw?

Umm, Chevis grunted non-committal.

We won't be here long enough, right Chevis? Pammy panted, her black T-shirt betraying black circles of sweat.

Umm…Chevis grunted again. We'll be here as long as it takes.

Or until the beer runs out, Lorne snorted.

Chevis, drawn tight as a trip wire, leaped over a vinyl footrest, poorly upholstered, and grabbed Lorne under the armpits, pinning all two hundred plus pounds of him to the buckling aluminum wall.

You're a bad Soldier. Don't forget The Mission.

Pammy and Jimmy watched without seeing. Junior didn't look up from the television.

Ashley sucked in her cheeks and whooshed out a low whistle.

Cuckoo…she said under her breath, rolling her eyes with a sardonic smile.

But Chevis dropped Lorne into a crumpled heap on the floor and the incident was forgotten as soon as it began. Two days without sleep, the string that held them together frayed into fuzz. They unglued and then stuck back together, their inner spheres revolving around each other and occasionally collided in the narrow trailer. The living room grew warm with body heat and the glowing coils of a space hater. Their cheeks took on a rosy hue, eyes glassy and blood red. The night sky blackened outside, far removed from city lights and hemmed in by tall pine trees and mountain silhouettes.

The beer was a benefit. It washed over them, filling in the cracks and smoothing down the rough edges. The stereo came alive, ricocheting double bass metal down the fake wood-sided narrow tube. The adults, as it were, huddled over future plans and talked in low voices. Ashley sat cross-legged behind Junior on the couch and absently braided his long black hair into cornrows as he flipped between the two grainy channels on the television. Between the black and white static was the remnants of an Arizona Diamondbacks game fighting its way across the airwaves.

Outside the wind picked up, rushing through the tall pines with a dull roar and whistling though the cracks and creases in the trailer, but nobody noticed. The pipe passed and the beer dwindled. Hours passed by like minutes. A pair of headlights illuminated the dirt streaked white aluminum trailer, stainless steel trim refracting yellow into the woods.

Chapter 11

Nothing fit. Tom turned it over in his mind. He sipped his second Sierra Nevada. He was sure he was being lulled, buttered up for the stuffing, led out to pasture. His own complicity irked him, an accomplice in his own murder, or worse. He could be in for a week of torture; a sodium amobarbital cocktail and he'd give up everything and everyone he knew. It could be in his beer already begun, or maybe it would be a quick bullet to the temple. One or two more beers at the most he'd be dulled enough to let it happen without so much as a twitch.

Through the windshield the rain varied between a frantic downpour and a misting drizzle. Adrenaline saturated his blood but it didn't show. This man hadn't been two weeks in the bush. His clean nails, floor mats vacuumed, the frame pack with zippers shiny like the day it was bought, his stubble easily planned, the trail maps and campground passes easily purchased and conveniently left in view on the dashboard. Nothing fit. The man not noticing Tom's vagrant stench which he himself found nearly unbearable. The freely offered beer. Believing in random generosity or coincidences could get you killed.

The man hit the brakes and angled the Tundra onto a dirt pullout. Tom tensed as the truck shuddered sideways on washboard ruts to a stop, wishing he had a gun, wondering why he didn't. The man turned to face him with a grin.

Gotta see a man about a horse.

Tom paused, froze.

Yeah, me too.

They exited the truck at the same time. Tom took half a dozen cautious steps. The man jogged to the edge of the pullout to take a leak where the ground ended abruptly in a few feet of grassy ravine and then a steep canyon with sandstone walls smoothly curving to an unseen bottom. The man untucked his shirt and unbuckled his belt, not even a backward glance at Tom. He was a cool customer. A pro.

Time elongated. Fractions of seconds seemed like minutes. Tom weighed his options. He could start running now down the highway in the opposite direction and hope to flag someone down. But the man would simply flip a u-turn and gun him down. The man was at enough distance that he could dash to the driver's side of the truck and speed away. It was an automatic, so no chance for a nervous stall that would seal his death. But the man would call 911 and he'd run into a roadblock ten miles down the road. Nowhere to run out in the desert.

No, this man had to die. He had to die quietly and unnoticed, without time to call for help.

The sun momentarily peeked under the blanket of gray cloud cover and turned the sandstone red, the cliffs worn sheer as a millstone by eons of rain and winds. The man's long arch of piss free fell into the canyon. Tom had to act fast. Now. Push him into the canyon. One shove and his was safe, and with the truck to boot. Innocent lives counted on it, and this man was not innocent.

He broke into a run but his mind was working faster than his body. He put too much weight on his front foot and slipped in the dirt, which had turned to paste in the rain. His knee hit first and then his hands. He rose with both palms full of mud, and as he did he froze for two reasons. One, his fall had caught the man's attention, who seemed to be suppressing a belly laugh, and two, an unmarked cruiser rounded the bend in the road and seemed to be barreling straight toward him. Through the tinted windows he was sure the woman driving was staring right at him.

The man loped back to the truck.

Easy old-timer. Beer getting to you? Not your first sip of the day?

It wasn't until Tom was back in the Range Rover, wiping the mud from between his fingers onto his pant legs that he thought, Old-timer? He was thirty-six years old. He must really look like shit. What happened to me? Tom kept his head down until the first intersection with another road, Route 7, running south just shy of Tonalea, and he abruptly asked to be let out.

Suit yourself, the man said, holding out his hand and then thinking better of it.

Tom opened the door, conscious that he would be vulnerable exiting the truck, willing himself to expect a bullet to the back of the head, but he wasn't sure anymore. He almost wanted it to happen. He stepped onto the soft muddy shoulder. The red clay sticking to his boots. He watched the Tundra disappear down the two-lane road until it was out of sight. He'd almost killed a civilian, and in a horrible way. The look of terror and confusion as the man free fell three hundred feet to a gruesome death. The image of the murder that hadn't happened burned into his brain. He physically slapped himself in the side of the face, but it wouldn't go away. And then he had seen the unmarked cruiser. Coincidence or timing? He walked down the pavement on the painted white line, gravel crunching under his boots. The wind blew in the chaparral. A strange feeling grew. The man had been an operative. They let him live because it was more useful to watch him, flush out other agents. Maybe that's what they did. The woman in the cruiser. She could have been his backup. They wouldn't tell him of course, how could they? Jesus, she was probably already dead. The thought sent an involuntary shiver up his spine. He found the sensation disturbingly exhilarating.

A time passed before he realized that a red Honda Accord had pulled onto the shoulder ahead of him. A woman took him to Leupp, a reservation town, a hundred or so tightly circled government built houses braced against windswept desert. The chaff from an abandoned strip mine dusting over the town. Since there were no gas stations, or businesses of any kind, she left him at the chapter house standing next to a forty foot yellow backlit road sign that read nothing. The wind rushed long and low across the empty expanse. San Francisco peaks to the East, yellow sand cut by sporadic dirt tracks leading into the far reaches of all the other directions.

The first vehicle he saw, a rancher in an eighties era F-150, took him an hour south to Winslow. Rather than trying to hitch on I-40, traffic moving at 85 miles per hour, he walked through town to 87 South, back to two-lane blacktop. To his surprise rides came fast, faster than they had since he started out. He realized it was because he was still wearing the poncho even though the rain had all but stopped, and it masked his disheveled appearance. The smell, however, couldn't be masked, at least not for long, and the rides were generally short.

The air grew muggy and warm as the road descended though canyons of carved rock, each one looking like the Grand Canyon, and off the plateau, out of the high plains. On the valley floor the rain had left fields of hearty yellow flowers flowing out from the highway, dazzling, feverish, they were probably more accurately described as a weed, a virulent dandelion perhaps, with thick green stalks and curved green barbs, rippling like an ocean to the distant hard scree and volcanic slabs. At the lower elevations the landscape grew increasingly insane. Rock formations dotted the horizon like Hershey's Kisses a half mile high, like cookie dough flicked from a giant spoon onto a sizzling pan. Tom thought of Dr. Seuss, and of how he too was probably crazy.

By nightfall he found himself in the outskirts of Phoenix, the last ride speeding away unapologetically. The night was phantasmal. A gentle breeze felt like the darting tongues of a thousand cats. The air, thick and humid, made the light sticky, and it clung to street lamps forming white balls against the black sky.

After a few minutes the heat became unbearable. He stripped down to a dingy brown T-shirt that had once been white, and piled the remnants onto his pack. With the poncho, wool coat, hooded sweatshirt, and long sleeve thermal strapped onto the top of his pack, he looked like a Sherpa beginning an ascent as he started out toward the glowing skyscrapers in the center of the valley of light.

He hopped over a guardrail and crossed a sterile dirt field studded with a few clumps of bunch grass and creosote to the nearest clutter of street lights. Like everything in the desert, distances were longer than they appeared. An hour later, Tom pulled himself over a concrete wall into a subdivision. He aimed toward the city center, planning to hitch north again when it was feasible, heading toward the dam, always to the dam.

The streets curved and spiraled. He followed the contours of the sidewalks, passed yards landscaped with gravel and cactus, getting lost in cull de sacs and enjoying the randomness of the streets. He found his way out of the maze, the entrance marked by a boulder engraved with the words Skyview Estates in a manicured rock garden.

An empty road stretched a good two miles without a single traffic light. He cinched up his pack and walked. Atop a small rise, the valley stretched out below. An orange moon, almost full, hovered above the downtown florescent pillars, the radiant orb barely squeezing between the barren mountains, ringing the city ablaze with pinpoints of light like the stars in the sky if they could been seen. Once in a while a late model sedan or a new SUV buzzed passed on the straight stretch of road. He felt his legs winding down, the product of a long day and many miles without food. A mile in he could make out a set of gates and a glass enclosed booth. He uncinched his pack for minute and paused to catch his breath, trying to gauge if the guard booth was manned or not. It seemed likely it was. He hopped a low concrete curb and bushwhacked through a stand of chaparral onto a dirt field dotted with cactus underfoot. He skirted a few conical anthills by the light of the orange moon using the distant freeway as a guide. He caught a trail used by animals and migrants and came upon a burnt black fire ring a good distance from the wall of the next subdivision. He let his pack fall without ceremony. He took a deep breath, feeling his chest free of the weight. He gathered some bramble off the ground to make a fire in the fire pit. He snapped off two handfuls of twigs close to the twisted dry truck of a stunted Russian Olive and plucked another handful of undersprigs of sage to use as kindling. The light was still pretty good from the moon. He watched a prairie dog rear on its hind legs, sniff the air, and dive into its hole. He pushed the kindling into a pyramid in the center of the oft-used fire pit and lit it with his lighter and eased in the thin branches and knotted limbs of the Russian Olive to build a small fire. The night suddenly contracted, and his peripheral vision shrunk to the small circumference of the firelight. It was quiet save for the echo of the eighteen-wheelers on the freeway, strangely rhythmic and calming. A blackness that could be seen surrounded the fire pit. He listened to the twigs crackle. He could hear nothing from the subdivision.

He opened the pack and pulled out his clothes and his emergency cans and his bag of change. He had a can of corn, a can of green beans, and a can of chunk light tuna. The tuna, he thought, was doubtful. It had been in there a long time. He set the can of corn and the can of green beans atop the fire. He smelled the clothes from the pack for mildew, detected it, and decided there wasn't much to be done other than try to shake out the wrinkles by snapping each piece taut and then laying them out on the desert floor and hanging his skivvies between the sticklike branches of a scraggly desiccated acacia. He did his best to pull his pack inside out to give it some air. When the cans were blackened and the labels burnt, he ate the green beans and the corn with a spoon and drank the water at the bottom of the cans once it was cool enough to drink. The corn was delicious. He stood and looked into the distance letting his eyes adjust to the darkness and then walked a circle with his back to the fire around the perimeter looking for any sign that he'd attracted attention. He stood still and pondered the night for some amount of minutes and returned to the now dying fire and sat down crosslegged on his outstretched coat and counted the bag of change. Most of the silver was nickels. Dimes were valuable and quarters were little nuggets of gold. He had fistfuls of pennies. It amounted to twenty-six dollars and ninety-seven cents. He ziplocked the bag airtight, stuffed it under the coat, and went to sleep.

He awoke just before dawn, the night sky slowly drawing away at the edges, the silhouettes of mountains appearing against an emerging band of pale blue. He became aware of the familiar sound of tractor-trailers on the interstate. A line of headlights consolidated from the east down valley along I-10 from Tucson. The pale blue light cast the desert in a soft blue hue. He stood, stretched, and lit a half-smoked GPC. He watched a trickle of red bulbous ants brave the white and gray ashes of the fire pit to get at the spent cans. The wall surrounding the subdivision was closer than it had appeared at night. His clothes were strewn about like the remnants of a house sucked into the heavens by a tornado. He flicked the cigarette into the fire pit and gathered up his clothes and shook them out and folded them neatly like they'd been freshly laundered. He counted out three dollars of change for his pocket and replaced the bag of change in the bottom of the pack. He packed the backpack tightly and fit everything in except for the coat, which he lashed onto the top, and his canteen, which he let dangle off the back by a nylon cord. The desert lightened from blue to pink to yellow, and the sound of traffic on the freeway intensified, and the freshness of the morning air dissipated, any crispness gone humid. He drank the last of the water from his canteen, saddled up the pack, and started walking. He followed the wall of the subdivision, meandering around the dust-hidden cactus, thorned shrubs, and partially subterranean agave, invisible in the flat graveled gap between the interstate and the outer suburbs.

The wall ended at a road that led to another walled subdivision with a guard and a gate, and he stayed out in the wasteland, walking past that subdivision and yet another until the sun was high in its arc and thirst drove him to climb over the eight foot concrete block wall and enter back into the world of men. He pushed his pack over the wall and heard it land with a thud and then dropped himself over. He landed on the yellowed lawn of a backyard of a three bed, two and a half bath ranch style. The house had an empty feel. He lifted his pack off a now crushed viburnum and walked around the side of the house and looked in the windows. No furniture inside. A for sale sign in the front yard. He shuffled back to the backyard and searched through some tall weeds alongside the house for the water spigot. It was dry and rusted around the wheel. He twisted it open but no water came out. He walked out into a wide cul-de-sac. He followed the streets watching for signs of life. There were for sale or foreclosed signs on about every third house and only one or two parked cars on each block. He checked the spigots on the side or in the back of the houses that had padlocks on the front doors and were clearly empty, and the water had been turned off on all of them. His face pulsed with his heartbeat. It felt red.

On a street with no cars in any of the driveways, he chanced going into the backyard of a house without a for sale sign. The yard was covered with white crushed stones, no weeds. Under the stilts of a white painted back porch, he found the spigot and filled his canteen from the metal tap. The water was warm as bathwater. He stuck his head under the tap and let the water make its way through his hair and beard. He drank from the canteen, filled it back up again, and scuttled into the backyard of the adjacent house that appeared abandoned. He stretched out in a thin strip of shade next to the house and drank deep and heavy from the canteen. The pounding in his temples subsided. He put his head on his pack and lay flat and smoked a cigarette.

Midday. The rectangle of shade narrowed and then disappeared. He slung the pack and started out again across the subdivision. He was immediately sweating, his skin growing blotchy and irritated. The heat did something to his clothes so that they gathered and bunched in the wrong places. Within a few blocks he began to tire again, but he plodded through, caught a second wind, and kept walking. Sweat dried and ran again fresh. It was inefficient going, the streets curved purposelessly. He followed the pattern of the plat, stamped onto the earth by a long gone developer, the circular streets filtering to a wide divided boulevard with stunted dust covered palm trees planted in a row on the median. A car came up behind him, a purple Chevy Cavalier with dark tinted windows and muffled bass. It sped up as it passed him, leaving a cloud of grit hanging in the air that swirled and stuck to his sweat creased skin. The boulevard tapered to a narrow entrance lane and exit lane with gates locked in the up position and an empty guard house with realtors' fliers taped to the windows.

He followed the road outside the subdivision for at least a mile before coming to a scaffolding of traffic lights at an intersection of two nondescript roads, seemingly too wide at six lanes each. He bore to the left and walked the road most parallel to the interstate that seemed to be heading in the general direction of Phoenix, although both roads were barren of homes and businesses and only led to the brown distance where homes and businesses presumably were. He walked along the wide empty street with occasional cars blowing by at sixty miles an hour. After a few miles he came to another display of heavy yellow traffic lights mounted on huge metallic silver steel poles at an intersection with no cross-street, only a dirt parking lot to a construction site with some cleared lots dedicated to some past or future construction. The light turned red nonetheless.

He kept walking, feeling his legs wind down. His steps were small, footing unsure. He wasn't so much hungry as weak. He sat the pack and rooted around in it for the can of tuna. His fingers shook as he opened it with the can opener. He ate the oily meat with his fingers. The grime from his hands ran down his forearms, the tuna juice acting as a solvent. He ran his fingers around the inside of the can to get the last shredded fish particles and then tossed the can on the side of the road. He saw no reason not to litter here. Everything here was litter. He slung the pack and continued.

He walked for the rest of the day. The road was a treadmill, a straight shot to nowhere. Distant objects, the mountains, buildings, and bridges were not getting any closer, instead they rotated like stars in the night sky, moving along the periphery so each time he looked up they looked different, appearing at new perceptions, until he wasn't even sure he was looking at the same thing or something totally new and unexpected. After some miles he passed a fortress wall of a neighborhood with only one gated entrance. He hoped for a gas station or a shopping mall, the start of the city, but when the wall abruptly ended he saw that it was another stretch across barren desert to the next signs of civilization. As the day waned, traffic increased, people coming home from work, but there was no sign of the heat letting up. It was the hottest part of the day. Each breath scorched his lungs. He had never inhaled heat before. The asphalt seemed to be giving off its own fumes, adding fire to the air. He felt like he was swimming in a thick oxygenated batter. He watched his arms moving slowly through the dense air, as if they were buoyed on thermals rising up from the ground. Ahead there was a long crack in the desert, a fissure that ran the breadth of the valley. It was an eroded creek bed from years when the water still ran. The road ran over it as all roads did. It took nearly an hour to reach. Tom stumbled off of the road and skidded down a red sand embankment into the riverbed and crawled onto the concrete escarpment of the overpass and into the shade. On his hands and knees, he climbed up the cool concrete incline under the road and rolled over on his back, breathing hard. He felt his face pulsing red, skin tight, peeling and flaking off. He lay there for long hours as sun went down. He was out of water. He thought he might die. But he did not.

He awoke, or at least became aware that he was awake. It was night. The sky was black. He saddled the pack and scrambled up and out of the culvert on his hands and knees, grabbing brittle weeds that easily pulled free, roots insecure in the sand. He gained the road and walked until sunup. Another dawn. It lightened imperceptibly until all at once he could see his surroundings. Traffic was lighter, maybe it was a weekend. He was into long blocks now, with streets and long walls with houses behind them. Far down the road he saw a sign perched on a staff high about the road that could only have been placed there by a gas station.

The blocks were long. He walked slowly. Crossing the long black parking lot of the Conoco station, he found he could not pick up his pace and simply had to endure the last minutes it took to get to the glass door and the air conditioning inside. He bought a plastic gallon jug of water, a tin of sardines, a box of crackers, a microwave burrito, and a Slim Jim. It cost $8.74. He sat on the curb of the parking lot and drank half of the water and ate the microwave burrito.

He rested a long while, although there really was no such thing as rest in the nuclear heat, just a slow sucking of life force. When he at least had his breath, he walked the parking lot, paying extra attention to the curb gutters and the row of newspaper boxes, and collected 17 cents and a half dozen usable butts. He sat back down and smoked two of the butts, mildly disgruntled that he had found not a single quarter around the row of newspaper dispensers, a row half as long as it should have been or once was and most of the metal boxes dispensing free rags advertising cars or hookers. No loose change around those. The decline in newsprint was bad for everyone.

He shouldered the pack and moved on. The road he traveled became marked by traffic lights at regular intervals. The sidewalk was wide, white, and uniform. The blocks were long. On each block there was some sort of strip mall, single story tubes of building divided up internally into individual shops occupying either a street corner or a rectangular box if in mid-block. Cars pulled in and parked directly in front of the building, and people went into the shops and then returned to their cars. Other than that there were no people to be seen. The sidewalks were empty. The stores had tinted windows so no one could see in. The side streets were quiet.

He walked the long street, not even attempting to hitchhike since he knew it would be futile. But he was glad to be in the city where he could find food and water when he needed to. A bank clock read 118 degrees. Its black digital screen rotating slowly on a tall pole reflected a blinding metallic glare when its corners hit the sun with each rotation. A line of cars idled at the bank's drive though lanes, windows rolled up, air conditioners on high.

He kept walking. Impossibly, the blocks grew longer, a half mile between cross streets. By late afternoon the business along the road had dwindled, replaced by industrial parks and glass encased suburban office complexes and then began the long concrete or faux stucco walls hiding unseen housing developments. The gaps between revealed alleyways to open desert. Reluctantly, he let the reality seep in that he was not in the city at all.

He stopped and looked back from where he'd come and then forward down the wide street. Nervously he finished what was left in the plastic gallon jug of water. He felt light headed, shaky. He wasn't even sure he could make it back to the last convenience store. What was it, two miles back? Four? He kept walking forward, now just hoping for shade, thinking it was ridiculous that he should die of thirst surrounded by millions of people in some nameless suburb. Not ridiculous but pitiful. Pathetic. But his next thought was that people die like this every day. The thought scared him. The immediacy of death, the unpredictability of it, the thousand little decisions that cause it. He actually started walking faster, not sure how a death like this would work. Would he suddenly die of heat stroke, or slowly wind down, feverish and delusional, not aware of what was happening to him, like a mountain climber so hypothermic he takes off his clothes like he was at the beach as the snow piles up around him. He suspected the latter. He wanted to act while he still had his wits. He needed refuge. He walked another mile, the early rush hour traffic thundering past. If he collapsed here would anyone notice? He knew the answer. Not until it was too late.

He came to a bridge over a canal. It was bone dry. At least there was shade. He made his way down under the bridge. He could hear his joints creaking, as if his limbs were held together by rubber gaskets that had dried and cracked and were on the verge of crumbling to powder.

He was not alone. Across the dusty debris strewn bottom of the dry aquifer a group of migrants clustered in the shade. Beneath the near side of the overpass a man sat on the cement incline with his elbows on his knees. He wore a floppy canvas hat with the drawstring pulled tight under his chin. He had a narrow face tanned to the color of copper and bright blue eyes. A scraggly beard revealed that he was neither young nor old. He absently searched for something in the deep pockets of his cargo pants and, not finding it, brought his knees up to his chest and refolded his hands there.

Tom lay prostrate on the concrete.

The man held up his arm in greeting like he was waiting to be noticed or called on.

Tom raised his arm and kept it perpendicular for a few seconds before letting it fall flatly outstretched at his side.

The man asked if he wanted some water. Tom's eyes lolled in their drawn sockets in the general direction of where the man was sitting. He rolled onto his shoulder and propped himself up and crawled slowly toward the man. The man tossed him a waterskin and they both drank, passing the skin back and forth.

Where you headed?

Right now?

Is there any other time?

Yeah, could be.

Okay then, right now.

North. Making my way north.

Got business to attend to?

Something like that.

People waiting on you?

I hope not.

The man nodded thoughtfully. He spit over his lower lip and wiped his mouth with a handkerchief.

Where are you heading?

The man flicked his wrist like he was shooing away a mosquito and looked absently across the aquifer.

I'm already there.

This is where you want to be?

Yup. Well, that's not entirely true. I'd like to go back to the spot under the 51 right by the church kitchen, but Eduardo told everyone I shorted him and now he wants to cut me. Got everyone pissed off at me or else I'd probably stay in the city.

Isn't this the city?

This isn't the city, this is just where the people live.

I'm trying to get through the city. Been walking for miles.

Many miles to go.

I've never seen a city like this.

Aren't they all like this?

I don't know, maybe they are nowadays.

They sat silent for a while, outstretched on the concrete slope, propped up on their elbows. A hot breeze funneled through the culvert. The migrants had a small fire going heating up coffee and a clay pot of something. The sound of the traffic overhead gradually increased to rush hour intensity without their noticing it.

Tom rested and surveyed the dry manmade concrete basin, a once natural arroyo cemented over for predictability.

Hell of a place, Tom said.

Hell of a place, the man said.

How'd we end up here?

In this place or in this life?

In this life.

It's not so bad this life. It's real. The other one is an illusion. This flask of water is real. The heat, this cement, that cockroach. Those Mexicans, they're fucking real. Up there it's just an illusion. Temporary. Imaginary. You know you don't own land. You rent it. You may have a deed, but it's not yours. You'll die, or sell it, or lose it, and then someone else will have it. For a while. But you can't keep it. There's a neighborhood called Venado Ranch less then two hundred yards from here. Look.

The man pointed to the other side of the canal where above the retaining wall there was another wall, taller and ringed with razor wire.

If you cut a straight line through that wall two hundred yards from here there's a guy sitting on a couch in a million dollar house with a patio and a pool and he doesn't even know that it's just a blip in time. He thinks that life is a series of decisions. But he's wrong. I haven't made one goddamn decision in my life.

What do you mean? You decided to stay here under the bridge, didn't you?

Yes, yes. I did decide to do that didn't I? I do get to make decisions here. You sir, are in a good place, maybe the right place.

Tom feigned a laugh. I'm fucking nowhere. I need to be four hundred miles from here.

No, no, you don't listen to what I'm saying. It's all an illusion. You're still living in that other life. You think you're up there. The man pointed with his thumb.

There's only one world.

Yes, there is only one world.

I thought you were going to tell me there are many.

No, there is only one. That is what I am saying.

So why are we separate from them?

We are because we see it for what it is.

And what is it?

It's right here. This.

And that's it.

Yes.

Don't you think some things need doing?

Is it about a woman?

No, nothing like that.

Then no.

Let's say you could do something that would help thousands, maybe millions of people. Now that's real, not some make believe alternative reality, actual people's lives. I know what you are getting at, they're all automatons up there living in ignorant bliss, pay no attention to the man behind the curtain and all that. Lab rats in a maze or hamsters spinning the wheel. Pick your metaphor. But if you had the power to save them, that wouldn't be worth doing?

The man shook his head. Can't be done. They get what they deserve and they deserve what they get. Let's be honest, mankind is destined to eat itself. If you save them this time they'll just find a way to destroy themselves a year or two from now. They'll never see the forest for the trees. It's in the nature of people to take something and run with it until either it gives up or they do. They'll use the water until it runs out and then scream and cry like the world ended and they couldn't see it coming. Like it just up and stopped raining. They'll grow so much food the land can't grow anything anymore and then fight over what's left. Trying to save mankind is an exercise in futility. It ends the same way every time.

Again, how can you say it's not worth trying?

People who try to change the world are the last people

who should try and change the world. Who knows what's best for everyone? I mean, take those Mexicans. How are you going to help them? They've got food, they've got each other, hell, they probably have jobs. Look, they even built a little fire. They're cooking food on it.

They live under a bridge.

You're not listening. Let's say someone gave them a house. Then they forget how to live under a bridge, or feel they're too good for it. Then they lose the house and have to go back to living under a bridge. Are they better or worse?

Tom squinted at them. The concrete had shaded fuchsia in the evening sun. The air hung hot, laced with downcurrents of exhaust from a thousand idling cars.

Why do they have to lose the house?

The house is always lost.

Tom digested this. He felt his skin prickle at the heat, the muffled roar of traffic, the rhythmic squeaking of brakes, the drone of cicadas deep beneath.

They have the memory of the house.

But they live much longer without the house.

Only God knows if it's worth it to them then.

The man looked toward him but not at him. He shifted his field of vision to refocus on something closer in the middle ground.

Do you believe in God?

No, I guess I don't.

But you believe in something.

Yes.

Or you wouldn't be going north.

Yes.

He shared the sardines and the crackers with the man. The man was well stocked with canned goods, not just green beans, creamed corn, and canned yams which always flooded the food banks at Thanksgiving and remained on the shelves most of the year, but with Spaghetti O's and Dinty Moore beef stew. But the man accepted the oily fish and salty crackers out of courtesy.

When Tom had fully rested, he shook hands with the man and climbed back up to the road. He would have preferred to spend the night under the bridge with someone he trusted to watch his back while he slept, but the mission was his priority and it was better to travel at night.

Freshly hydrated and fed, it was easier to travel, to live, to be alive. His sight was actually clearer. The tunnel vision was gone. In this way he stopped when what would have been lost on the periphery as some fuzzy colored blob came into focus as a real object with defined edges, a bus stop it appeared, although he couldn't recall having seen any actual busses in his time here. A bench and a post with a cryptic sign. Preposterous in the day time under the blow torch sun, it now seemed plausible to sit on an exposed bench and wait to see it a bus would come. He didn't know the time. It could have been too late for busses to run, but in any event the sitting was nice with the sun safely behind the earth's crust. After what could have been an hour or a day, a bus did come. The door swung open and something akin to cool air rushed out. It felt like luxury, how the rich travel.

The bus was empty. An empty vessel floating upon the asphalt. The driver insisted that Tom have some sort of swipeable card. He had no such card. He only had nickels and dimes. The machine did not accept change. He was directed to a card dispenser that might as well have been on the moon for how he would get to it. If he could walk to the card dispenser he could walk to his destination. After some negotiation in which Tom proffered a dollar in change in what amounted an attempt to bribe the bus driver with what would have been close to the standard fare, the bus driver refused his offer but let him ride anyway. Perhaps for the company. Perhaps so there would be a point to driving the bus at all. Tom was the only passenger.

It felt good to be moving, but he was nervous; one turn and the bus could undo days of walking and take him back where he started. Or worse. The bus appeared to be moving in the right direction, north with the distant skyscrapers almost parallel.

Gradually a few passengers got on. Sad people, burnt and tired. The movement created an optical effect like an open shutter, lights blending together into beams of light and color. The black night outside the window was a clear, deep blank slate, something so touchable you could stick your finger in if you tried.

Party people started getting on the bus. He could tell by the look in their eyes, the night with possibilities, expectations. Their legs bounced with casual energy. The girls wore skirts that left their thighs bare. Thin thighs, smooth and white. Latinas, tan and muscular. The men wore long pants and black leather shoes in spite of the heat. A girl tattooed on her back and down one arm like a sleeve, the new sign of demarcation. Tattoos on skinny arms. The non-party people mostly ignored these newcomers. Tom stared. Transfixed. He didn't know why. When the party people got off the bus he followed. This must be the city.

People were out on the street. Lights were everywhere. Neon emblazoned the night with reds and greens. Ringlets of white light outlined the buildings and spiraled up the traffic lights. Of the group of them that got off the bus, he followed one girl in particular. She was like a lion, or more like a maned deer, with her mantle of warm hair. She moved slowly, slovenly, an affected indifference that made him wonder what she wondered, if her mind wandered. She must be thinking about sex. She is sex. Lips parted in slack jawed boredom, an act, a dumb look that was practiced, just absent minded enough to leave possibilities. What filled up that mind and those thoughts now infiltrated his mind.

He didn't know what was happening to him. He walked too closely behind her, following the hem of her skirt against the back of her legs, and then he realized what he was doing and backed off. He needed a drink. There were lines outside the bars. Women with shiny handbags and tight sequined dresses milling in rows, accompanied by gangs of heavily cologned men in long pleatless pants and collared shirts open to the nipples. He got in line. The red velvet rope ended outside the club doorway, but the line went down the street. A boy turned to him, taking a step back to steady himself.

Hey man, who are you?

The boy wore a knit skullcap and a short sleeve shirt. Who wears a wool ski hat when it's a hundred and five at night? The boy had around him a cluster of boys that might have been girls and girls that were definitely girls.

I'm Tom.

Hey Tom, you partying tonight?

I just need a drink.

Hey motherfuckers, this is Tom. He said it to the line. The line turned to look back.

He needs a drink.

A contagious roar verberated through the crowd from one ear to the next. A chorus of 'me toos' roiled up the front door of the club and rippled back.

Tom understood being made fun of. Let's make fun of the bum. It felt good in a perverse way. A guilty good. What had he become? People appeared to shake his hand, or fist bump, or back hand slap, and someone pressed a flask into his hand and he drank heavily from it, bourbon, probably Beam. People cheered him who he'd never seen and would never see again. The line moved forward. When he got to the front the line two doormen in headsets turned him away without saying a word. They just crossed their arms. No one said anything as Tom peeled off the line and kept on the sidewalk.

He walked down the block to a Circle K at the corner and bought two Budweiser tall boys for two fifty plus tax. He went into the alley between the Circle K and what appeared to be a frat house and sat next to a thick plastic recycling bin and popped open the first tall boy. He watched the street traffic from the alley coming and going from the bars, the party people, the stumbling teens, the trained predators. At one point he thought he saw the girl from the bus with the pouty lips and the bored stare. She was clinging to an older man, watching her footsteps, indifferent. He felt like puking. But he finished the second tall boy and laughed to himself. The night was miraculous.

Chapter 12

The trailer's hollow plywood front door opened sending in a blast of cold mountain air.

Honey, I'm home!

Frank smiled, making his neck balloon like a pelican swallowing a carp.

The girl made no move to get up.

He stepped inside resembling an oozing mass. His body moved one way and the goiter shifted the other, his huge frame filling the room. He slammed the door behind him with a flick of his wrist. Everyone turned to watch him. With deceptive speed, Frank laid a giant paw on Lorne's shoulder and wrenched him to his bosom.

Didn't think I'd see you again after last time, buddy.

Frank said it as he hugged Lorne uncomfortably tight to his bulbous pectorals. Lorne struggled to keep his balance on his one good foot. Lorne started to say something but stopped, catching something in Frank's jaundiced eyes, blue in a sea of murky yellow. What had happened the last time he was in Alpine?

So, what did you boys bring me?

He turned to the others, still holding Lorne to his breast in a sort of headlock, Lorne's head sandwiched by a bicep the size and consistency of a Christmas ham. Chevis was jittery, sweat beading on his shaved head. Pammy and Jimmy backed away instinctively; everyone was too close. The room seemed small, like a cage.

Two hundred for two thousand. Double your money at least. Chevis straightened up and took his hands out of his pockets.

Frank smiled again, the same jack lantern grin.

Well, let's see it.

Chevis reached inside his jacket pocket and took out a plastic ziplock bag filled with little plastic ziplock bags. Two hundred of them. Just holding it made his palms moist and his nose run.

Eight hundred bucks.

What?

Eight hundred.

Come on, man. You gotta at least come back at a thousand.

I don't have to do shit.

Chevis shook his head. Sweat flickered down onto the carpet. Ashley looked at Frank for the first time. Junior uncrossed his legs and stood up.

I don't know. You're not even gonna try it?

Don't need to.

Why?

Not for eight hundred. Don't need to.

Chevis squinted at him. Too much meth. Meth meth meth, Meth meth Meth meth Meth meth Meth.

You hunt?

Frank turned to face Junior.

Junior turned toward Frank, flicking his newly braided braids.

Sometimes.

Whacha you use, 30-30, 30 ought 6?

Bow.

Bow and arrow?

Yeah.

Well that's fucking ironic.

I got my first last winter. Jimmy's got many.

He nodded blankly at Jimmy. Jimmy was watching Frank's eyes.

What do you hunt with?

Let me show you something.

Frank spun quickly and slid back a defunct Lazy-Boy which hid a dented footlocker with a padlock flopping by a steel fob. Frank deftly slid off the lock without ever producing a key and spun back around holding a crossbow. The polished wood and steel bolts gleamed in the florescent overhead light. The handle was nickel plated and engraved with the initials BFF.

You ever get a deer with one of these?

Nice.

Junior said it almost involuntarily, stepping forward and petting the shiny titanium shaft of the loaded crossbow bolt with his fingers.

This can't be good at distance.

Frank gently brushed the boy's hand away.

No. It's not. But in close quarters it's okay.

Frank leveled the crossbow at Chevis and fired a bolt into his chest, pinning him against the aluminum trailer wall just above the fake fireplace.

Chevis didn't exactly scream, he just spat out chunks of what could have been lung. The blood flicked out into the living room and splayed across the crusted lamp shades and makeshift curtains and the vinyl siding.

The crossbow had a chrome cylindric cartridge loading mechanism that reloaded fresh bolts like a semi-automatic. Frank calmly swiveled half a click and had a primed three-pronged bolt aimed directly at Pammy's forehead, but before he could pull the trigger a tremendous boom stunned the cramped room, and Frank went flying into the far wall, denting it before he collapsed, a six foot smear of blood arching up the vinyl siding and onto and across the ceiling. Jimmy had been quick, smoothly pulling his .44 from his back waistband and firing by reflex. The black barrel smoked, filling the room with the smell.

Ashley's big blue eyes grew even bigger. She held onto Junior's arm. Junior stepped away from the couch. She let his arm drop. Junior looked at Frank, who lay motionless, legs propped up on an overturned TV table, back to the floor, and then he went to Chevis.

It will be okay.

Chevis swore and swung his arms wildly, trying to pry himself free from the wall. He screamed in pain and rage and kicked his legs against the plaster fireplace. The bolt wiggled in his chest just below his shoulder and in his back just above his shoulder blade, the tip firmly punctured through the trailer wall.

Pammy rushed to Junior's side and laid her weight against Chevis, holding his arms to the wall.

Don't fucking move. You'll make it worse.

Fuck that, pull me off. Chevis spat.

Jimmy nudged Junior aside and put a hand on Chevis's shaved head.

She's right. Be still. We're going to pull you off but we have to leave the arrow in.

Give me a hit.

Junior went to get the glass pipe and held it to Chevis's lips. He lit the bowl underneath and rotated it back and forth as Chevis inhaled. Pammy braced herself against the wall and gained leverage with her elbow and yanked out the bolt with Jimmy holding onto Chevis. Chevis staggered forward with the bolt in place below the clavicle.

Give me another hit.

Junior handed him the pipe.

Lorne stroked his beard and grinned madly looking down

at Frank lying on the floor and then at Chevis standing up and then back again. Ashley wordlessly disappeared into the back bedroom. She went directly to the mirrored floor length closet doors facing a bare mattress and box spring. Behind a tangle of plastic coat hangers she scooped up a pile of rubber banded rolls of bills and a black 9mm and tucked them into a tiny velvet backpack with shoe string shoulder straps. She slipped back into the box car living room as they were pulling Chevis from the wall. She looked at Junior but spoke to the others.

Take me with you.

Chapter 13

Nineteen-year-old girls smell like hope. He had been good looking once, was good looking although he never knew what to do with it, didn't know how good looking people were supposed to act, but he used to see it in the eyes of some women, a penetrating look that just couldn't have been given to everyone, to the world at large. How to respond to such a look? He had never been taught, or had never learned. Now, at some level, he knew rot had set in. Not just in the obvious places, the gums, the feet, in between the toes, but deeper, internal perhaps. And yet he was suddenly certain that he would know what to do if he was ever given that look again.

He woke next to the recycle bin in the alley, his head momentarily stuck to it, not melted to it from the heat but affixed by superheated beverage remnants that had impossibly vaporized and condensed on the outside of the plastic bin with their sticky qualities intact. A liquid outflow trickled to the center of the alley where it pooled and steamed, refusing to evaporate entirely, a beer and wine reduction simmering on one hundred and thirty degree asphalt. The smell congealed in the humid air, which was thick as pea soup. The larval life, he did not care to think about.

He got to his feet with less pain than expected, the sauna of the alley loosening his joints to rubber. He emerged from the mouth of the alley to a bright street awash in sunlight. The bars were shuttered, but the sidewalks were crowded.

Students, backpacks slung, migrated in the same general direction. The human flow had its own gravitational pull. The momentum carried him to the ASU campus, broad sidewalks, neat squares of green lawn and manicured rock gardens and desert 'scapes, sandstone academic buildings and institutional dorms. But the sickness from the night before was still with him. He could see nothing but the women. The girls. It was like entering a world he didn't know existed. A world told about by drunks in bars, and foretold in the most firebrand Southern Baptist churches and beer commercials. These were simply not the girls he had gone to college with. Their bodies were different, toned and tight, shiny and hard, tanned or alabaster, with good posture walking with purpose, straight ahead, shoulders back and bare in spaghetti straps, blanketed and caressed by silky hair that left a trail of perfume in its wake to do its work on the world. Calf muscles. Bellies everywhere, taut and muscular or young and doughy, they all looked good exposed to the sun between shirt and skirt. The thigh had an entirely different shape then it used to. The secret milky flesh of the dreams of Tom's adolescence replaced by the firm smooth legs of athletes. He drank them in, their health, their life, their innate goodness, and he desired to touch it, hold it, to know it was real. How could the world go on with these creatures? How did it not grind to a halt in admiration, in desire, in madness? He wanted to touch, to feel. It would break every moral he held and lived by, would break the law. But he could do it. Just reach his hand out. In this very instant nothing was stopping him from grabbing that ocean of skin. Is this how men became rapists? The lack of money had made him an outcast, a leper, untouchable, but had it made him something worse? There were no more lines. Somewhere on the hot and desolate road they had melted away. Where nothing was possible, everything was possible. A girl strode by, white halter top and a frayed jean skirt, a rope of straight blonde hair slung over her long thin neck. He held out his arm, birdlike, a parrot doubtful about the strength of a skinny branch. Could he stop himself? How did he know what he was? Was one not a murderer until one murders? Or was one always a murderer, the act latent, the committal of the act coloring everything that had gone before? She walked past him, elegant shoulder blades visible though the thin sheer fabric. He watched her until she disappeared in the crowd, his arm still half-cocked, as if asking a question to the air.

He felt faint, dehydrated, delusional perhaps. He walked back to the Circle K and bought a bottle of water for $1.89. No food. He reemerged uncomfortable. His reflection in the tinted window revealed a red-faced stranger, skin peeling and blistered. He wanted to hide. It is a problem of the homeless. Nowhere to go to hide, to rest, to regroup. With nowhere to go he began walking. Soon he came to train tracks and began to follow them instead. At least he was off the street, out of view. The tracks cut through the city but in most places cinderblock walls backed the yards of houses and buildings to dampen the noise from locomotives. It formed a tunnel through urbana, a hobo highway he thought, as he walked on the tracks, rust brown colored above crushed gravel and weeds. When the tracks crossed city streets, the drawbridge gates open, he shuffled across dodging traffic. The tracks traversed through neighborhoods and industrial warehouse districts with no discernible pattern or concern. The tracks were here long before the city he guessed. When he had just about stopped paying attention to what he was doing and had settled into the draining numbness of the march, thankful that mind had separated from body, feeling a certain elation, like a runner's high, conscious of nothing except the sweat and a high altitude buzzing in his brain and a fuzziness of vision, his detachment was so complete that at first he didn't take the vibrations of the tracks for what they were, an oncoming train. A thunderous blast of the whistle jolted him from the tracks and sent him rolling into a ditch.

Chapter 14

US 62, outside of Battleboro, Arkansas.

Soft evening air smoothed the edges out of the day. A layer of pink hung above the treeline. A light mist permeated lush green marsh grass and hovered indecisively in tall reeds with white tipped cattails. Somewhere nearby a rooster crowed. Traffic was sparse on the two lane road. His boots on the faded yellow line, kicking pebbles off of the narrow shoulder. The confused lowing of cows carried on the breeze from an unseen pasture. The smell of manure and fresh cut hay bales after an afternoon rain.

A figure walked along the road in the direction he had come from. Heavy plodding steps like a pack mule, a hitch-hiker, a pilgrim, or a prisoner. He kept a steady unhurried gait. A pickup truck approached preceded by the rumble of a V8 with at least one piston misfiring. The man turned to face it with an outstretched arm. The truck didn't slow down for the man, so Tom didn't bother sticking his own thumb out, just watched the truck pass by. The truck flicked on its headlights as if suddenly reminded that daylight was fading.

The man put his arm down and kept walking. No other cars came. When he reached where Tom was standing, he stopped and put his pack down and stretched.

Evening.

Evening.

Tom smiled, his pack shifting awkwardly on his back with over a hundred dollars in change in a thick sack at the bottom.

Not many cars.

Not many.

It took a moment to adjust in the dimming light but Tom could see the man was a young man, maybe a kid with a three week beard. What came off as long hair was really just three weeks late on a haircut. He was thin, but not hungry. Dark blue t-shirt, good quality, thick, not made to shrink. His khakis were made out of some modern polymer, thin but light, drawstrings at the ankles to form a seal over the boots to keep the bugs out. He took out a joint from a crumpled pack of American Spirits and lit it, took three drags scoffing on the side of the road and offered it to Tom. Tom held up his hand, declining with a grin. It was long before he had lost his discipline. The kid gave him a suit-yourself-smile.

Where you headed?

West.

How about you?

The end of the Earth.

Tom watched him with a patient look.

Tierra del Fuego.

An eighteen-wheeler rattled by with the air break on. Neither man noticed.

Tierra del Fuego. You mean in South America?

As far as you can go.

Sounds like a long way.

It must be.

Tom nodded.

Well, that's a new one.

The boy seemed satisfied. He pulled heavily on the joint. He looked somewhere in the unfocused distance.

You mind if I ask why?

You can ask, but I won't have a good answer.

Tom smiled and scratched his beard.

Why are you heading west?

Tom snorted and shook his head.

You can ask…

But there ain't a good…

Yeah.

Yup.

They stood in silence for a while listening to the chatter of the birds reaching a crescendo as the air cooled and objects grew fuzzier in the changing light.

The kid snuffed out the joint and put the roach back in the cellophane cigarette pack while simultaneously pulling out a fresh American Spirit.

Not much chance of us both getting a ride out here. Hard enough for one, what with night coming. But the two of us. No chance.

Providence.

Tom lit a GPC and held out the match. The kid cupped his hand to protect the flame and lit his Spirit.

Providence?

You don't believe in Providence?

No, I don't. I believe in reality.

Providence happens.

Maybe, but not to me.

You're too young to talk like that.

The man exhaled squinty eyed.

I'm a Jew.

What's that got to do with anything?

Here's what the Jews know.

As he began to speak he gestured with his hands expansively as if waiting for the void to fill with words.

One...people are evil. The overarching myth of the Holocaust is that there was an oppressive government that committed atrocities and that the citizens of this government were led into committing those atrocities. In fact, it was exactly the opposite. It was a million tiny individual acts of barbarism that accomplished the Holocaust. The result of a permissive, laissez faire government.

I don't think you're using that term right. The Nazi government wasn't exactly permissive...

For some they were....Whatever. The important thing is that people operating in a moral void will revert to their evil nature. It is how Abu Ghraib happened and would happen again if this kind of freedom over other people were given to people to act out as they please. The people running that war either didn't understand the evil nature of people, or they were aware of people enjoying their government sanctioned permissiveness and didn't care.

Tom frowned, noncommittal.

Two...people are good. When outside the rule of law as created and enforced by people, who are evil, people will act altruistically and even sacrifice themselves for their fellow man. That leads to...three...there is no natural rule of law. There are only people who are evil, and people who see evil and respond to it.

So what does all this mean?

There is no God. There are only people who, if allowed, will be evil, and people who witness this evil and are sufficiently moved to rebel against it because of our latent altruistic nature.

So it's more or less every man for himself?

Someone once asked me if Jews believe in God. I said no. All Jews are atheists, except for the Orthodox who are fanatical like the Mormons or the Evangelicals or anyone who will believe something with no hint of proof at all. This person was a Christian and she indignantly said that she had no proof of the existence of God but she believed in him. That is called the leap of faith and it is a tenet of the religion. I said that is the difference. While I cannot prove that God exists, all Jews have proof that God does not exist. She said, the Holocaust? I said yes. No God would allow half of you to be murdered. And if there is such a God, well, he isn't really worth worshiping, is he? I mean, wouldn't he just damn the other half to hell? The first half certainly didn't deserve to get murdered. She said there is a glorious afterlife that would certainly be better than the murderous one they have left. I said Jews don't believe in the afterlife. She had nothing to say to that.

The Lord works in mysterious ways.

Look, I'm not saying someone isn't going to pick us both up, but if they do, it isn't Providence.

What would you call it then?

Luck.

All right, luck then.

I mean it would be pretty insulting if God let all the shit slide that goes on in the world but intervenes to give us two jokers a ride.

Okay then. I get your point. So what now that we are foreclosed from getting a ride except by an extreme stroke of luck?

I'll tell you what. You stick your thumb out now, and I'll hide in the tall grass, and when someone stops I'll sneak up and bludgeon them to death.

Tom stared blankly, but suddenly his pulse quickened, his mental sensors twitched uncontrollably.

I'm just fucking with you. I'll go catch a train.

A train? Tom struggled to shake the feeling off.

Yeah, there's track that crosses the road a mile back. You never ride the rails, jump a freight train?

Isn't that dangerous?

Of course it's dangerous. Just remember one thing. Run along side it and grab on to something first, then jump. Never jump if you don't know where you're going to land.

They crushed out their cigarettes. The illusion of pink in the clouds had faded to deep purple and then disappeared. It was night. They stood listening to the croaking frogs that had announced their presence and a carpet of cricket chirps that laid down a baseline of background noise.

All right then.

Good luck.

The kid smiled, teeth showing in the night.

Good luck to you to sir.

They shook hands and then the kid walked back the way he came and was soon invisible in the blackness. When he was gone Tom felt strangely alone and noticed how dark it had gotten.

Chapter 15

There is a moment on every commercial airline flight, during the descent, about five to ten minutes before landing, where if you are sufficiently disconnected from Ipads and laptops, headphones and LCD screens of any kind, you are struck with the reality that you are incased in a metal cylinder that is literally barreling toward the earth at five hundred miles an hour in a loosely controlled, jet-thrusted free fall. The cabin rattles and shakes, rolling like a ship at sea, the overhead compartments strain against their latches, the seats jostle against their bolts, the giant riveted wings bend in unsettling ways, almost flapping on powerful air currents. The noise, if you allow yourself to hear it, is a deafening roar. A scream. You cannot escape this reality, that you are plummeting toward the ground. You know that technology usually saves you from certain death. The correct angle of the nose raised just right, the hydraulic landing gear, the billions of calculations and the firing circuits and switches and properly charged ions that make them, should bring you once more safely to ground.

But not always.

The night appeared to Lorne in a series of still life images, movie frames in no particular sequence. Pine trees lit by headlights surging out of a pitch-black sky. Tall grass marking the boundary of the highway. The quiet town, Alpine, unlit, dwarfed by mountains too dark to see. Felt but not seen.

The florescent devil eyes of some nocturnal ground animal scampering across the road to watch from the underbrush. Angry, mad, feral. A police car that only he and maybe Jimmy noticed, parked behind a stand of poplars with its snout faced toward the road, the occupant either asleep or engaged in some private interlude. He didn't pull over the Malibu or even tail it even though Lorne knew they looked sketchy as hell. The night was disjointed, out of order. Flipping pages too fast to read.

Lorne drove, bad foot and all. There was surprisingly little talk. Not that Lorne supposed the others were lost in thought, or thinking at all, except for how many hits was too many. Chevis sat erect in the front seat, no indication that a crossbow bolt bisected his chest. Pammy anchored the back seat with Jimmy, then Junior and Ashley half on Junior's lap and half on the door's peeling vinyl armrest.

Ashley shifted an ounce and a half away from the door and onto the boy, and when she looked into his eyes and saw herself there she felt good, and then for a split second she faltered, she doubted herself and was surprised. She brushed a bead of sweat from the left side of her chin and looked away. She knew she was an illusion. Did he see? She was what men wanted to see. Did he want to see? She self-consciously twisted a strand of hair and tucked it behind her ear, felt her cheek, started to speak and then didn't, not knowing what she'd say and aware that she didn't know, and then she looked back into those black pools of his eyes and saw nothingness, a deep rich bath of empty, a warm chocolate custard of numb that she could go to sleep in forever. If only she ever slept.

Out of the mountains and back into the desert. The desert at night was a vacuum. A cold blanket. There was no time in all that space. That was the hope. The hope of the desert was non-existence.

Just before dawn, the Malibu pulled into a gas station at

the intersection of Route 191 North and U.S. 60 West outside of Eagar. Halos on the floodlights above an empty parking lot. Lorne got out and tried the pump, but it needed a credit card to operate. Chevis twisted out of the passenger seat. The wind blew at his shirt but it was held in place by the crossbow bolt. The others watched like they were witness to Jesus's resurrection or a mummy rising from its tomb. Red and black stained his shirt and ran down his pants in streaks. They watched him lumber past the pumps toward the convenience store. He pulled the glass door open and side stepped inside so he wouldn't bump the projectile sticking out of him. They watched through the floor to ceiling windows. The clerk seemed frozen. Words were passed. The clerk stood motionless. More words were passed. The clerk made an imperceptible motion and the pump turned on with an audible clunk, and gas flowed into the tank from the pump handle Lorne held. Lorne watched the pump. Everyone else watched the store in silence. The florescent light inside was brilliant against the black emptiness of the desert. The pump handle clicked when the tank was full. Chevis pulled the .44 from his waist and shot the clerk in the head.

Nobody spoke. Ashley thought about saying something, but everything in her experience told her there would be no point. She didn't know if the others were silent because they were surprised, they expected it, or they were Indians. She looked down into those black pools and was calm, awash in a sea of obsidian.

Chapter 16

Tom picked himself up, secured his pack, and jogged alongside the moving train. The whistle blew again, shaking him to his core and jolting him a yard eschew as he ran. The train coked back and forth with a sickening creak of metal joints. The hulking metal frame lumbered deceptively fast, and he could barely catch up. He reached out wildly several times and grabbed onto a metal ladder at the connection between two boxcars. He held on as he ran next to the train before he jumped as his friend had told him so many miles ago. But there was nothing for his feet to grab on to. He swung his legs around frantically and lodged his feet against the beveled frame of a boxcar door, holding his legs by centrifugal force so that he dangled horizontally over the tracks. Hanging on, face skyward, his pack was dead weight, dragging him to the ground. He sank until his head was eye level with the giant steel wheels grinding loose stones to dust on the tracks. One leg broke free and wandered under the boxcar and out of sight. He didn't know if he'd see it again or if a stump would reemerge spouting blood. Would he even feel it? One errant jostle of the behemoth or a crick in the track and his body would be halved. The pack dipped and scraped and bumped against the weed and dust strewn ground speeding past below. His hand burned but he wouldn't let go, terrified of being sucked into the meat grinder or hitting the ground and bouncing under the train. He wanted to live. It was crystal clear. He wanted to live.

But he had made a horrible mistake. The weight of the pack made it impossible for him to pull himself up in his current position. This was why hobos in movies threw their bundles tied to the ends of sticks into an open boxcar before they jumped on board. A thick thatch of weeds pulpified between the top of his pack and his neck like a human combine harvesting thistle and ragweed. His pack spawned a cloud of dust, a plow blade set to fallow earth.

The hot metal seared his hands, and he slipped another inch, the pack now grating the ground under the pressure of his body weight. The fabric frayed, polymers decoupling. He heard seams pop and actually felt the pack tear as if it was his own flesh. He saw dirty cloths flutter behind, snagging on bramble and little ground cactus and blown against barbed wire bordering the tracks. And then the plastic ziplock bag of change saw daylight. It dragged behind the pack and then broke free. It skipped once and then exploded like fireworks on the Fourth of July. The coins shimmered in the sun, streaking across the sky in a starburst pattern, like foam from a backlit cresting ocean wave crashing against a rocky shore.

Not more than thirty seconds later the train clamored and stopped at a rail crossing. Tom let go and fell to the ground, his fingers frozen in their death grip, staring upward at nothing like roadkill. And then his lungs filled with hot air and dust. He rolled onto his stomach, brought himself onto all fours, and then pushed himself to his feet with much effort. He stared down the tracks at the wreckage of his belongings. His meager traveling companions strewn across the wasteland. Defiled. Dead where they lay.

He spent the heat of the day stooped like a field worker, scavenging the change from the twigs and thorns and ground clutter weeds, tough and stringy, more like twine than any recognizable plant phyla, his fingers dirty, calloused and blistered, claw-like, mechanical. He recovered six dollars and forty-two cents. He put it in his pocket. He tied up the ragged ends from the gaping hole in the pack so it was now more like a satchel. He rescued a flannel shirt, a pair of boxers, and a balled up pair of dirty socks, and of course, the long wool coat. He used his pocket knife to cut strips of the black vein-like weeds that spidered across the desert floor and used them to tie the satchel.

He slung the satchel and sat down and waited. His throat was parched. He had no water. The heat was infernal. But he made no move to start walking. He sat in the dirt and waited.

At some point in the afternoon, although it was hard to tell with the daylight stretching fifteen hours into night, another train came and stopped exactly where the last one had at the rail crossing. Tom stretched his legs and climbed up on a small platform between two boxcars. The heat had grown throughout the day until now it was almost intolerable. He could feel his brains cooking. When the train began to move there was no relief. The heat radiating from the two boxcars was like a toaster.

The ride only lasted ten minutes. The train came to a metal on metal stop at a rail yard downtown. Twenty sets of tracks. Rows of iron husks. Tom walked out looking over his shoulder, stepping carefully over the ties, the satchel slung over his shoulder. He eyed a white pickup with a rectangular orange light strip on the roof but no rent a cop in sight. No people of any kind.

Even downtown the streets were six lanes across. The skyscrapers that seemed bunched from a distance were really islands each taking up a city block, surrounded by fenced vacant lots and concrete parking structures.

The streets were empty. The first person he saw was clearly a meth head or one of the deranged homeless, a woman with pink skin like an albino left out in the sun, with hair the color and consistency of uncooked spaghetti.

That fucker. That fucker. Condescend to me motherfucker. Police suck my dick!

She steamed past him muttering to herself, wild eyed.

A family came out of the mirrored glass doors of the downtown Grand Hyatt Convention Center. They crossed the street to avoid the woman. So did Tom. When they saw Tom also cross the street, they walked faster, the woman clutching the little boy to her breast, the man walking on the outside, pink polo shirt, white slacks, brown leather loafers. He pushed his wife forward with a hand on her back. Her summer dress was short over tan thighs, sculpted calves, thin strapped sandals. They got to the corner of the block and then stopped, looking up and down the wide cross street. They let Tom pass by and then turned around and walked back to the hotel.

The sun was orange and low on the horizon. It reflected off of the glass skyscrapers in an apocalyptic glow, giving everything an irradiated hue. The buildings' mirrored windows reflected pillars of fire. Towering neon stalks planted in the desert by man imitating God. He walked not knowing where he was going or what he was looking for. No cars were on the streets. A group of Mexicans a couple blocks ahead hopped a low chain-link fence and crossed an empty lot. He turned right for no reason and walked between the concrete buttresses protecting the service entrances to two tall buildings. A man crossed the street on a path to intersect him. He was the only one on the street. The man moved like a slug, one foot protruding and dragging the body behind. In spite of the heat, which had only increased with the approaching sunset, the man wore pleated slacks and a blue cardigan over a pressed oxford shirt. Tom thought of a creepy Mr. Rogers. And he used to like Mr. Rogers.

Excuse me, the man said as he got into earshot.

Excuse me. Would you like to go somewhere? Somewhere cool. We could go somewhere. I could take you somewhere.

His face was pasty white. There was something lecherous in the slanted grin. Thin lips. Something evil. Tom walked hurriedly passed him holding up a hand as if to shield himself, trying not to notice the man's hand brushing against the front of his trousers. Tom was disgusting even to himself, caked in dirt and grime and sweat. Who could view him as a sex object? Only the truly depraved. The man apologized as he sidestepped away as if to confirm it. Ahead, a man with hair as bushy about the face as on top of his head so that atop his neck bobbled a spherical sun bronzed Brillo pad, rooted in a festering metal ringed trashcan for lord knows what. Tom turned into an alley just to get off the street, although there was no one of consequence about. The alley was flanked by tall buildings, and it bowed in the center like a miniature culvert, and down the center ran a thin stream of putrid liquid, the sun spoiled remnants leached out of trash heaps and funneled into a trickle of stink. It was the wrong alley. A man sunburnt red, face peeling and raw with pink blistered skin open to the sun for further debasement, rounded a dumpster and was unavoidable. Yellow pustules ringed his lips, and his face bore the scars of the meth itch that must be scratched to the point of bleeding and scabs and new bleeding and new scabs. He surprised Tom completely and he gripped Tom by both shoulders as if to embrace him, eyes crazy, an acrid evil stink coming off him like burnt plastic mixed with sweat.

The speed and shock of the attack stunned Tom for a second, the man squeezing him, eyes bulging like a frog alive but paralyzed by some predator's venom, nerves twitching ineffectually, short of breath, almost hyperventilating. Then he reacted spastically, suddenly repulsed more by the pustules and stench then the threat of impending violence. Desperate to get distance between himself and the man, he flung his arms wildly, but the man had drawn him in too close so his blows glanced off his shoulders and back. The man leered at him with crystal blue pinpoints straining against yellowed eye whites. His frozen grin seemed involuntary, stretching from ear to ear as if the corners of his mouth were rigged to the strings of some mad puppeteer. He hissed an eerie lock-jawed whine through clenched jagged teeth and blackened gums.

Tom finally forced himself to speak.

Let me go.

The man grunted and formed words through his teeth.

Go? Go where? Yes let's go…let's dance!

And he gripped Tom even harder, lifting him totally off the ground, and began to twirl. Tom lost all of his leverage. He felt his legs lift off the asphalt with centrifugal force and felt the man's hot, rancid breath on his face, and the next thing he felt was his hand pushing against the man's stomach and into the man's stomach. Something in the man's eyes changed; his grin seemed more pulled tight across his face then ever. Tom was surprised to find his Swiss army knife open, the flimsy three inch blade going into the man's abdomen and pushing through so Tom's hand was in the man's guts and then rooting around as if fumbling for the off switch, jabbing this way and that, until he felt the dull little blade hit what must have been his spine. The man shrieked and drew back his already protracted grin in a death scowl, a runover dog curling his lips in instinctual panic or a coyote caught in a snare lashing out at anything close, his already mottled face bubbling and distended like a vampire in the sunlight. The man convulsed and took Tom to the ground, his hands still gripping Tom's shoulders. Tom withdrew his hand from the man's innards and pried loose the man's fingers from him one by one.

The man lay prostrate in the alley, a river of blood mixed with the putrid stream of trash juice running to the street. His lips coated in blood, his jaw finally seemed to relax enough to speak clearly for the first time.

Why?

The man's eyes seemed almost sane.

Tom closed the blade on his knife, gummy and viscous. His arm was coated in blood to the elbow. Death is sobering, he thought ruefully and amazed. And then he picked up his satchel and ran up the alley. When he got to the corner he looked back. The man hadn't moved except to hold up a quivering hand as if still asking the question.

Chapter 17

The world has gone insane. Tom walked through the night in a vaguely northernly direction, as much as the streets and sidewalks would allow. It was hot and strangely humid. Glistening sweat mixed with the blood on his arm and clothes that somehow refused to dry. The world has truly gone insane. He walked up Central Ave., across the gigantic overpass with traffic hurtling bumper to bumper on I-10 below. On the other side of the overpass, he found a second downtown, fake somehow like a movie set, with skyscrapers just as tall as the ones he'd walked through but spaced further apart. The streets were wide. At first he walked afraid the cops would pick him up, staggering and covered in blood, and then he realized nobody noticed. He was invisible. Traffic raced by. He came to think that the cars were moving too fast for the people inside to see him. But the more he walked the more he came to believe that it wasn't that nobody noticed, it was that nobody cared.

He was used to being weak and dehydrated, but that didn't mean he wasn't sick of it. He saw the neon glow of a Taco Bell a block up, but it still took him fifteen minutes to reach it, crossing a six-lane street, endless curb cuts, and a generous parking lot. He went inside feeling the blast of air conditioning and ordered a number three—three taco supremes and a large coke for $2.99 plus tax. A large Hispanic woman mechanically punched his order into a touch screen, her fat rolls straining against her tightly tucked in purple Taco Bell shirt. He loaded up the tacos with fire sauce and then scooped up the loose lettuce flacks and tomato cubes with his fingers. He sat in a plastic chair at a plastic booth crusted in dried blood and smiled. A family of six ate noisily in the next booth speaking Spanish in short bursts. He took the 44-ounce plastic cup of Coke with him on his long march, and when he'd finished it he pissed right into the street and kept walking.

Noon the next day found him sitting on a curb in North Scottsdale. He had three dollars and change left, and he was trying to figure out if it was enough for another number three from Taco Bell, if he could find one, but he kept getting the count wrong, the change falling through his fingers to splatter on the asphalt—first $3.16 which wasn't enough, and then $3.65 which was. He just wanted one more meal. After that it didn't matter. He counted again and had $3.15. The streets were wide. Cars flew by at sixty miles per hour inches from his feet. Endless traffic. The world had gone insane. He could no longer tell which was worse, the people he chased, or the people he was trying to save. It seemed either could kill him at any moment. And the good ones, the civilians if there were any, he could kill without even realizing it. When had he become a murderer? The answer was yesterday. He decided to call his sister.

The streets were wide. He walked a mile into a cul-de-sac and had to turn around and then crossed the wide street and did the same thing. A mile and a half up the road he found a wayward strip mall with a pay phone. It was an older strip mall, brick instead of stucco, and it was losing its battle with the desert. Sand swept across the mostly empty parking lot. The heat beat into his brain. Sweat trickled down his body and into every crevice. The phone was hot to the touch. He had to hold the receiver away from his ear and mouth. He was breaking a cardinal rule. He knew he would pop up on the grid within seconds of dialing the number. Still he spun the quarters into the slot and listened to the click of their acceptance. He dialed the number on the metal keys reflecting sunlight like mirrors scoring his eyes. In the stillness the heat intensified. He listened to the monotone electronic bleating indicating a phone ringing somewhere on the other side. He pressed his forehead against the Plexiglas phone booth and felt it sear his brain.

Hello?

Janey.

Silence.

Oh my god.

Janey.

Oh my god, David, is that you?

Silence.

It's me.

David, you're alive.

Apparently.

David, where are you?

I can't say.

You can't say because you don't know?

I can't say. You know why.

David.

The mission.

David.

I'm not crazy. You are fucking crazy.

David come here. Come here now.

I can't.

Do you need money?

Tom laughed. He pressed his head back against the burning Plexiglas. It felt right.

David come here now.

I can't now.

David.

I have to go. I love you Janey.

David, come here now, we'll…

Tom gently hung up the phone. He walked until he found a Taco Bell and ordered a number three. With tax it was $3.17. After counting out his change he took two cents from the penny cup next to the register to pay for it. Now he didn't have a penny to his name.

Chapter 18

Tank full of premium unleaded, the Malibu pulled onto US 60 West for a five-mile jog back to AZ 191, the Old Coronado Trail. They crept through Springerville and then headed north. The town was quiet. For the second time in one night, it surprised Lorne that nothing immediately happened when a man was murdered. In fact, the world carried on much unchanged.

A long low stretch of 191. They passed a sign shaped like an arrowhead that said Apache County. This struck the Navajos as odd since the only Apaches they knew were around Dulce, New Mexico, several hundred miles to the Northeast, living good off their royalty checks from the oil wells that blanketed their reservation, bobbing up and down like drunken whores sucking black jizz from the earth. It was daylight now and the blanched desert naked in the scorching sunlight was eerie with its emptiness and wind-strewn sterility. Sometime in late morning they reached Sanders and decided to stop.

The Aztec motel was a cinderblock dogleg along a stretch of Old Route 66 between Sanders and Chambers with boarded up motels on either side, maroon and turquoise paint chipped and fading, a long dead neon sign and a giant concrete Indian with a giant concrete feathered headdress. Across the street in an empty field stood the remnants of a drive-in movie theater, the windblown plastic bags and trash collecting against the rows of metal poles that once housed speakers. Beyond that a barbed wire fence, a half-mile of sand and scrub brush, and I-40, busy with the day's tractor-trailers and speeding cars, silent from this distance like a moving diorama behind glass.

The sun had been up for hours, but those still scratching out a living on the vestiges of Old Route 66 had no need to be up at this hour, and there was no one in sight and no cars on the road. They parked away from the office, and Lorne went in to get a room alone. The window shade rattled as he pulled too hard on the glass door. There was no one waiting behind the counter. He slapped at the little brass bell with the palm of his hand. A few minutes later, a large woman in a flower print dress shuffled in from a back room dragging with her the distant sound of television. Lorne rested his giant paws on the counter. She frowned at his long greasy hair and four-day road stink, but she accepted thirty-five dollars cash for a room. He walked back to the car slowly, checking to see if she peeked through the blinds, but if she was, it was too bright outside to tell.

The carpet was an indeterminate color between green and purple, thick and crunchy but with give underfoot, like layers of dried soda. The room was hot and musty. The air was old. Lorne turned down the plastic thermostat on the wall unit, and the crusted vents exhaled gritty warm air that slowly cooled. Jimmy was parked at the peephole, looking at a fisheye view of the outside world. Ashley and Junior stretched out on one bed, heads on the pillow, skinny, young. Chevis awkwardly sat up on the other bed. Pammy wedged into the only chair, and Lorne paced, loading the pipe.

We should come down, Jimmy said.

Lorne paced faster.

Not here, all of us cramped up like this. No way.

Jimmy thought about this, nodding stoically.

All right, well let's get some beer then.

Lorne took a turn at the peephole, and when he was satisfied he emerged into the sunlight and walked hurriedly to the Malibu. He returned with a case of Busch Light, a family-sized bag of Cool Ranch Doritos, and three packs of Winston Lights. The kids had showered, but Pammy, Chevis, and Jimmy hadn't moved. Pammy emulsified in the one chair, sweating, her layers collapsing, Jimmy with his eye pressed to the tiny glass doorhole, and Chevis sitting straight up, paling, mouth red as if he were bleeding from his lips and gums instead of from the steel shaft in his chest cavity.

It feels good to throw your life away doesn't it?

Lorne was looking down at the pipe he had just taken a hit from, shaking his head and smiling. The others were vaguely paying attention, as much as could be expected.

I don't mean that, throwing it away really. I mean actively destroying it…tearing it apart…. It feels…like freedom.

Do you know what it feels like? Junior spoke unexpectedly, hands behind his head luxuriating on a propped up pillow, looking down through his eyelashes. Like how your gums ache just before you bite into a rare venison steak.

Lorne wheeled and pointed at him.

Yes.

He shook his finger and spun and shook it at the television. Yes.

Like ripping your cuticles, Pammy said. You guys don't do that? It hurts but it feels good. Sometimes I fuck with them until they bleed, get the nail under there and push it back and then bite it off. It hurts but I can't stop myself.

That's because you're a freak, Jimmy said.

She thrust her chin out at him and he returned the gesture, teasing.

Ashley rolled her eyes and let an arm fall absently onto Junior's stomach.

I've felt like this my whole life.

You're young, Chevis said. They were surprised to hear

from him. He hadn't said anything since the killing at the gas station. He coughed and a tendril of blood looped out onto his chin.

You all right?

Chevis grinned, showing blood-streaked teeth. He nodded his head.

I've never felt better. It's like this guy said.

He nodded gingerly toward Lorne.

Blood tastes like freedom.

The afternoon was a blur. They drank and smoked and felt much improved and much insane, the pipe erasing the lack of sleep, the rolling of the days and nights on top of each other like an undertow of consciousness. The others eventually took showers except for Chevis, who would not move. They lost control of the volume, in one moment shouting over the television broadcasting an incomprehensible blend of scenes from sitcoms and the local news flipping over each other and blending into one and in the next huddling together in whispers with the lights turned out, paranoid, afraid they could be seen through the curtains, and then raucous and grinning with glassy eyes and shiny cheeks.

In the night Chevis took a turn, becoming melancholy and then angry and panicked. He cursed Bullfrog Frank, and white people, and then he made them promise to kill the terrorists, continue the mission at any cost. They had largely forgotten about the mission, even Lorne, and they nodded dutifully, already comforting the dead, but then the page would turn, the drug take hold, breathing life into an idea, any idea, and they remembered why it was so important, why they had killed, how they were important, how this was their chance, in this moment, in this motel. And Lorne told the story again, of Tom the drifter, the savior, who'd taken his vow of poverty and still would not be defeated, would not be deterred. And they were rapt.

Sometime in the night Chevis died. At some point in the early morning hours they noticed Chevis was dead. Pammy had sat on the corner of the bed, and the bounce in the box springs tottered Chevis awkwardly onto his side, partially propped up by the protruding crossbow bolt. He stayed that way, already stiff. It was not dignified. Junior crouched down and studied his dead brother. He was not surprised. He felt like they had entered this death cult sometime ago, although he couldn't be sure when the initiation occurred, and this was the natural result. Still it was weird though, seeing the husk that used to contain his brother and now was simply a beacon for his brother's ghost. He couldn't explain it, but he felt like Chevis was just the first of them to go, and the order of death didn't really matter. Ashley put her hand on his shoulder. It felt odd to both of them.

They carried his body to the bathroom and laid him gently in the tub. Ashley and Lorne waited in the outer room while the others washed his body, the water from the lime-crusted faucet melting the dried blood into a rusty stream that ran to the drain. Lorne hobbled to the front door and looked out the eyehole.

I'm going out for a smoke.

You're not going to take off are you?

No.

Cuz you know we'd be fucked.

He squinted back at her. Something caught in his beard.

I mean, if you did.

I just want to go outside for a smoke. Don't you?

Do you think that we should?

I have to.

Yeah, I need to breathe.

Ashley picked up her skinny backpack and crept to the door behind Lorne. The hinges creaked loudly as Lorne cracked the door open cautiously. The night sky was inky black. Lorne peered down the row of vacant rooms with tangerine bug stained lights demarking the doorways, each encumbered by a small army of moths. They closed the door an inch at a time, cringing at every squeak, and sat on a rectangular concrete parking space bumper affixed to the ground by two rusty stalks of rebar. Lorne lit two Winston Lights and handed one to Ashley. She took a long drag and exhaled in a cloud that spiraled into the black night like dye in brackish water, hearing only the sound of cicadas, a deafening rattle drowning out all background noise. Occasional headlights appeared on I 40 across a dark Old Route 66. She watched the faint pinpoint beams silently turn into red taillights fading into darkness. She looked up at the black sky but couldn't find the moon. She spoke in a whisper.

Hey, why didn't you leave?

What?

Lorne was looking here and there, his head darting to lights or sounds that caught his attention or to the flickers in the corners of his eyes that were either real or not.

You've got the car keys.

Lorne pinched his cigarette between his thumb and forefinger.

Look at the sky.

Lorne spread his arms wide extending his fingers up to the unseen heavens.

Have you ever seen anything like it?

Ashley looked up at him with all of her energy in her big blue eyes and tilted her head so that the orange light illuminated her hair and looked to Lorne like tracers of fire dancing against the blackness.

It's beautiful here, the desert, can you feel it in the air? It's everywhere.

I'm just saying.

Lorne slapped at his arm.

I don't want this to end.

She looked at Lorne and smiled a little.

Dude, it's going to end.

Lorne snorted and grinned back at her.

Shit.

Ashley crossed her arms across her breasts and hunched over. She nodded at the door behind them.

What do you think they're doing in there?

Lorne dug a finger into his ear.

I don't know, some kind of ceremony or some shit.

Nice.

What? The fuck do I know about Indians?

Racist.

Fine. I mean I don't know shit about Native Americans. And their burial rituals.

Actually, I think they call themselves Indians.

Does that mean we should?

I don't know. Fuck it.

At that moment the door opened and Jimmy, Pammy, and Junior carried Chevis's body rolled up a comforter from the bed. They took him to the trunk of the Malibu. They gathered around the trunk and took long look before they slammed it shut.

Let's go before someone sees us.

The Malibu crept through town on Old Route 66. The only traffic light in sight was flashing yellow. They turned left and bounced over a railroad crossing and then through a not oft used underpass beneath I-40. The road twisted up the side of a mesa and then flattened on the high plateau. The humidity dropped and stars became visible. The air coming through the passenger side window was less soupy than at the lower elevation back in town. A lone floodlight and a lonely swatch of sumac marked Wide Ruins trading post, now empty. An hour later they reached Klagetoh with dawn approaching. The Klagetoh trading post was open with a small assemblage of pickups already in the parking lot. The Malibu creaked to a halt at a pump, and Junior went inside to pay for gas. He walked past two rows of snack foods of both the salty and sweet variety and a display of handguns under a glass countertop toward the cashier. Some fine Navajo rugs hung along the wall behind the register—red, black and white zigzag patterns on a gray background. The old woman behind the counter asked him if he liked the rugs. He said that he did. He liked the gray background, different from the red background that the weavers he knew used.

You're from the north then?

He nodded.

And how are things up there?

They say times are hard.

They do say that, she agreed.

But these are the only times I know.

The old woman laughed.

Me too.

He paid for the gas with two twenties Ashley had given him. He put the change through a slot cut in the lid of a plastic pickle jar that purported to be collecting money for a scholarship fund.

Hey, travel safe young man, she said in English.

Okay.

When he returned to the car the glass pipe was being passed freshly loaded. The woman watched from the window as the Malibu turned onto 191 headed north.

The sun rose over the Chuska Mountains to the east above the Defiance Plateau that the Malibu traversed at a cool ninety miles per hour. Halfway between Klegatoh and Ganado the Malibu abruptly braked and took a hard left onto Navajo Route 28, a dirt road the locals called the Klegatoh Loop. The road was grated dirt, the desert topsoil scraped clean, and the yellowed thistles and grasses temporarily plowed asunder by a recent bulldozer blade. The road ran a short distance to a low ridgeline that followed the valley where it became a rutted singletrack punctuated by rocks dried and worn smooth by the sun. The track thread a series of scattered and discordant hills and rises populated by juniper and pinions, twisted and stunted, and few white spruce taking solace in waving bunchgrass and grama bowing to the wind. On the leeside of the sierra the desert spread out before them. The Malibu bounced over a dry arroyo, bottoming out on the ruts of once running currents. Lorne ignored the sound of metal undercarriage scraping against sand and rock. If he once cared, he didn't now. On the other side of the arroyo the Malibu left the track and spun its wheels up a talus slope, the engine revving up and down with the reflex of the shocks, and angled to a stop partway up with its nose pointed downhill.

Ashley, Lorne, and Pammy waited in the car. Jimmy and Junior climbed close to the top of the hill and scraped out a shallow grave for Chevis using greasewood and a tire iron to break the hard earth. It was hard work. The trench was only a foot or so deep. They walked back to the car and carried Chevis up the hill and laid him in the trench. His body was even with the land. They set about gathering rocks to cover him up. Ashley, Lorne, and Pammy watched in silence. The wind moaned outside the car, and ribbons of wind whistled through the window seals. When Jimmy and Junior had covered up the grave with a low burial mound they stood for a moment and then walked back down to the car, their long hair blowing wildly in the wind.

Is that it? Lorne said.

Jimmy sat heavily in the passenger seat and slammed the door.

Best not to dwell too much on dead, or else they follow you around in life.

Pammy emptied three little baggies onto a spoon and cooked it to liquid. The wind rocked the car at odd intervals. Dust sifted through the vents, flecks of earth destined for the blood. They took turns shooting up. The effect was immediate and overwhelming. The desert spread out before them. To the northeast, dark clouds gathered over the canyon lands. To the southeast, a hundred mile view, red sand ribbed with whites, yellows, and faded gold. The sun was a pale circle in a white sea, the land blanched under it. The Malibu was back on the dirt road, dust billowing behind it like a mushroom cloud. After some miles the Malibu hit blacktop running south.

Ashley's cell phone vibrated in her backpack. She pulled the phone out from underneath the gun and flipped it open. There was an incoming text message. The message was from Bullfrog Frank. It read:

Where are you

Her blood ran cold. She looked around the car. No one was paying attention to her. Junior was distracted by something out the window in the distance. Reality slapped her like the crest of a wave. It hit her so hard she actually jumped in her seat. But the meth made it hard to gauge reality. Like stepping stones across a fast flowing river or the dotted centerline of the two-lane highway at cruising speed, reality was intermittent, coming in drips and drabs. She texted back:

OMFG!
Thought U were
dead!

She waited a few minutes, feeling her legs tingle, rubbing her smooth thighs together. Her pussy felt wetter than it had ever been, but she was bone dry. She squirmed in her seat, horny and terrified at the same time. She knew she was seriously high.

Chapter 19

Am I poor because I am crazy? Or am I crazy because I am poor? Here's how it begins. You are driving to work one day, to a job you hate, where you will spend the next ten hours doing work you don't like and eating shit from people you don't like, as you do every day, and as you will do every day for rest of your life, or for the next thirty years, which ever comes first, and you see a homeless guy lying in the grass underneath a bush, and you realize you actually envy this guy. I mean it's not a passing thought you laugh off. You're stopped at a red light on your way to work weighing the pros and cons of this guy's existence, and you envy him. You envy his freedom, his mobility, his selfishness, his self-reliance. He has no shitty job to go to. And you think my God, I truly envy a vagrant, probably mentally ill bum. It's actually come to this. And then something happens. Something that changes the trajectory of your life. For me, it wasn't like I lost a child in a car accident or a spouse in the 911 attacks. For me, it was a word and an idea. The idea was that the foreign born owners of the biopharmaceutical company I worked for may have been up to no good, were at least unethical, and very well may be producing our product for some nefarious purpose (I had read the research and there was certainly no good application for the drug we produced). The word was a pejorative term I used in relation to those foreign born owners of our company, a term with an ethnic/racial connotation, a slur really, that I used only once and never uttered again so I will not repeat it here. The transgression was reported to my supervisor who reported it to the corporate ethics officer and resulted in my termination. The word I disowned. That I could never get rid of the idea I cannot explain. I became obsessed with surveillance, with monitoring my former company and its Network. One lead led to another. The investigation of my company led to its parent company and then back down to the parent company's subsidiaries and affiliates and then to other transnational corporations and their subsidiaries and affiliates and then to certain individuals and their agents and operatives and then to their cronies, thugs, and bagmen. At some point I became aware that I was under surveillance. A street sweeper with an earpiece and a white van with tinted windows parked a half-block up. The same face one too many times on the metro with the brim of a hat low over the eyes looking at you without looking. That was when I knew that I had to drop off the grid, that I could be tracked even by microtransmitters embedded in the money. At first it was easy. Well, if not easy it was certainly novel, a game, an adventure. Disappearing. Sleeping in bus stations. Eating in soup kitchens. People seemed generous, or at least I had a generous view of people. I made intense if brief friendships. The kind I never made before. Life was more colorful, vivid. Food tasted better. The land looked more beautiful. The air smelled better, at least when there was a breeze. But then it doesn't end. You realize it doesn't end. There is no waking up. There is no waking up in your own warm clean bed, batteries recharged, time to plan out your day. It becomes a struggle. Finding food, a place to sleep, a place to shit. The grime, the filth, the stench of the streets, of your own body, the ragged company you keep, the mentally ill or the just plain crazy, the violent, the thieves, the perverse, the predators. It becomes a grind. A grind that stretches day after day with no end in sight except death. A grind just like the one you left.

Chapter 20

The windows were rolled down. The air rushed at them like a firestorm. The cell phone vibrated again.

where r u

She texted back:

Dunno

She pressed the buttons deliberately; her thumbs felt numb, the keys sticky. If the others saw her, they said nothing. She could have been texting anyone, the police, anyone. They either trusted her, or they just didn't care. It was hard to care.

WHERE ARE YOU!!!!

At that moment she saw a sign for I-40. The Malibu crested onto a wide sloping on-ramp, its last hubcap shot off into the scrub brush. Lorne watched without interest. She texted:

I 40

east or west?

She held the phone loosely in her lap, taking deep breaths

and feeling her molecules bind and twist. Whatever it is that makes up consciousness revolved somewhere outside her body.

West

She snapped shut the phone and put it back into her backpack. The interstate spread out before them. A million shards of light danced in the roadway, beautifully stretching into oblivion.

Chapter 21

Bullfrog Frank's eyes opened to the ceiling of the trailer. He'd never seen it from this angle before. Water stains. Cobwebs. The loose filaments from some disorganized spider. It was daylight. He could hear the chatter of birds outside and the rustle of the wind through pine boughs. His orientation to the world came slowly. He was flat on his back, his legs propped up by an overturned card table. Blood splatter coated the wall and ran up to the ceiling. Little circles of matter with their own red streaks streamed like tear drops of blood down the Virgin's checks. He did not connect this bloody effluvium to himself until he noticed the wetness around his neck and he probed gently with his hand and lifted it to his face and saw with horror that his hand was covered in a serum of blood and pus. It came back to him in a flash. His eyes darted to where the Indian should have been crucified to his trailer wall. There was only a bloody hole where the crossbow bolt had been. He lurched to his feet, kicking the metal card table into the TV, shattering the picture tube. The trailer was trashed. He could still smell the gun smoke and meth.

Ashley!

He yelled it, but he knew the trailer was empty. Enraged, he brought a giant fist down on the kitchen counter, snapping the pressure treated plyboard in half so the mold-spotted sink collapsed and dangled to the floor by a rust colored pipe like a plucked goose with a kinked neck. He kicked down the door to the back bedroom. It exploded off its hinges, spraying wood shards all over the bed. The mirrored closet door was open, and he knew what that meant. The money and the gun were gone, along with the girl. He slid the closet door along its rail until he was face to face with his reflection in the full-length mirror.

Jesus Fucking Christ.

From his ears down half his chest he was coated in a thick sticky syrup, the color and consistency of sweet and sour sauce. The shot had blown his goiter clear off. The wound on his neck looked like charred ham drowning in pineapple glaze. A long flap of skin dangled from one side. A yellow ooze ran down the flap and mixed with the amalgam like a popped water balloon filled with piss.

He went back into the kitchen and pulled a bottle of Jack out of a cupboard and emptied it into his mouth, swallowing half and letting the other half run down his neck, flushing the gaping wound. It stung like a son of a bitch. He injected a syringe full of meth into his hand for the pain. He was suddenly sky high. He found his first aid kit in the closet with his hunting gear, and wrapped his neck in gauze, tucking in the loose flap of skin as best he could. He looked at himself in the mirror again and laughed like a maniac. He looked younger, he thought. His face was thinner. The thought made him laugh again. He didn't look pretty, but he never had. At least they'd have to call him something other than Bullfrog.

He grabbed the sawed-off ten gauge from the bottom of the footlocker, the crossbow, and his stash, and headed out into the sunlight. He didn't know what day it was and he didn't care. He could have been in a coma for all he knew. Outside the sky was a crisp clear blue like the day of creation. The pick up, a '78 Ford F150, started up on the first turn. The 350 V8 rumbled beneath him. The cab smelled of the plastic and vinyl dash warmed by the sun and the cloth seat cover steeped in old cigarette smoke. He gathered his fraying ponytail and smoothed back the loose strands of greasy hair. He took a snort of crystal off the back of this hand and lit a Winston. His eyes felt like razor blades. With one hand he wheeled the truck through a patch of thistles and wild flowers and started down the narrow dirt road, with the other hand he flipped up his phone and texted Ashley.

Where r u

The truck barreled down the jeep trail, two ruts in the weeds, the trees darting in and out, closing in. He could do it with his eyes shut, the wheel moving even faster than he could think about it, the truck floating through the woods like a leaf down a stream. He hit the county road and fishtailed wide. Unexpectedly, a pickup was coming the other way on the usually empty road, and he swerved onto the far shoulder as the oncoming pickup honked its horn and braked hard to the inside just missing him. The other driver extended his finger out the window. Frank flushed with rage and reached for the sawed-off. Then he eased back onto the northbound lane and laughed.

That was my bad.

He laughed and said it again.

That was my bad you lucky fucker.

Almost got you kilt.

He punched the radio and got Kenny Chesney coming out of a Tucson station. The road snaked the valley ahead, the sky was dazzling, too bright for his gelatinous eyes. Greens, yellows and blues. It was all beautiful. He checked his cell. Ashley had texted him back.

That's cute he thought. Fucking adorable. I love that little girl. I'm going to kill them all.

Chapter 22

The Caprice cruiser glided along 160 West through much of the Navajo Nation and around the red mesas of the Hopi much like an escape pod launched into deep space by some dying spaceship. It was under Hailey's control, but she was barely aware of it. A steady flow of cool air from the sixteen dashboard vents kept the interior chilly even as the green digital readout next to the tachometer measured the outside air temperature at one hundred and ten. Hailey felt like she was enveloped in bubble wrap, the Caprice a metal egg effortlessly transported hundreds of miles to her unseen destination. She was the yolk in the egg.

She was briefly roused from her trance rounding a curve, when she couldn't help but notice the pickup parked in a turnout, her police instinct never totally muted by the pills. Not the pickup but the man next to the pickup. Not his general unkempt appearance, his unplanned beard, hair wild, ratty even, which she regarded in an instant, but the way he stared at her, as if he made her for a cop before she rounded the bend, as if he were looking for a cop. As she sped by she saw the second man, better dressed, urinating off of the side of the road, and then she glanced back to the disheveled one, eyes still locked on her, his head swiveling as she passed, frozen as if unable to look away. And then the curve finished its aperture and there were only smooth sandstone cliffs in the rearview, and she was already wondering if she'd really seen something in the man or if he were just another fool too fixated on discerning unmarked vehicles. And then she flinched from a sharp jabbing pain in her hip and became aware that she had been sitting frozen at the wheel for the last four hours since Bartonville. She fumbled through her purse, and with one hand she twisted off the cap to the Vicodin, rattled two of them out and swallowed them dry.

The Caprice was quiet. Air tight. She could tell there was a wind outside by the dust devils and the bobbing antenna and the rivers of sand swimming across the open desert, but nothing penetrated the cruiser and the ride was steady. She was close enough to Flagstaff to get the NPR station crackling a benign conversation about the significance of San Francisco Peak to the native community and how snowmaking with reclaimed water was seen by some as spraying raw sewage on the sacred mountain. She felt the Viks merge with the Perks and the Demerol (had she taken Dems today?) and the pain receded along with her interest in the case and the strange way that hobo had stared at her as if he saw her coming (wasn't she looking for a bum? No, she was looking for two bums) and she once again enjoyed the drive with a passing appreciation of the scenery, the desert unfolding beyond her tinted windows,and the dark looming mountains of Flagstaff thick and green with dense pine forests under a liquid mercury sky. The mountains rose even higher as she approached Flagstaff so she was actually craning her neck. Silver clouds swirled above the peaks, and she felt her scalp tingle. But that could have been the Ephedrine she took to counter the Viks and stay awake. Still, she felt alive, insulated in her metal football. The land could still do that to her. She figured that was why she lived out here.

She took the business loop to downtown Flag. Main Street had the feel of the old western mining town it was, two-story brick buildings with wooden balconies, saloons, historic hotels, a railroad depot still functioning, and rusty tracks running right through town. But on closer inspection most of the store fronts housed coffee shops, bead stores, tourist T-shirt emporiums, or sold snowboards or mountain bikes or climbing gear and the associated apparel. The streets were full of college kids from Northern Arizona University looking like they were either going to or coming from the ski area even though it was summer. There were fliers up in all the store windows and taped to telephone poles for concerts, classes, and every manner of festival from the High Plains Chile Cook-off to the 25th Annual Flagstaff Bluegrass Jamboree. She wondered why she didn't move to a place like this, where something was going on. She watched two girls pass a group of boys on the street, and they stopped to talk to a sleepy looking kid with a beard and a nice smile. Someone they knew from class. They punched numbers into each other's phones. They'd meet up later.

Hailey parked the Caprice and found a seat on a crowded patio of a trendy bar and ordered a chicken Caesar salad and a microbrew from a wispy little college girl in a tight T-shirt with La Estrallita tattooed on her tit. She was bright and perky, full of what she was going to be. Hailey suddenly hated her. The patio was a jumble of people in animated conversation. A cluster behind her were talking about last season's ski conditions. Another group were planning a climb in Escalante. A couple talked abstractly about the war.

The salad was perfect. Fresh, locally grown vegetables. The air carried the crisp cool scent of mountain pines. The beer was complex, brewed with care and full of bitter flavor. A troop of dreadlocked hippies with guitars on their backs walked past, and a tall one with white teeth smiled her way, but she didn't know she was supposed to smile back. She could never live here, she realized. Maybe she could have, but that time had passed. She just couldn't take these people seriously. They didn't have problems. She liked people and places with problems. She needed problems. Didn't know how to live without them.

A half hour later, cruising south on the divided four-lane highway down from Flagstaff, tall pines on both sides and the vistas opening up below with breathtaking views of the lower mountain ridges descending to the desert floor, her mood lightened. She was a career woman, she told herself. She had accomplishments, accommodations. Besides, she wasn't ever going to snowboard, or rock climb, or mountain bike farther than the bar down the street. After her accident, one of her girlfriends emailed her an article about an Iraq vet who'd lost his legs and had gone on to climb Denali. But that was other people. She was no soldier, no athlete. She had a job. People with jobs don't have time for that shit. And she still had a nice ass, she smiled to herself.

For the final descent to the Valley of the Sun, she rolled the windows down and put on the hip hop station. The cactus flew by at ninety. The heat blasted through the open windows. Her mouth was dry. In front of her a gigantic city rose out of the fiery desert. She couldn't help but feel optimistic.

She took the 51 to Camelback and drove straight to Scottsdale, through faux adobe old town with its galleries, antique shops, and sushi bars, to the Embassy Suites adjacent to Scottsdale Fashion Mall. She parked the cruiser in a spot away from other cars and stepped out into the twilight. The heat stunned her. She stood straight and stretched and felt the heat work through her. It seemed to flush away all her thoughts. She felt the heat relax her joints, her bad hip, her contorted back, and gave her a head rush as if the heat relaxed a few extra molecules of pain killer in her veins.

Parking far away had the disadvantage of leaving an expanse of superheated asphalt between her and the entrance to the hotel. If she had been wearing heals, she was sure the spikes would have sank into the pavement, so relaxed was the blacktop under the oppressive sun. As it was, she felt uneasy in her flats. A layer of heat puckered the air a few feet off the ground so that it shimmered, and she worried that black asphalt would stain the white soles of her shoes.

Inside the hotel safely behind the tinted windows, it was three shades darker and fifty degrees cooler. The air smelled of chlorine and whatever's in filters used in industrial dehumidifiers. The center of the hotel was occupied by a lush terrarium and a swimming pool ringed on all four sides by seventeen floors of rooms. She looked up like a child gaping at a full moon. Bougainvillea hung from each floor like a cascading waterfall. The ceiling was a glass pyramid protruding from the roof with four smaller glass pyramids on each corner for a total of five. She vaguely recalled an ad campaign the hotel chain had running, something to do with five, five stars, or five diamonds, something to denote quality, and she wondered if they built the roof around the ad campaign or the ad campaign around the roof. She guessed the latter, but she had a sinister suspicion it might be the former. She didn't know why that felt sinister to her, that a corporation would build a roof to suit an ad campaign. But she did know that she was easily distracted.

She checked in for two nights and was pleased to get the government rate of $99 a night. At the granite counter, the hotel receptionist, a man in a denim-looking shirt with a tie that matched the color of the carpet, studied her government I.D. for longer than she thought necessary. In turn she studied his carefully manicured 5 o'clock shadow and heavily styled hair.

You're too pretty to be an FBI agent, he said brazenly.

She should have been taken aback, but this was Scottsdale

where everyone was judged on appearances, so she smiled inwardly, almost giggled.

You're too cute to be bellhop.

Concierge, madam, concierge, he said with a fake accent that was neither French nor English, Australian perhaps. She laughed nonetheless, then felt embarrassed, then worried that she'd offended the man by calling him a bellhop. She finished initialing and signing and hastily took the glass elevator to the eleventh floor. The sensation gave her vertigo. She thought about what she should have said back. Clearly you're a man of many talents or something like that, but then she thought that might also sound condescending, and then she thought fuck this place. FUCK THIS PLACE.

She put it all behind her with a flick of her hair and slid the key card into room 1117, grateful to see the light flash green and hear the door click unlocked. The room was cold. The door slammed shut behind her, and she felt safe. She dropped her roller in the center of the room and went instinctively to the windows. She fought through at least two layers of curtains to the hermetically sealed windows and pressed her forehead against a view that was higher than any in her half of the state of Utah. It was unnaturally silent in the room, as if the scene outside was on television. She halfheartedly unpacked, throwing her things into two of the six drawers and leaving her shoes in the roller and then returned to the windows, an eleventh story view of now unsellable houses and the Scottsdale Fashion Mall and a vast parking lot with cars as far as the eye could see. She was suddenly depressed. She wished she'd kept driving south, straight to Mexico. She locked her service weapon and her laptop in the room safe, grabbed her key card and her handbag and left, afraid of what would happen if she stayed.

The Embassy Suites was connected to the Scottsdale Fashion Mall by a glassed corridor with a moving walkway, so she didn't have to go outside. The heat of the day was far behind her. She wore flip-flops, and that made her feel better. She smiled at her beautiful and sedate surroundings. The moving escalator ended at an ocean of marble flooring punctuated by the first of no less than seven fountains spouting water twenty feet in the air and splashing into turquoise pools. Although none of the spray hit her, she felt the coolness of the water evaporating into the air like a childhood summer day wasting into adulthood, unnoticed and taken for granted. The mall was bright. The marble, glass, and water reflected light back at her like a mirror and gave her an almost euphoric feeling, but one that was constantly leaving. She kept her sunglasses on.

When Hailey went shopping she never bought much. She was particular. The mall was considered upscale: Tiffany's, Max Maura, Gucci, and the obligatory Victoria's Secret. The mall was crowded, and few looked like they could afford the shops, but it was impossible to tell. This was a town where teenagers in shredded jeans and wife-beater tank tops drove Hummers. She was amazed at how crowded the Louis Vuitton store was. She waited twenty minutes to get the salesgirl's attention at the counter. She looked at an oversized handbag for $980 but ultimately passed. She had something special in mind, and she found it at Neiman Marcus on the mall's ground floor. A pair of Christian Louboutins, black satin platform pumps with the signature red soles and five-inch stiletto heals, costing almost $800. She put them on her MasterCard, admired the pretty package and the merlot colored bag that she would carry proudly with her the rest of the day. She left supremely satisfied.

She wandered into Ra, a sushi bar with outdoor seating covered by misters which made the outside habitable, and took a bar stool at a small round table. She ordered tuna sashimi and a sake bomb. She people watched for five minutes, busying herself with her Blackberry and feeling self conscious until the waitress brought her a small white jar of sake and a twenty ounce Kirin beer that she'd ordered and made it all better.

She allowed herself to put the Blackberry in her bag and let her eyes drift to the flatscreen over the outdoor bar where SportsCenter silently fought a losing battle against the sun's glare. A creature came out and stood flat against the doorframe. She was in a knit cap with earflaps and a dated windbreaker and looked for someone who wasn't in there or never existed. Anyone who noticed avoided eye contact. The creature paced awkwardly, ducked her head, looked ashamed, and left. Afterwards a kitchenman followed her out. She had not gone far. He said something to her and she stood dumbly, comprehendingly, waved a meek acknowledgment and continued into the wasteland.

Something to love. Wasn't that it? Hailey filed her little ceramic cup with sake and drank it in long sips.

She watched two men in suits sitting just outside the perimeter of shade the umbrellas provided, the man farthest from the misters looking clearly uncomfortable. One man shoved a clumsily folded wad of bills at the other to cover the check safely ensconced in a black leather valet. The other man held up his hand and threw down his plastic. The first man stuffed his bank roll back into the pocket of his cramped slacks, barely concealing his relief.

Two young women with tattooed arm sleeves and various metal studs gleaming in the sun took a different approach to the check, gesticulating wildly, arms crossing and uncrossing, hands running through heavily gelled hair. Hailey busied herself with her beer chaser. Nothing more depressing than lesbians arguing about money.

The scene made her more uncomfortable then she already was. If a casual observer could innocently watch this scene and read those people's thoughts then what were people thinking about her? She could hear their thoughts. Poor sad girl, alone, with the weird walk. Sad. Sad. And she thought she was hot. She'd been told she was hot. Was it a lie? Did it matter? No, it didn't. Hot and lonely, hoping one of these red-faced recently divorced lawyers with man-boobs nipping through sweat damp polo shirts would offer to buy her a drink. Sad. She realized there must be some here who wanted to but wouldn't because of the sheer awkwardness of the situation. Sad. And that she wanted one to. Sad. Only the biggest asshole would hit on her in a place like this. Someone who didn't care if they were bothering someone else or not, if they looked like a fool or not. Like inverse natural selection. She was doomed to only meet the biggest assholes. That explained a lot.

She shook her head involuntarily and left dangling a shoe by her finger. She walked quickly through the mall and down the tinted glass encased walkway to the hotel. In the artificial cool and quiet of her room she left the lights off. In the half-light of the approaching night, she stood looking out the floor to ceiling windows at the auburn swath of sky between the dolloped mountains where the sun had been. Scottsdale Boulevard filled with headlights, and the overhead halogens cast conical tubes of white light on the pavement.

Even from the height of the hotel in the fading light, she could see the goings on across the Boulevard. She watched some young prostitutes slovenly congeal in a group and then fan out into the night. That was how it had to be she supposed, one must be coveted and one must covet. Could just as easily be the other way around she supposed, women pulling up in cars and paying the men. It just turned out this way instead. And then she thought of her own situation. She wanted to get laid, but she didn't want to be paid for it. She didn't know what to make of the irony.

Chapter 23

The Malibu was not aerodynamic. Even less so with the windows down, hot air vibrating the metal hulk, periodically shifting the internal pressure like a helicopter was hovering just overhead. It battered its way through wind resistance at eighty miles an hour by sheer brute strength, the engine roaring louder than the stereo so a blanket of noise enveloped them in an ever growing numbness. The world was being born, reborn, and destroyed every second. Pammy, Jimmy, and Lorne had ridden benders before and knew the only thing to do was to see where it goes and assess the damage later. It would end eventually. Or it wouldn't. Ashley and Junior in the backseat weren't thinking about it at all. Besides, there was no place to get off this ride anyway.

The scenery along the interstate was somehow blander than the dramatic spires of playdough sandstone, red rock gorges, and cactus forest desert scape that they'd burrowed through on the narrow two-lane state highways, but on the interstate the spaces seemed three hundred and sixty degree wide open, infinite, impenetrable, so that after three hours of hard sunburnt driving, Lorne felt like they'd travelled nowhere, even though in reality, or at least the dim indicia of it, they'd covered over two hundred miles and were solidly in the western part of the state, not far from the Grand Canyon. With space and distance immeasurable and lacking consistency, time also lost its structure, and if not for the ancient yellow gas gage indicator light and its irrefutable logic, they may have kept driving until their innards exploded and buried them in their own piss and shit.

Lorne saw a town up ahead. A brown spot off the interstate identifiable by a cluster of sickly palms. At least a gas station and a motel. Two of the three essentials. The third being meth, prodigiously smoked. Which they had. And they smoked. Prodigiously. The Malibu braked unevenly on one pad down to the quick, and the other slick with leaking brake fluid. The feeling mimicked Lorne's heartbeat, three beats on, one beat off, as the car took the off-ramp at a fifteen degree angle off-center due to the beating the alignment had taken in the last three days, the last thirty years. The Malibu coasted the long arc of the off-ramp with precision, Lorne's concentration heightened by the immediacy of purpose. The sun hit the windshield like a razor blade pendulum illuminating the rock-born spider bites in the shatterproof glass.

The narrow frontage road was lined by tall yellow grass brittled by the sun. Each gap in the grass was marked by a red swath of dirt, dust, and sand blown across the road by a constant crosswind. The road was calm compared to the chaos of the interstate, but it only served to punctuate the strung out edginess palpable in the Malibu. The gas station was a rickety affair off the frontage road with a rusted Pennzoil sign that slapped against a metal pole with the wind like a door being slammed in anger. They spilled out of the car and drifted aimlessly in the parking lot. A twenty appeared in Lorne's hand for gas, at least it seemed to him that it had just appeared there, but after a moment he thought that it might have come from Ashley. He didn't think about where she'd gotten it from or why she'd given it to him. He put twenty in the tank and paid without making eye contact with the clerk. Out the age-smeared window he saw Junior standing in the middle of the parking lot, staring at something in the distance. Jimmy walked in little circles while Pammy squatted and took a piss by the side of the building. Ashley waited in the back seat of the Malibu, her pretty face staring straight ahead. He could still hear traffic from the interstate, but mostly he heard the wind.

On the road again, Lorne felt an intolerable jittery twitch in his legs and fingertips and a sudden feeling of dread. He needed a drink. The frontage road intersected with a county road, and at the corner was a motel with a crushed quartz rotund encircling a stand of palm trees. The Malibu crunched over the white shards of fill with a satisfying sound as it pulled into the driveway. A Budweiser sign hung in the lobby window. The motel was two stories, yellow stucco with a Spanish-tiled roof, decorated with cow skulls and cactus. Old tires had been sunk halfway into the ground to mark the parking spaces. Two wagon wheels flanked the lobby entrance. The palm trees circled a faux oasis, a kiddy pool sized brackish pond filled in with weeds and grass. The desiccated palm fronds rustled rhythmically in the wind. Lorne got them a room on the second floor with more of Ashley's money, and they went upstairs. Lorne silently thanked God the place had a bar, but first he needed to party. He was sure they had one last gasp before whatever crash was coming.

In the room, the pipe was passed and the weight was lifted. They took serious hits, the hits of no return. Lorne went outside and set his arms on the railing of the second story slab. Inside the motel room, Jimmy and Pammy were taking hits and blowing the white smoke into each other's mouths, recycling. He bet Junior and Ashley were somewhere doing the same. He didn't know when, but the sky had turned a rich lavender. The silhouette of arid barren mountains cut black against the darkening pastel sky. Lorne lit a cigarette. The air was soft and almost moist. His skin tingled instead of itched. Cast iron lanterns came on below. Amber glowed from the glass-encased bulbs meant to mimic candlelight. The rustle of the palm trees seemed exotic, like he was being transported. But he was here, and not here. He inhaled deeply and watched the cigarette smoke fan out into oblivion. He laughed once, liked the feel of it, and then laughed full out loud. He'd done it, he'd gotten away with murder. Of course he hadn't murdered anyone, but that's not they way the law would see it. But here he was, feeling the expanse of the night, every cell tingling. The stars came out like blurs there to make you dizzy, points of reference whose only purpose was to show you that solid ground did not exist. Expecting the motel room door to be the thick hacienda black stained wood it pretended to be, Lorne pushed too hard on the cheap plywood and it flew back against the doorstop and bounced back at him but he caught it. He was ninja fast. Pammy and Jimmy looked up with vague recognition, the pipe in mid pass. He didn't have to say anything. Jimmy took a hit and then beckoned him forward. Lorne spread his lips, and Jimmy blew a fountain of smoke into his mouth. Lorne inhaled and then stumbled with thumbs up around the room and into the bathroom. To his surprise, Ashley was just finishing on the toilet. He grabbed the back of her neck and pushed his mouth on hers and forced the smoke from his lungs into hers. She inhaled and held it there with a look that gave both reprimand and hope. Lorne tried to finish the transfer by leaving his lips on her mouth, but she put a hand on his chipmunk chest, pushing him away without actually pushing. She looked up, her eyes a cold gray blue that made Lorne's stomach drop with ache. Her beauty was physically painful. It occurred to him that the only reason he was this close to such a beautiful girl was the meth, and he thanked God for it, again. This was what life was all about. The validation of all his drunken philosophies. His bullshit. He knew it was bullshit. But she was real. Probably not legal, but real. He tried to kiss her again, and again she put her hand on his chest. Her hair had lanky curls with highlights that shown iridescent in the florescent bathroom light, an unnatural sheen that smelled great, like rich people's spa treatments. He touched her arm just below the shoulder. It was silken skin. He outlined the faint trace of a tricep with his middle finger while running his thumb across the more defined bulge of her bicep. She stared involuntarily at his crotch. He tried for a third time to kiss her, and this time she stopped him with just one arched eyebrow and a little knowing smirk. He took a half step back and followed her gaze to his own crotch. He stared at it with her. He felt like she was talking, but she wasn't. She was laying bare the mysterious well of horniness and shame. Daring him to go there. And his cock felt like the touchstone of life. He felt it through his jeans and it made him weak in the knees.

Yeah, she said.

He unzipped and took it out. At least as best he could. It was all shrunken and withdrawn from days of meth but it felt great. Suddenly, out in the open he couldn't stop touching it. She leaned back against the toilet and smiled. He started pulling it in earnest.

That's it.

She looked in the mirror and laughed.

Lorne was too far gone to stop. This was no erection whatsoever, but somehow that added to the thrill of it. Just a little bald head and bunched up skin. Like a clitoris. He rubbed it with his palm and it felt better than any purple rocket he'd ever had. It actually made his legs buckle. He groaned involuntarily. Mewing in spite of himself. He didn't want to take it that far. Nobody wants to mew. But he couldn't help it. He couldn't help anything now.

For some reason she focused on the cheap motel soap sitting slimily next to the faucet that someone had unwrapped and used and then she looked into the mirror at Lorne masturbating furiously and felt her hips rocking back and forth on the toilet seat. She caught Lorne's eyes with her stunning grays and guided them to the soap. The bar of soap was pink and deeply cracked and ridged, more like a luffa or a pumice stone. Lorne put it under the faucet and rolled it in his hands, noticing for the first time that his palms were desiccated and calloused from the days of partying, and skin that should have been soft, or at least smooth, formed deep valleys and was as rutted and hard as the long suffering bar of soap. He worked up a thin lather and used it to rub his drug-shrunken cock. The girl watched this display with a sardonic smile. Her big eyes and arched eyebrows said 'really?' but there was nothing in the look that said 'stop' or even 'slow down'. The greasy trail of lube from the soap felt like a hot wet mouth to Lorne, and he moaned like a woman.

The bathroom door opened unceremoniously, and Junior took a step in the dim yellowed room, unbuckling his jeans to piss when he saw them. He saw them in the mirror first upon entering, and then he looked at Ashley sitting on the toilet and Lorne with the cock in his hand and then looked back in the mirror, not really sure what he was seeing and trying to decipher reality. Lorne buttoned up quick. This was weird, even for him. He ducked out of the room without washing the slime off his hands.

Ashley looked stunned, her supple pale face blanched a degree whiter if that was possible, her demeanor totally changed. Reality hit her in an instant — this boy — the murder, Bullfrog Frank, her phone buzzing and vibrating with texts even now, Chevis with an arrow sticking out of his chest, Lorne masturbating like a deranged chimpanzee, and these Indians and the glass pipe and wherever they were going and whatever apocalypse they were trying to stop — this boy.

Before Junior could say anything stupid, or worse, do anything stupid, Ashley stood up off the can and with her panties still around her ankles shuffled to Junior and threw her arms around his neck, and she kissed him harder and deeper then he'd ever been kissed.

Lorne went straight through the room, passed Jimmy and Pammy spooning in the bed and opened the door out into the night. It was hot and humid in the room and hotter outside. The sky was purple with thin orange clouds and stars that blinked like the Christmas lights strung loosely in the palm trees lining the driveway. He lit a cigarette and hung his arms over the balcony railing and exhaled deeply.

Fuck.

He walked across the balcony and down the stairs and pushed open the door to the hotel lobby. As promised, there was a bar in the back guarded by a black curtain and a sign that read 'Caballeros'. Inside it was a single room with three booths along one side, a mishmash of tables in the middle, and a sturdy oak bar with a long bottle-lined mirror on the other side. One of the booths was occupied by a Mexican couple sitting next to each other on the same side of the booth and talking in whispers. An old guy at the end of the bar picked his head up when Lorne walked in and then looked back down. The bartender dangled a cigarette out one side of his mouth. The only other person at the bar was a leggy blonde stabbing a cocktail straw into a vodka tonic like she was trying to punish the lime wedge for all the crimes of her past.

Chapter 24

Bullfrog Frank hit the I-40 and stopped for breakfast at Tony's Truck Town. He pushed open the glass door and was startled and then annoyed by the bell that tinkled overhead. The clatter of forks and knives on plates slicing through eggs over easy and flapjacks stopped when he entered. He felt for the dying flap of skin dangling from his neck and tucked it into the bandage he'd made for himself. He sat at one of the fake wood tables and pulled out a metal chair so violently it almost eluded his grip and flew across the room. He ordered what everyone was eating—eggs, bacon, wheat toast, potatoes, and coffee. The waitress, a chubby girl just out of high school reluctantly took the order. She stood two yards back, her mouth agape, staring at the oozing wound on his neck.

How do you want those eggs?

He pushed his sunglasses onto his forehead. His eyes were red.

How do I want them? He smiled wide.

That's funny.

What do you mean, mister?

The farmers and truckers shuffled in their seats.

How do you recommend?

Recommend? Eggs?

Yeah.

The girl looked out at the flawless blue sky and the freeway with traffic moving at ninety miles an hour.

Scrambled, I guess.

Frank smiled wider and his neck oozed watery puss.

Scrambled is good.

A few minutes later the waitress filled his white ceramic mug with coffee from an orange plastic football-shaped coffee pot. She was careful not to look at him. When the food came, he took a bite of the eggs but couldn't swallow them. He held them in his mouth for a long time, but he couldn't make his throat work. He took the mug of coffee and walked out into the parking lot and spat out the eggs.

He took a slug of coffee and spat that out too for good measure.

Chapter 25

Walking past the entrance to the parking garage of the Embassy Suites, Hailey smelled weed. The smell was unmistakable. She followed the smell around a concrete pylon. The concierge, with the same polished hair but now changed into street clothes, was holding a joint and talking to a friend. He smiled when he saw her.

Hey FBI, wanna hit this?

He held the joint out to her. The friend, a college-aged kid with expensive slacks, an unbuttoned and untucked French cuffed shirt, and a trimmed beard, also smiled and held out his arms like her table awaited.

Jesus, not very subtle are you?

She walked over but held up her hand, passing on the joint.

You don't know if you don't ask.

I mean you're not too worried about getting caught.

He passed the joint to his friend who took a hit.

What, we're not breaking any laws?

Actually, I think you are.

Well, not any that are important.

The friend eyed the Christian Louboutin bag.

Very nice.

She smoothed an errant strand of blonde hair behind her ear.

I couldn't resist.

Is she really FBI? The friend exhaled a funnel of smoke.

Yup.

Cool.

Yup.

She's one cool lady.

I'm really not that cool.

She's one sorta cool lady.

She turned to the friend.

You work here too?

He laughed and shook his head, smoke venting from side to side as he did so.

He doesn't work, said the concierge.

But you do.

Yup. I do all kinds of work.

I bet you do. Jesus, did I just said that?

I'm off work now, do you want to go to a party?

She shrugged.

Apparently I have nothing better to do.

She got in the back seat of an ageless Honda Civic. The friend with clothes more expensive than the car offered her the front seat, but she let him have it. She was oddly comfortable in the backseat. The car rode a few inches off the ground. She liked being a passenger for a change. The back windows were tinted, and she relaxed into the seat cushion, no idea where they were off to.

The streets were wide. The sky was burnt orange. At speed the city itself seemed like a scenic highway. Large saguaros and mesquite lined driveways. Glass office buildings and shopping malls. The city's skyline was mesmerizing; she'd seen it countless times before, but now the city's skyscrapers seemed as alien and as beautiful as the scattered rock formations in the desert canyon lands.

They didn't talk much, couldn't talk much over the music the concierge played, some impossibly new band in an impossibly new genre, afro-beat techno if she had to give it a name, the type of band or genre that Hailey couldn't keep up with because she would never know where to look for it again, even though she was enjoying it.

Scottsdale, Moon Valley, Peoria, Glendale, the city was suburbs and the suburbs were the city. The streets were wide. The new football stadium hovered over the west valley like a spaceship, its base obscured by a dusty haze. Built as an homage to the barrel cactus, it looked more like a metallic mushroom landing on top of suburbia, squashing the citizenry below.

They entered a subdivision of faux adobe single family homes with identical red tile roofs and floor plans. Young palm trees no more than ten feet in height were interspersed one to a house. The Civic saddled up to the curb in front of a house with the door propped open. A jeep and two new pickups were in the driveway. Several cars were parked haphazardly on the street, one on the lawn.

The concierge clenched her fist in his and helped her out of the backseat. They went through the open door and another genre of music that she couldn't name took over and again she liked it. They said hi to a few people in the kitchen and went though the sliding glass patio doors to the backyard where a few girls caught the last orange-red rays of sun by the pool and a cluster of guys manned a grill billowing with smoke.

The concierge handed her a Corona with a lime and then disappeared for a while. She chatted with a few of the something somethings. Two girls in bikinis said hi. Nobody ignored her but nobody paid her much attention either and that was fine. She kicked off her sandals and dangled her feet in the pool. She was glad she wore her cute yellow sundress. Nobody was partying hard, no crack pipes or needles, just beers and burgers. She felt relaxed and realized it had been a while since she'd done anything like this. She figured this was a pre-party for the dozen or so something somethings before they hit the town. Even just sipping beer, she knew she wouldn't last until the real partying began and that was fine. It had been a long day and this was a nice turn. And then she looked up and the sky was black and the stars left little traces when she moved. Her bare feet felt good in the backyard grass. The pool shimmered an iridescent blue. Still, it might have been midnight when she sat on a kitchen counter and watched through a haze of cigarette smoke as the friend kissed a brown skinned brunette and whispered something in her ear and she laughed and punched him in the chest, at least a dozen something somethings crowded in the kitchen and the concierge by her side whose name was Tony although most folks called him ZPak, and she casually wondered if it was a reference to herpes or some other STD, not the STD but rather the antibiotic cocktail that cured it, although his real name was Antonio which surprised her because he hadn't looked Hispanic until she stared closely at him now and could see it; it was in his dark eyes and stubbled jawline, and it somehow made him suddenly more attractive. She smiled at him then, and he smiled back at her and then looked away, satisfied with something. She held the kitchen counter with her palms and swung her legs playfully and they both watched the crowd.

The drive back to Scottsdale was fast this time of night. The sky was black, the streetlights, white and orange, floated by like tails of comets. The drive felt ethereal, hard to tell where the road ended and the sky began, quiet but loud with the stereo at the same time.

The streets were wide. The Civic skated across the empty lanes effortlessly. The Embassy Suites rose like a glass beacon, a luminescent green E emblazoned in a white pyramid cast down on the dark city below. She thought of the Wizard of Oz, like they had traveled long to reach the Emerald City, and wondered if this too were a marketing ploy.

He took her up the service elevator to her room on the

eleventh floor. They made love, and it was not at all like she had expected it to be, drunken hook up and all, sweat and bad breath and pawing. Instead it was nice. Slow, only a little awkward, and that made it kind of sweet in a way.

When she woke in the morning he was gone. She was relieved in a way, but she didn't quite know what to do with the day and thought it odd that he could be working the front desk at that moment—at the very least he was probably somewhere in the hotel. She took her black government laptop out of the safe and powered it up. The Dell blinked once and flashed the FBI logo and seal across a blue screen. She had a moment of panic when she couldn't find her secure ID token, a pager sized device that gave her a passcode that changed every ninety seconds. She rooted through her bag and found it amid a bramble of spare keys, sugarless gum wrappers, and outdated gym memberships and coffee shop punch cards. She logged in with five seconds to spare before her computer would have locked her out and she'd have to call the IT administrator in Salt Lake City. Once into her computer, she logged in to her government email account. It usually had several hundred unread messages, and she was surprised to see fewer than fifty. Not a good sign. Maybe they'd actually started to forget about her. She scrolled through her inbox looking for anything urgent or that would give a clear indication that her services at the FBI were no longer welcome. A dozen of the messages were from one thread from her dwindling group of work friends. The chain began with a message with a YouTube video labeled WTF, isn't this your neck of the woods Hailey? The video was dated from yesterday and already had over one hundred thousand hits. She clicked the link to the video, and a grainy black and white security gas station camera freeze frame came to life. It was night. The sky was black. Everything was an overexposed white. The screen was split in four, each quadrant showing the view from a different security camera. The upper left quadrant showed a well-muscled man in a tank top with what looked like an arrow sticking straight out of his chest cross a parking lot and enter a gas station convenience store. In the upper right quadrant, the man in profile now, with a projectile clearly heaving up and down with the pulse of his breathing, raised a large caliber handgun and splattered the clerk's head across a wall of cigarette cartons. But it was the bottom right quadrant that made Hailey say holy shit. Barely in the frame was the back half of an ancient model Chevy Malibu with the gas pump handle fully depressed and buried inside the car's orifice, the lower half of a man in jeans shuffling from one foot to the other, except that one foot was encased in a dingy and apparently decomposing cast.

Chapter 26

State Route 89, outside of Kaibab, Arizona.

Tom sat in the middle of a dirt parking lot next to a gas station. The sun beat down. His arms over his knees, he hunched motionless staring at the scrub hills beyond the blacktop. An RV towing a small car blew by on 89 spawning a mini dust devil that spun across the parking lot and through the gas pumps and barbed wire fencing over a rambling ephemeral wash and into a thousand miles of desert. The tattered remains of the wool coat covered his head and shoulders like a shawl shading his eyes. He spat dust, a drab of spittle stuck to a desiccated lip, cracked, bled, dried, and calloused.

The Great Hoover Dam was some hundred and fifty miles northwest. He looked that way and then looked south at the empty stretch of highway. A few birds circled a patch of roadkill a mile back. He looked at his hands. They were clean. He pushed up his sleeve and ran his hand up his arm, which should have been coated to the armpit in blood from the gut of the guy he'd stabbed. Had his sweat washed off the blood, or had it ever happened? He felt like he was waking up from a dream. He felt suddenly elated. Unmoored. He hadn't killed anyone. Or he had. I didn't kill anyone. Had any of it ever happened? He looked back in the direction of the dam. Was there a terrorist attack he was supposed to stop? If so, how? The signs had stopped coming. Or he'd misread them. Why couldn't the instructions come from a Blackberry—a

Blackberry wouldn't lie. Unless it was hacked by the Network. The last sign he had seen told him to set fire to a mine with someone inside, or was it the sign that told him to push someone off a cliff? Or he hadn't. I didn't do it. Maybe he was just a homicidal maniac. That made him laugh. A dry cough. He looked straight at the sun. It was barely moving, muted by a gray sky.

He looked at his hands. His hands were clean except for the permanent black rings under his fingernails. He held his hands up to the sky and stretched out his fingers, the black fingernails like claws, and pulled apart the gray sky to reveal a dazzling blue sky and yellow sun smiling down on the world as it was supposed to be. He was reborn. As if he'd pulled himself out from a gray cobwebbed womb to a fresh new world. He stood up and pulled the wool coat off from his head and flung it behind him in the dirt. He shook his head free and felt the air in his pores and started walking.

He walked past the single pump gas station, ramshackle houses, and scattered trailers and followed the highway north out of town, the possibilities opening up to him like the endless desert in front of him. Money. In this new world he could carry bills like anyone else. No one was tracking him through embedded biosensors in the watermarks. It was preposterous! What was I thinking? It was crazy to live without money. I was seriously fucked up there for a while, huh? The highway had no shoulder, and he walked on the sun-bleached weeds blown down, trampled, and half-drowning in sand. Cars blew by him but he barely noticed. How can I get money? Day labor maybe, enough for a hotel room so he could clean up and apply for something minimum wage. Without the wool coat there was nothing to contain his smell, a ten-foot halo of air gone sour, like his body had turned bad, been salted, spiced, and seasoned and then died and turned bad again, fetid and rotten, even outdoors and in the wind. A tractor-trailer barreled past, blasting him with powdered earth that stuck to his sweat and invaded the crevices of his dried and cracked lips. Maybe the coating of dirt would damp down the stench. Earlier today you squatted in an irrigation ditch and blew Taco Bell out of your ass. There's shit splatter on your pants. Even day labor may be out of the question for the time being. He didn't care. There were possibilities now. He walked. The sky mellowed into pink and orange. The sound of the wind traversing the desert was thrilling. Panhandling. Enough for a cheap hotel room was possible now that he didn't have to reject the dollar bills and only accept coins. Or a homeless shelter. He had no qualms about that. But a city big enough for a homeless shelter was at least two hundred miles away. He crested a slow rolling rise and saw the lights of the interstate crossing the desert below. He stopped to take it in, picking up the faint din of traffic reflected off the land. By the time he closed the distance it was night. He was drawn to the lights along a frontage road, hoping for a good place to sparechange, sit with a cup outstretched and reap the rewards of a generous society, let it trickle down in ones and hopefully even fives, be the change dish of civilization, or maybe it's pool filter.

The first gathering of lights and palm trees turned out to be a hotel. There were more lights a mile or so down, which he thought might be better harvesting grounds, when something stopped him dead in his tracks. His stomach jumped straight to his throat, and the edges of his new universe pulsated inwards. Parked in the hotel's white crushed quartz horseshoe parking lot in front of a red painted hitching post was a Chevy Malibu Tom knew very well.

Chapter 27

Another vodka tonic?

The blonde at the bar smiled faintly to herself, staring at nothing like she was somewhere else trying to grasp something that kept slipping away. She shook her head. The verdict of an internal debate.

Please.

The bartender was a big barrel-chested man with his hair pulled back into a ponytail. He exhaled smoke through his nostrils and set his cigarette to rest in a groove in an ashtray beneath the bar. The blonde fished through her purse for a cigarette, careful not to expose the Glock 9mm she'd bought for herself her second year on the job. She liked its weight. The feel was good. She fished out a Marlboro Light, lit it and took two drags before she realized she didn't have an ashtray.

How come there are no ashtrays?

They outlawed smoking in bars. Took effect the beginning of the month.

He set her drink on a cocktail napkin in front of her. He pinched his smoldering cigarette butt out of the ashtray beneath the bar, took a drag and flicked it into a trashcan. Then he set the ashtray on the bar.

Thanks.

No problem.

Can I ask you a question?

Shoot.

How come you're still smoking in here...I mean, is there a bartender loophole or something?

No, I just figure no one's going to enforce it. I mean, you're not going to bust me are you?

She was truly stunned. Bartenders were notoriously good at sniffing out cops but people usually didn't get that vibe from her.

No, I'm not...I mean...I'm a Fed...I don't even know if I could bust someone for smoking. Seriously, I have no fucking idea.

I'm James.

Hailey.

They shook hands.

Even if you could though, you wouldn't right? It'd be a waste of time. You have more important things to do, I'm sure.

No, not me. You know, in my experience, people are going to do what they're going to do. The law doesn't stop anyone from doing anything. The law just cleans up the mess.

The day I can't smoke behind the bar is the day I'll quit bartending.

Really? That seems a little extreme. You can just smoke out back.

Wouldn't be the same.

Hailey stuck a bar straw into the pulp of her lime at the bottom of her glass.

The door jingled and a man hobbled in, one foot anchored in a damp cast. He bellied up to the bar leaving one barstool between himself and Hailey. She could smell him from where he was, and she guessed the bartender could too by the way he hadn't moved, kept his arms crossed, looking down, all six foot five of him, like some impassive Buddha. The smell was acrid, like singed hair or renal failure. Meth. She pegged it right away.

Beer and a shot of Jack.

The Buddha stood still as stone.

Come on, man.

The shadow people had come. The little people that live in the corners of your eyes and appear as shadows so you don't know whether they are real or not. They usually came around the fourth or fifth day. The man spun ninety degrees to his left and stared at the wall until determining nothing was there. He spun back around to look at them. He was jumpy but Hailey saw that he had soft brown eyes. Kind eyes.

Did you see that?

The bartender shrugged.

Hailey scooched her stool back a few inches.

Shadow people.

Shit.

They're here.

The bartender poured a pint of PBR and a shot of Jack in a rocks glass and set it in front of the man.

This will help.

The man took a long pull off the draft, something greasy on his hand making it tough to grip the glass, and then took the shot, shaking as he did it, sloshing the bourbon around his mouth like mouthwash. He laid out a twenty and ordered another round. This time the bartender poured himself and Hailey a shot of Jack too. They bottomed up. Hailey gasped and slapped the bar.

Set 'em up again. On me.

The bartender gave her a spurious look.

I think I like you.

He poured three more shots of Jack.

To the river! the man shouted, holding up his glass.

Hailey shrugged at the bartender.

To the river.

They clinked glasses. The bartender asked the man which river he was toasting, and he replied the Green and laughed his ass off because the river's name was perfect, but it was also the Delores, or the Colorado, or the Arkansas, or the Gauley. They'd both been boatmen to some degree, knew the towns, Salida, Cotopaxi, Buena Vista, Leadville, Steamboat Springs, Gunnison, Green River.

You know the Tavern there on Main Street in Green River? I live above the Tavern.

No shit.

Against his best judgment the bartender shook hands with the man.

James.

Lorne.

You guiding this season? The water's running good I hear.

No, just working at the bar.

Yeah, me too.

You know they make you piss now?

To be a guide?

Piss test even to work in the gift shop.

No!

Dude.

Use't be you'd light a big fatty as soon as you launched and brought extras to sell to the tourists.

They don't let you do that no more.

Hell no.

Those were better times.

Yeah, they were.

Hailey laughed.

Listen to you guys. Oh no, I can't smoke pot at work anymore. Seriously?

Oh, I still smoke pot at work.

Yeah, me too.

Fantastic.

Hailey put her hands up in defense and then rummaged through her purse and set a bottle of Oxycontin on the bar.

This is what I take at work.

She shook out a pile of pills in her hand.

I think I really like this girl.

The bartender put out his hand and she placed two pills in his palm.

She slid two pills across the bar to Lorne.

God bless you.

Lorne shook his head and smiled to himself. His philosophy was right again. The Lord will provide. He swallowed the pills with a mouthful of whiskey.

The quiet Mexican couple had paid their check and left a while ago, leaving the three of them alone in the bar.

Hailey tried and failed to brush her hair out of her eyes. She put her hand on Lorne's arm to steady herself, and then looked around to regain her balance.

Lorne is it?

Uh yup. That's me. The man smoothed out his beard.

Good. She slurred. You got a light?

Uh, yup.

She held a Marlboro Light between her lips while he struck a match and lit her cigarette.

Did you recently start a fire at a mine back in Utah?

Lorne squinted at the TV and thought deeply for long time.

You know, I think we did. Lorne shook a finger at her. Oh, you're good, how did you know that?

I didn't really, I swear, it was just a good guess.

Wow.

Yeah, wow.

The bartender clapped two giant hands together.

Hailey shrugged.

Sometimes you just get lucky.

Lorne looked at the bartender.

Is she for real?

Yeah, man. She's a cop. You didn't know that?

Wow.

Lorne looked at her with curiosity.

Are you gonna bust me?

Hailey ordered three more shots.

Probably, but I really just want the shooter. The one who did the clerk. At the gas station outside of Eagar on U.S. 60. You remember. Just give me his name.

The bartender laid three shots on the bar.

That's a good deal, right?

Hailey blew the flagging strand of highlighted hair out of her eyes.

That is a good deal, the bartender nodded.

Come on, Lorne.

She leaned over and gave Lorne a hug.

Chevis. Chevis did the clerk. But he's dead. Dead and buried.

Who killed Chevis?

The door jingled. They all turned their heads. A stranger stepped inside the bar room. There was something wrong with his face. He had a strap of skin dangling off of his jaw and a bandage tied beneath his chin soaked through and crusted with dried blood and yellowed with pus.

He did.

Lorne pointed at the stranger.

The stranger stepped into the bar room smiling like a jack-o-lantern. Viscous liquid oozed from his bandaged neck.

The bartender involuntarily backed up against the beer cooler.

Weird. This night keeps getting weirder, huh? The bartender turned to Hailey, but she saw what the others didn't because they were too transfixed by the dangling flap of skin and his mostly exposed trachea and esophagus—the man held a crossbow in one hand and a sawed off shotgun in the other.

Lorne, you motherfucker, you enjoying yourself?

The man chuckled, expectorating little red droplets of saliva.

Lorne was speechless.

I can't be kilt. Specially by the likes of you, you little bitch.

F...F...Frank.

Lorne sort of gagged, his eyes wide.

The sudden realization and vulnerability in Lorne's voice made Hailey's stomach hurt, even as she instinctually grasped the smooth form-fitting handle of the Glock in her purse.

In the second that passed, the bartender realized the man was not only oozing puss and blood from his neck down the front of his shirt, but he was seriously deranged and heavily armed. James felt beneath the bar for the .38 kept there for just such encounters.

No! Hailey shouted just as James found the grip of the gun.

In a split second Bullfrog Frank tilted his left hand to the right angle and fired a crossbow bolt into the bartender's neck. James flew backward and crashed against the rows of liquor bottles behind him and spasmed to the floor, writhing in shock and pain on the wet spongy bar mats.

Lorne was between Hailey and the chinless psychopath, so when she rose up to fire she inadvertently used Lorne as cover, reaching around him to jerk the Glock three times, firing two slugs into a wall and the third into Frank's left shoulder just as Frank was raising his right arm to fire the sawed-off. Struck in the left shoulder, Frank dropped the crossbow as he fired a pointblank round of buckshot into Lorne's belly. Lorne was opened up and blown back, taking Hailey with him in a hail of shattered glass and barstools. She crashed heavy on the floor and was knocked out cold.

Bullfrog Frank staggered back out of the bar room and into the small hotel lobby. He lay on the floor panting for a moment and laughing to himself. He felt the pain and laughed some more. He probed the shoulder wound with his finger and knew it had been a through and through shot. He wiped the blood from his hands onto his jeans and reloaded the shotgun. He emptied a twenty bag of meth onto his tongue and felt no more pain. Ashley. Where was that little piece of ass? Not like the other girls in the valley who were cracked out by the time they were seniors in high school. She was fresh. She'd texted him after all, so she was here somewhere.

From where he lay on the lobby floor he could see the upstairs rooms through the glass lobby door. There was only one room with the light on. He got to his feet and pushed through the door to the staircase to the second floor. One hand slid along the balcony railing. The other gripped the sawed-off.

He stopped in front of the door to Room 27. The light was on behind the curtains. He thought the curtains might have moved slightly, were still moving, as if someone had peeked out and the curtains were still settling back in place. The night was still. He heard birdsong. No time like the present he said to himself in a low whistle, and he girded himself to bust down the door when there was a roar like two cannons firing, and the curtained window shattered. Frank was hit by flying shards of glass, but the two .44 slugs fired from inside the room went wide and into the night. Frank kicked down the Mexican pine wood door and spun to his left where he guessed the shooter must be. His instinct was right, and as Jimmy spun and fired the big .44, Frank let go with the sawed-off, just about blowing Jimmy in half. Pammy sat on the edge of the bed. She didn't move and she didn't speak.

Goddamn.

He swatted at the gun smoke in the room as if that would make it clear. Frank held out the sawed-off with his one usable arm like Zeus about to hurl a lightning bolt. He put the barrel to her forehead.

Where's the girl?

Pammy looked up at the barrel pressed to her forehead making her eyes cross.

Dunno.

The bathroom door opened. Ashley stepped out.

I was hoping you would come.

Frank pulled the trigger, splattering Pammy's head against the wall and ceiling.

Ashley jumped.

It's okay, it's all over now baby. I gotcha.

Junior followed her out from the bathroom, buttoning his pants.

Frank wheeled the shotgun on them.

Step to the side baby. I'm gonna shoot this skinny Indian.

I've got the money. They made me take it.

I know they did, sweetheart.

Ashley held out the little blue velvet backpack.

This is yours, baby.

She handed him the backpack, one hand on the strap, the other hand clutching the 9mm inside. As he reached for it, she jerked the trigger through the fabric as many times as she could, peppering his chest with bullets. He stumbled back, a genuine look of shock on his face. She followed him as he did his awkward backpedal, knocking over the TV and stepping into the splintered doorframe. Her big blue eyes stared straight into his as she backed him all the way outside the room and against the balcony railing. She jammed the pistol into his gaping neck wound and pulled the trigger.

The shoestring-strapped little blue velvet backpack was shredded and singed from the muzzle flashes. It disintegrated in Ashley's hand, and she tossed the remnants onto the now headless corpse that had recently been Bullfrog Frank. She hurried back into the room and sidestepped a shellshocked Junior who stood motionless, staring at the carnage in the room. She went into the bathroom and gathered up the rolls of cash she'd stashed under the sink. The money she'd stolen from Frank's closet back in the trailer deep in the woods was rolled up tight and rubber banded in bunches of a thousand dollars each. And there were ten of them. She fumbled under the sink, brushing roaches out of her way, and finally corralled all ten rolls. Ashley was smart. There was no way she was going to leave the money in the blue velvet backpack and let it get all shot to shit if it came to that. And she'd known it would come to that. In fact, she counted on it. But now she had no way to carry the money. The pockets on her jean skirt were fake and couldn't actually hold anything. She held the money in her tank top stretched out in front of her and went back out into the room. Junior still hadn't moved. Nobody had a bag of any kind. Traveling for days and no luggage. She put the money and the gun in an empty Busch Light twelve-pack cardboard box, grabbed Junior's hand, and led him out the door. She ushered him along the balcony and down the stairs to the lobby where they were confronted with another horrible scene. There were at least three corpses in the barroom, maybe more; it was hard to tell with all the blood and body parts. Junior made a move to run outside, but Ashley tightened her grip on his hand and rooted him in place.

Wait here.

No, don't.

Just wait here.

She tiptoed into the barroom, conscious that she was stepping in blood still warm and sticky, not yet congealed. She found Lorne. He had been flayed but still seemed to be barely breathing. A blonde woman lay on the floor. Ashley grit her teeth and swore at herself for what she was about to do. She felt in the pockets of Lorne's jeans until she found a small bulge. She held her breath, and with just her thumb and forefinger reached in his front pocket and pulled out the keys to the Malibu. As she held up the keys, the blonde woman seemed to wake up. She opened her eyes and tilted her head toward Ashley and held it there for a long time, trying to focus, or trying to understand where she was or what had happened or what she was seeing.

You're a pretty girl.

She spoke in a whisper, Ashley barely heard her.

Thank you, so are you.

Ashley snapped up the keys, spun around, and never looked back.

Chapter 28

Tom stopped dead in his tracks when he saw the Malibu. A cloud of dust washed over his boots. He was crestfallen. The Malibu was proof that he was living in the reality he feared. He couldn't erase the past. It chased him. It was unavoidable. But how much of it was real? If the Malibu was real, were the murders? Was the Network real?

He heard the sound of gunfire. Instinctively he dove into a low drainage ditch running along the frontage road. He rolled through the weeds to the bottom of the ditch covering his face and head as best he could. More gunfire. He crawled up the side of the ditch clutching the long grass for leverage. His chin in the dirt, he brushed the weeds out of the way so he had a good view of the hotel. Just as he caught his breath, he watched as a large man backpedaled from a smoke filled room on the second floor to lean against a railing as his head was blown clean off. Tom ducked his head down and covered his eyes trying to wipe the image from his mind. It was all real. They were really after him. He breathed into the dirt. Felt the thistles in his hands. He pulled the tall weeds out by their roots, feeling them pluck from the soil, that little bit of resistance proving that nothing wants to die. He crept back up to the top of the berm. A boy and a girl ran out of the hotel. The girl dragging the boy by his arm. She pushed him to the passenger seat of the Malibu and then ran around to the driver's side door, opened it up and tossed a cardboard beer box into the backseat, got in and slammed the door. The Malibu roared to life, the V8 engine rattling the rusted hood. She backed it up and then tore out of the horseshoe driveway in a hail of quartzite gravel.

Nothing moved inside the hotel. When the Malibu was out of sight, the night grew entirely quiet. Tom climbed out of the ditch and approached the hotel cautiously. The lobby was covered in blood and shattered glass. A trail of blood led to the barroom. He slowly pushed open the swinging saloon doors and saw Lorne lying in a pool of blood that covered the entire floor. A woman lay on the floor next to him. Tom slipped on the blood, cursed and got up and shuffled his way through the pooled blood to Lorne. Lorne's eyes were open but his breathing sounded like a death rattle. The sight of Tom hovering over him seemed to register with Lorne. He tried to speak and mouthed something that Tom couldn't quite make out but could have been 'I'm sorry'.

You did good partner.

Tom put his hand on Lorne's forehead.

You did real good.

Tom saw the woman looking at him.

He said he'd call for help, found Lorne's hand and squeezed it, and then made his way across the blood-slick barroom floor and into the hotel lobby.

Tom didn't call for help. That would have brought the Network's assassins on him in a matter of minutes. Instead he went up the stairs to the second floor and searched the headless man's pockets for his keys. In the parking lot there was an old Nissan Sentra and an older Ford F-150. The keys unlocked the pickup. Tom put it in gear, hit the frontage road, and fishtailed as he lay down the gas. He took the long curve of the onramp onto I-40 heading west. A small army of police cars with lights blazing passed him on the other side of the divided interstate. It would be a while for the ambulances he guessed; the nearest hospital was a hundred miles away. He filed away a mental note that if he saw a helicopter it was probably Flight for Life, not the Network. Don't get paranoid. That had been a close call back there. But he was alive. And he believed in the mission stronger then ever.

Chapter 29

After Hailey had been debriefed by the Arizona State Police, the Coconino County Sheriff's Office, the Navajo Tribal Police, and the FBI, and she'd taken the obligatory ambulance ride to Memorial Hospital in Flagstaff to have her concussion evaluated and a half dozen shotgun pellets removed from her right arm, she drove back to St. George. When she opened the door to her little house, her beast of dog wiggled to her like a puppy and tried to climb in her lap. She laughed and squeezed his big soft head. He half-howled and nuzzled into her knocking her over on her back, and she laughed until she cried. The dog licked the tears from her face, and she laughed and cried like that for a long time.

I'll never leave you again, she said rubbing his fat belly.

He snorted and grinned revealing his huge canines.

Three weeks later she did leave him again to drive the four hours west to Las Vegas for her friend Stef's bachelorette party. The girls had booked the mack daddy suite at the MGM Grand, two stories, three bedrooms, and a beautiful patio overlooking the Vegas strip. After much champagne and an ill-advised visit from a male stripper, she sat in the hot tub looking at the lights from the strip with a couple of her girlfriends. She was glad she came. It turned out that her friends who she hadn't seen in almost five years didn't care what she did for a living, or where she lived, or how she'd screwed up her life, and that was just fine with her. They just wanted to have a good time. For the first time in a long time she thought about nothing.

Sunday morning she was massively hung over. Instead of taking a couple Percocets, she just puked and took a lukewarm shower. She hugged her friends at the cab stand in the blazing Vegas sun and watched as they took a van to the airport to catch flights back to the cities they had come from.

Hailey started driving on I-15 back to Utah but instead turned south onto Route 93 over the Hoover Dam and through Grasshopper Junction and Santa Claus and into Kingman, Arizona, and then east on I-40 to Flagstaff and south into Phoenix to the Scottsdale Embassy Suites. Antonio wasn't at the front desk so she went to the hotel bar and ordered a Bloody Mary. She noticed that there weren't any ashtrays. She lit a cigarette anyway. She blew a smoke ring across the bar and it floated into the top shelf liquor bottles in front of a large finely polished mirror. The bartender told her the hotel was non-smoking and she smiled, took a long drag, and ashed on the floor.

Chapter 30

County Rd. 172, Kingman Wash Access Road, Mohave County, Arizona.

The pickup followed the dirt road as far as it went, about five miles as the crow flies from the Hoover Dam, but separated from the dam by rugged mountains without trails that would take considerable work to cross. Tom let the truck skid to a stop, the chrome bumper slightly indenting around a wall of boulders that had slid there some time after the road's creation. Dust billowed over the cab and through dashboard vents. Tom checked the rearview mirror as he had every minute or so throughout the night but saw nothing except his own trail of dust scattering with the wind.

The cloth seats smelled of cigarette smoke and someone else's sweat. With the heat of the morning sun, the cab quickly filed with the scent of dashboard musk. Tom was desperate to ditch the truck. The Network would be using real time satellite images to search for the truck in an ever-widening radius from the hotel massacre. He'd parked under the mountain's steepest side in hopes that the truck might be missed by cursory inspection, but he doubted that would work, not when he was so close to their target. He quickly searched the cab for anything useful and became even more alarmed. Loose syringes, shotgun shells, and little baggies filled with white flakes that Tom guessed was methamphetamine. The truck was a mobile prison sentence. He found a little over three dollars in change under the seats and floor mats and buried at the bottom of the glove box. In the door panel under the armrest he found an old first aid kit with a few Band-Aids, gauze, tape, and a weathered tube of antiseptic ointment. The real find was a drawstring laundry bag that he used to hold his belongings instead of the homemade satchel made out of his shredded and soiled coat. He threw his half-full water bottle along with an empty one into the bag and started walking.

He walked slowly up the mountainside in a general northward direction, using his hands to press down on his knees to gain leverage and to steady himself. The mountains were as barren as any he'd crossed, rock with intermittent patches of sand that sifted into his boots through the loose seems and invisible pores. He skirted barrel cactus and rock-nettles as he worked his way up the slope, eyeing the summit and the endless blue sky beyond. He reached the top and instinctively crouched down. Below, the Hoover Dam shown white in the sun, its giant curve bulging out toward him. Lake Mead was dark blue with a green iridescence near the shoreline where the lake met the mountains. The four mammoth penstock towers rose a hundred feet above the waterline and several more hundreds below. So much concrete beneath so much water. The enormity of the structures filled him with exhilaration and dread. He felt at once insignificant and uniquely important.

He crept to a flat spot between the rocks guarded by a silver cholla and a patch of dune primrose. He took his green plastic poncho out of the laundry bag and hooked the hood onto the cholla and stretched it over to the rocks for a slice of shade. And then he waited. He watched and waited. A thin line of traffic moved in both directions over the dam. Otherwise the dam and the penstocks stood impassive, no sign of the massive hydroelectric generators whirling away somewhere beneath. No sign of any other human activity.

He sat almost perfectly still. He thought the adrenaline he was running on would wear off, but now that he was here, so close, after all this time, it didn't. He didn't feel tired even though he hadn't slept in days, didn't feel hungry even though he hadn't eaten and had no food to eat. He was mesmerized by the dam, hypnotized by it. As much as he stared, he couldn't understand it, its size, its importance, its domination over the huge expanse of deep blue lake which itself was made from the dam, born from concrete and existed because of it.

Every hour or so he sipped from his water bottle. At sunset, when the landscape seemed to flip colors with the sky, the land going through purples and blues as the sky went to oranges and reds, his water bottle was empty. He didn't necessarily feel thirsty, it was just reality that he'd need more water to survive another day.

The level of Lake Mead had apparently dropped at some point in recent years so that the entire lake was ringed by a fifty-foot band of rock that looked bleached white after decades spent under water, hidden from the sun. Tom started down toward the lake, but the closer he got to the lifeless band of white stone the steeper and more unsteady the terrain until he had to climb back up to the ridgeline and follow that down several miles to a sandy wash dotted with tamarisk and encelia that led to the lake. He filed his water bottles and took a long drink. Then he disrobed and waded into the cool water, fully submerged and scrubbed himself with bottom sand and pebbles to clean off the body funk. The sky was black, the water was black, and the stars were infinite. The dam was above him now, still visible in the darkness, always visible.

He emerged from the water and put his beggar's rags back on. He gathered his bag and noticed signs of fishing, kids most likely, tangled lightweight fishing line and pink bobbers and little orange marshmallows used to catch catfish and bluegill.

He spent an hour gathering the fish bait from the mud and rocks and rinsed them off in the lake and then hiked back up to his spot on the ridgeline above the dam.

He spent the next day watching the dam under his poncho tarp, every hour or so taking a drink of water and eating a little orange-dusted marshmallow. That night he went back to the wash and bathed and looked for more fish bait.

The next day he was thinking clearly. The Network had most likely postponed any attack on the dam. The melee at the hotel would have caused problems. At least three dead that he saw, if you included Lorne, who he thought would probably die. Maybe more, he hadn't checked inside the hotel room where there had been considerable gunfire. Whether the fallout from that bloodbath had postponed the attack or not, he had to concede that the attack could now be days, months, or even years away.

Still he repeated his routine for the next few days, and when the days began to run together in earnest and he could no longer tell what was a dream or a dream within a dream, he put his poncho in his bag and slung the bag over his shoulder and walked slowly down to the road that crossed the dam. He walked across the Hoover Dam on the sidewalk next to the road with a tall railing for the tourists to safely cross without falling to their deaths and continued walking all the way to Boulder City, Nevada. He walked through the endless traffic lights and strip malls and fast food joints of Boulder City until the shoulder of highway 93 narrowed and cars flew by at ninety miles an hour, showering him with grit. As night fell, a Deputy Sheriff from Clark County stopped him and asked him where he was going and where he'd been and when he couldn't answer took him to the Las Vegas Rescue Mission. Tom thanked the man and shook his hand when he left.

Tom spent three months at the homeless shelter. The staff

provided him with a new set of second-hand clothes, using rubber gloves to bag up and dispose of his old tattered garments. Every morning he showered and shaved and brushed his teeth until his gums bled. At night he slept well, having nothing of value to worry about anyone stealing. The days he spent mostly in the common room with the pay vending machines and the free coffee, reading what sections of the newspaper he could corral from the other residents, looking for the signs.

There was an unsettling air in the Las Vegas shelter, an anxious hum beneath the surface of the place that was different from other shelters in distant parts of the country. There was never a consistent rhythm to the day there. Instead of a calming regularity, there was a jumpy vibe that bread agitation among the population. Perhaps it was the smell of all that money circulating just outside the door, won, lost and wasted. There were more degenerate gamblers than other places to be sure, to whom just being in Las Vegas was a special kind of exquisite torture.

Tom was polite and friendly to everybody. He befriended a man in the bunk next to him named Terrence who spent two weeks at the Rescue Mission talking non-stop about how he hated Las Vegas and hated the Mission even more. Terrence was a poker player who felt he'd lost all his money in the worst possible way because he had no one to blame but himself, couldn't even blame it on luck, kept insisting he'd gone broke on a game of skill, and thus, he was unskilled. Tom never expressed an opinion one way or the other.

Eventually Terrence's brother came to pick him up and drive him the three hundred miles west back to Bakersfield, California. Terrence convinced his brother to take on an extra passenger and then convinced Tom to come along. Las Vegas is no place for good people he said. We're good people.

Bakersfield was quiet. Wide streets with low houses.

Long blocks, desert scrub and green bushes, spindly pines and distant sun-bathed mountains. Long sunsets and slow time. Palm trees.

The brother was not going to take Tom in, not even in the garage since that was where Terrence was going to put his life back together, but he did take him to Valley Baptist Church where Tom was given directions to the homeless shelter and told he could come back anytime.

The shelter gave him a bed but they could not help him get work since Tom refused to accept paper money, so instead everyday Tom walked to the church where he swept and mopped the floors and did whatever odd jobs he felt skilled enough to attempt. He was patient. When the giant GOD LOVES YOU sign out front blew a fuse and was alight no more, he spent eight hours sitting cross-legged in a hundred degree sun rewiring the thing even though he had never excelled at electrical systems during surveillance training. The pastor fed him at least one meal a day and often gave him donated food to bring back to the shelter at night. Over time the parishioners grew accustomed to seeing Tom working about the church, and there was a noticeable uptick in canned food donations. Every evening Tom filled his drawstring laundry bag with canned vegetables, powdered soups, and boxes of pasta and slung the bag over his shoulder for the long walk to the shelter. The donations were more than welcome at the shelter, and eventually a volunteer there gave him a proper frame backpack for his daily journeys back and forth from the church. The shelter had an easy client, and the church had a useful parishioner, and Tom fell into a routine like none other he'd ever had.

A year passed and then another. He spent Thanksgivings with Terrence and Terrence's brother and his family, a kind of flesh and blood life lesson to the children about charity and needing charity, but otherwise saw them little. Although he spent everyday at the church, he usually made himself scarce around church services, tinkering in the basement or manicuring the grounds, not because he had any particular aversion to religion but rather because he felt like the hired help, enjoyed feeling like the help.

One brilliant blue sky November day, he was picking leaves out from under the shrubs along the side of the church by hand when Terrence's brother tapped him on the shoulder and told him that Terrence had left town, was probably back in Vegas and up to old ways, but that Tom was still invited to Thanksgiving dinner. Tom nodded and thanked him for the invitation. He had Thanksgiving with Terrence's brother's family but said even less than usual. The children were busy tapping on mobile devices with their thumbs through most of the dinner, and the football game on the big screen high definition television was largely unwatched and thus even more meaningless than it had ever been.

Living off the grid Tom had never had a cell phone, but now he noticed people attached to sleek little devices everywhere. When he observed people on his daily treks back and forth from the homeless shelter to the church, they invariably had a transmitter in at least one ear. They were listening to music or talking on the phone or checking their email or linked in to a global positioning satellite or to a van down the street. It was impossible to tell. The Network had never had it so easy, he thought. Hiding in plain sight. That was his tactic.

He began running scouting missions at night. If anyone could be a Network agent, if everyone looked like one, then only diligence would reveal the truth. Patterns show themselves eventually. And they were there. The same man in a sweat suit on the same block three nights out of five preoccupied with his handheld device and the earbuds they were attached to, and on the other two nights the same woman walking two black Pomeranians and talking nonchalantly into a bluetooth affixed to her right ear. And then the pattern repeated. Sweat suit man three nights and dog woman the other two. It gave him a little thrill that they were still there, that he'd found them. Or had they found him?

He couldn't sleep at the shelter anymore. The bunk seemed to have narrowed. The breathing of the other men in the room at night in the dark, not knowing who they were, where their allegiances lay. When he shut his eyes, the movie he saw playing on his mindscreen was of the dam blowing, the water blasting through the fissures in the concrete, a tidal wave scouring the canyon walls, obliterating everything in its path, drowning them all. If they had found him then an attack was imminent.

Tom left the shelter and slung his pack and walked up Monroe Avenue a mile and half on his usual route, but a block before Valley Baptist Church he took a left so he wouldn't have to pass the church and continued up and circled the block back to Monroe and kept walking to Highway 99 and stuck out his thumb. He caught a ride almost immediately. Dressed in khakis and a blue button down he looked more than presentable—he was downright nonthreatening. Over the years the parishioners who'd grown used to seeing him around the church preferred donating their better cloths to him: not the dingy t-shirts and old college hoodies that made it to the goodwill bins, but rather barely worn slacks and shirtsleeves bought by a dear one who misjudged a size or believed some exaggerated weight loss. He thought of his current mode of dress as slightly used, business casual. Perhaps his new uniform was only given to him because it made him more palatable as a fixture of the community, but the advantage was the best hitchhiking of his life. His first ride took him all the way to Fresno. The next took him not just to Stockton but onto the I-5 exchange. Hitchhiking on Interstate 5 was unnerving with eight lanes of traffic doing 90 miles an hour, but a young couple in a Subaru Outback took mercy, mistaking him for a stranded motorist, and drove him to Sacramento. Sacramento posed the usual challenge of first finding the outskirts of town and then a suitable location to hitch from. Twice he got rides that led back to the interstate only to be let off a few exits up the road. Darkness fell, and not wanting to try the Interstate again he walked all night through town heading north until he found a two-lane county road and began getting rides at dawn. His cloths were rumpled now and not as crisp as they'd felt the previous morning, but he looked okay and he easily found rides through Yuba City, Live Oak, and Oroville on to Chico where he got back to highway 99 to Red Bluff. He headed north, now it was only north, to the Grand Coulee Dam in Washington state not far from the Canadian border, the biggest dam in the United States and one of the biggest in the world, holding back the entire Columbia River. He knew he was taking a huge risk. The Grand Coulee Dam was the second most valuable target after the Hoover Dam, but maybe the Network had given up on the Hoover Dam after nearly four years without an attack. Call it a hunch, but doing something was better than doing nothing. And if he were right he'd change history.

Chapter 31

US Route 97, near the Oregon state line.

The road was hemmed by trees on both sides with deep forest to the mountains beyond. The shoulder was carpeted in pine needles, wet and slick by mist and recent rain. Tom breathed in the cool humid air feeling the dampness cut right to his skin under his clothes as if he was naked to the elements. He breathed out white water vapor like some snowbound bison and stopped walking. He lit a soggy GPC and watched his exhale gray and take on substance, swirl and hover just overhead instead of disappearing into the mist. He supposed this was not what would classically be called cloud forest, but nonetheless the clouds hung so low they obscured the tree tops and left moisture glistening on the lower branches and on the rocks, lichens and mosses, and saturated the leafy forest undergrowth. He knew Mt. Shasta was close by to the south, Mt. Hood farther away to the north, and the dam even farther away to the northeast, but he couldn't see them. All he could see were trees and road wrapped in a gray shroud.

Tom heard the heavy throttle of a big rig and then the throaty reverberations of a fully deployed air break, and he instinctively stepped a couple paces off the shoulder. Visibility was down to a few dozen yards. He looked back the way he'd come but could see nothing beyond a white wall of clouds at the base of a mountain pass, hiding the twisting road above.

There was a second of warning when headlights reflected eerily in the surrounding fog and then a tractor trailer materialized out of the mist barreling passed him; running lights outlined the entire frame, a neon rectangle slicing through the vapor. A line of cars followed closely behind the eighteen-wheeler, headlights refracting off the bumpers, glass and taillights of the cars in front of them. The convoy sprayed a fine particulate mud splatter across Tom's khaki trousers. He walked with his thumb out long after the convoy had passed, feeling the cold water squish in the bottoms of his boots.

He slowly became aware of the world darkening. The casing of fog and cloud grayed to charcoal, shading down imperceptibly as dusk fell. It began to rain in earnest, the drizzle turning to big heavy drops drove stinging by the gathering wind. He dawned his green poncho, but it did nothing for his khakis over his lower legs which soaked almost clean of mud in the deluge and clung to his shins as fastly and translucent as Saran Wrap. As he walked on, he felt that he was swimming through some interstitial space, neither day nor night, wet nor dry, awake nor asleep, crazy nor sane.

After a time he came to a lone street lamp broadcasting from a telephone pole marking an intersection that no longer saw much use. He huddled directly under the light watching the sheets of rain from under the brim of his hood. Runoff from the road ran in rivulets and pooled at his feet. After several attempts he lit a GPC and hunched his back against the weather.

Headlights approached from the south, and he uncreaked his joints to get to his feet and shuffle onto the shoulder, his foot on the painted white line, thumb outstretched. A van passed him and then slowed and stopped on the shoulder. He froze for an instant and then grabbed his pack and hustled toward the red break lights. He slowed as he came close, eying the satellite dish on top of the van. He walked up to the passenger side door, cataloging the name of some obscure telecom company he'd never heard of on the side.

The passenger side window lowered as he approached.

Hey buddy, where you heading?

Up the road, anywhere really to get out of this.

I hear that, get in.

Tom quickly flipped the poncho over his head and shook it out and then climbed in the passenger seat and set his pack at his feet with the balled up poncho. He slicked his hair back with his hands and wiped the water off his face.

Thanks for stopping.

Dark night, almost didn't see ya.

The windshield wipers slapped against their moorings, leaving semi-circle arches of water in the field of vision. As the van sped up, the water arches streamed upward against gravity and blurred up and over the van. It was suddenly quiet in the van. Dark outside.

You coming off a job?

Yep, trying to keep people connected, you know how it is.

Do I?

The driver looked at him.

Well, thanks again for the ride.

Against company policy to pick up hitchhikers, but on a night like this, just seemed like the Christian thing to do.

Well, you are a good Christian then.

The man looked at him again.

Tom warmed his hands on air from the dashboard vents and nonchalantly looked back at the cargo hold of the van—rolls of fiber optic wire, heavy cable, satellite dishes, modems, receivers, and connectors of every kind. Coincidence that this was the ride he'd found? If it was against company policy to pick up hitchhikers, why had he stopped then, just this once, to pick him up? Another coincidence?

The reflective paint of a road sign suddenly illuminated

white by the headlights read Klamath Falls, Oregon 12 miles. The road snaked through unbroken forest. No lights ahead or behind.

Not many folks out here to connect with all this stuff, I suspect.

Not many but they're out here, just gotta know where to look.

Tom nodded. His right hand dug deep into his coat pocket, gripping his pocket knife.

Where you headed again?

North, Washington.

Seattle?

No, more like Spokane.

Ah, gotcha... long trip then.

Yep.

The man picked up his CB radio and mouthed something to a dispatcher. The other end crackled something unintelligible and then went dead. The van was again silent, except for the sound of the wind, which occasionally blew the van momentarily over the double yellow striped center line. The man flipped on AM talk radio. The stereo cast a florescent green light in the cab. The talk show host was energetically making an argument, but the words all seemed to have double meanings, as if he was speaking in code.

The van abruptly pulled off the road and stopped. He turned off the radio leaving just the sound of rain pounding on the roof.

Sorry to do this.

Tom's fingers adroitly flipped open the blade of his pocket knife under his coat.

But I got to let you out. Headquarters just up the road, and like I said, I'm not supposed to have anyone riding in a company vehicle with me so I can't let 'em see you.

No problem, bless you for the ride.

Godspeed. See you on the other side.

Tom smiled and gathered his pack and poncho and gently shut the door behind him. The van sped off leaving him again alone in the rain. He watched the van's red taillights go up the road a quarter mile and then turn up a long driveway. Tom walked to the spot and saw that the driveway led to a small office building surrounded by a chain link fence. Half a dozen satellite dishes and antenna of various sizes were on the roof. A huge satellite dish with its needle pointing skyward was visible in back of the building. The whole installation was cut neatly out of the dense pine forest. From the lack of regrowth in the clearing, the construction looked to be recent.

Tom walked a few hundred yards up the road and then cut into the forest. He picked his way through the underbrush, ducking under low branches and climbing over long downed and decomposing trees. The ground became muddy and bog-like with mosquito-infested brackish water up to his ankles. He reached the tree line adjacent to the chain link fence alongside the building and hunkered down with his poncho covering him and his pack completely, the hood low over his face.

He waited for the office lights to go off in the building, leaving just the lobby lit and visible from the outside. He watched the last civilian vehicles, a Ford Taurus and an older Chevy Silverado, leave out of the parking lot and turn onto the highway. He ditched the poncho, took a plastic water bottle filled with kerosene out of his pack and scaled the fence, gaining the top in two moves and then dropping to the ground on the other side, landing in a crouch. Moving close to the ground he doused the kerosene on the massive satellite dish in back of the building and led a trail of kerosene to the front of the building. He smashed a front window with a rock, spread kerosene all through the lobby, making sure there was a connecting trail to the satellite out back, and tossed in a lit match. The fire gathered slowly, but by the time he reached the highway the entire building as well as the giant satellite dish were ablaze.

Chapter 32

An hour later he was picked up on the outskirts of Klamath Falls, Oregon. A Sheriff's car lit him up and he turned to face it. He spent the night in county jail and was arraigned the next day. The digital surveillance feed from the security cameras was simultaneously beamed to an offsite private contractor and preserved even though the cameras themselves had melted in the blaze. There was unmistakable footage of him committing arson. The public defender had little to work with. Tom would not give his name, date of birth, occupation, place of residence, prior criminal record, or any identifying information. He did not speak at all. Because his fingerprints had been apparently sanded off, damaged to the point of uselessness for identification purposes, he was entered into the court's docket as John Doe.

The trial took one day. He was convicted of first-degree arson and sentenced to one hundred and fourteen months in prison. After another three weeks in county he was transferred to the Oregon State Penitentiary in Salem, Oregon to serve out his sentence. He was a model prisoner, quiet and respectful, helpful to prison staff and friendly with his fellow inmates. But because he never expressed remorse for his crime or even revealed his true identity so they could make an assessment of his criminal proclivities and chance of recidivism, he received no credit for good time and had no chance for parole. He served every day of his sentence.

With roughly two thousand inmates in the facility, almost three were released a day. Warden Yates hardly attended all the discharges, but he made sure that he was there to say goodbye to Tom. Warden Yates had never had an inmate stay a John Doe for his entire sentence, at least not one as long as Tom's, and the Warden had dropped in to visit with Tom over the years, finding him surprisingly pleasant and intelligent, well educated, he guessed. Over the last few years of Tom's sentence they'd had occasion to chat every few months or so, discussing wide ranging topics from literature to law, military history to ecology, physics to philosophy. Everything except anything personal about either man. This was an unspoken ground rule. It made for relaxing conversation.

Because Tom served his sentence in its entirety, there were no conditions to his release. No parole officer to appease, no piss tests, halfway houses, job interviews, counselors, or sheriff's departments to check in with. He was free to leave the state, or the country if he chose.

The day before Tom's release, Warden Yates did him a favor. For reasons the Warden couldn't even guess at, Tom refused to accept the fourteen hundred and sixty-two dollars he'd earned working in the penitentiary garage for nine and a half years. Instead he asked for a bus ticket to Boulder City, Nevada, ten rolls of quarters, and for the rest of the money to go to the prison indigent fund. The Warden personally drove to the Greyhound station in Salem and bought him the ticket and then to his credit union for the quarters. He would have driven Tom to the bus station, but that would have crossed some line of professional responsibility that he wasn't prepared to cross, someplace that if he went he wouldn't know again where the boundary was, a line that once erased couldn't be redrawn. So he just shook hands with Tom at the gate and wished him luck out in the world. Under an overcast sky Tom walked the eight miles into town on Oregon Route 22 to the bus station, the pack on his back, his donated windbreaker drawn tightly over his shoulders against the dampness, and emerged into the hundred degree Nevada sun two days later.

He walked across the street from the bus depot to a 7-ll and bought a pack of GPCs with some of the quarters. He packed the smokes against his knuckles, sat on an empty concrete parking space bumper and lit one up. His first cigarette in nearly a decade. He inhaled deeply and looked at the four-lane traffic on Canyon Boulevard speeding back and forth in both directions. Big cars mostly. Barren mountains in the distance. Cloudless blue sky. Billboards selling bankruptcy attorneys and bail bondsmen. He knocked the cherry off the half smoked cigarette and put the butt back in the pack. He went back inside the 7-11 and bought a gallon jug of water.

He walked Canyon Boulevard, strip malls and traffic lights, landscaped curb cuts with green grass smelling of fertilizer and spindly saplings propped up with wire, and empty dirt lots with realtor's signs advertising prospects for development. At an army surplus store he bought fishing line, lures, weights, a bedroll with a foam sleeping pad, a tarp, a green plastic poncho, and a kerosene lantern. Further down the road he stopped at a dollar store and bought two boxes of Triscuits, a pocket knife with a can opener, and a dozen cans of tuna fish and an equal number of canned spam.

He found the onramp junction with US 93, the Great Basin Highway, and started walking toward the Hoover Dam. He did not attempt to hitchhike. He did not want to have to explain to someone why he wanted to be let out in the middle of nowhere. He walked a dozen miles through the early evening hours into darkness. He walked slowly. Head down, hands in pockets. Inconspicuous.

When he saw the distant glow of floodlights atop the dam, he left the highway walking straight into desert scrub and up a hillside where he settled in among the cockleburs and watched the traffic below steadily thin until daybreak. In the morning, when the sun had risen over the canyon rim, he continued up the hillside and, reaching the summit, appraised the jagged rock-faced mountains guarding the dam from this approach. Lacking the gear for a technical climb, or any rock climbing gear at all, he had to find a way around the worst of the rugged mountains. He descended a ravine and climbed up the other side to a ridgeline from where he could see Lake Mead. He walked toward the lake picking his way over and around windswept dunes and bunchgrass berms. When he reached the water he followed the shoreline until he was only a few hundred yards from the dam. Although the mountains on the Nevada side of the dam rose sharply, he found a level patch of ground in an elevated cove protected from the wind but safely above the waterline. He unstrapped his pack and set about clearing away a space for his bedroll by kicking away rocks and bramble deposited there when the rains washed down debris from the canyon above. He unfurled his newly purchased army green tarp and stretched it between two rock faces that met at a crease filled with sand, pebbles, and tiny cactus running up the mountain. He used this joint where the cliff faces met as an anchor for the tarp and made a shelter with an awning he could tie back in strong winds.

He finished as the sun was setting. That first night he did not make a fire. He ate a cold meal of canned tuna and Triscuits. There were stars but no moon and it was very dark. He lay down fully clothed on top of his bedroll under the tarp and went to sleep almost immediately. He woke up sometime later and saw only blackness. He stilled his breathing and listened for the world around him but heard only the gentle lapping of water on the rocks below. He slept a deep dreamless sleep. When he woke, the sun was high and the sky was a brilliant blue.

The day was hot, and he stripped off his windbreaker and long sleeved shirt leaving his prison pale skin exposed to the sun from the waist up. He rigged his fishing line with a lure and carefully picked his way down to the water and fished for a few hours with no success. He circled the shoreline back the way he came the day before and climbed on top the mountain he camped under until he overlooked the dam less than a quarter mile away.

He sat down on the coarse scoured earth on the barren mountaintop with his legs stretched out before him. The rocks, volcanic but brittled by time, had been crushed by the elements like desiccated coral underfoot. He watched the traffic creep across the dam. To his left he saw the mountains on the Arizona side of Lake Mead where he'd foraged in desperation all those years ago. He looked at his boots, one of the few items from his past they'd returned to him upon his release from prison. The sides blown out. The soles had come loose and clacked when he walked. He wondered how many miles those boots had crossed.

Tom was forty-nine years old. It had been almost fourteen years since the massacre at the hotel. Fourteen years since he'd last killed someone. The rot he feared back then had since metastasized. He'd lost roughly a tooth a year in prison, the state dentist pulling those teeth he suspected of harboring the seeds of infection. His mouth whistled when he inhaled. Preventive dentistry made sense. Tom bore the dentist no ill will. He appreciated and respected anyone associated with law enforcement. Everybody plays their part.

Toward sunset he crept back to the shoreline and fished until nightfall. Catching nothing, he felt his way back to his campsite in the darkness and fell asleep.

Chapter 33

Tom's skin reddened and then browned. The lures were useless, at least in his hands, but he caught minnows in a low eddy with a homespun net and used them as bait and eventually caught some bluegills and sunfish. He picked clean the skin and filaments of meat and ate them raw and then crushed up the heads, tails and bones and mixed them with cactus meat, stripped yucca, and scavenged flowers and herbs and cooked them into something eatable. After a month the Triscuits were gone, but he still had half his store of canned tuna and spam. Each day he spent time on the hill overlooking the dam, watching for the signs.

The days shortened and the sun dulled its assault as the cool desert night sharpened its bite. Some mornings he would wake to a thin layer of frost over everything, and he would build a small fire and cook slices of spam, charring the sides black, to give him the strength for the chores of the day ahead, fishing, gathering wood, hauling water. He ate watching the water and the mountains beyond. From parts of his campsite he could see the dam, but as the days pressed on he usually looked out on the endless lake opening the canyon lands and stretching out of sight for a hundred miles.

One afternoon he was quite near the dam, almost right up against it down not far from where traffic passed, gathering dead muskrats and other unfortunate creatures that tended to get stuck in a grated off overflow pipe, when he heard the screeching of tires and then the telltale pregnant pause when everything could still turn out okay before the dull thud of heavy metal and plastic objects colliding. A second and third thud followed closely behind.

Tom immediately climbed out of the pipe and scurried up the embankment alongside the dam and emerged onto the road still holding a dead rat by its tail. Although this could have been the terrorist attack he'd been waiting for, his quick reaction owed more to his instinct that there had been a bad car crash and someone might be hurt. Just after the road crossed onto the dam, at least three cars and a large refrigerated cargo truck were entwined at odd angles, and smoke was beginning to rise. He ran past the first two cars where the occupants were fighting through seat belts and deployed air bags to exit the vehicles to the third car, which was pinned to the thick steel side rail by the cargo truck. The car was kinked in the middle like a crushed beer can. On one end the driver appeared unconscious. In the back seat, separated from the front by the truck's front grill and engine block, was a child's car seat, and in it, a wide eyed little girl. Gasoline trickled out from the back end of the car and ran in a stream to Tom's boots. A first responder appeared and dragged the woman out from the driver's seat, but the back seat was completely pinched off and pinned against the retaining wall. Tom climbed on top of the wall, gripping the steel railing. He dropped the rat and it skittered along the dam to the water below. He shimmied along the railing until he could put one foot on the roof of the car. He reached through the shattered passenger side window, lacerating both his forearms, and unclicked the child safety restraints on the car seat. He used his fingers to pick out the remaining glass in the window, oblivious to the cuts on his fingertips, and pulled the girl out. He held her with one arm, her tiny waist snuggly in the crook of his elbow, while he pulled them along the railing with the other arm. Don't look down, he said, but the girl wasn't looking at anything.

More first responders arrived and took the girl from Tom and helped him back onto the road. The back of the car caught fire and people scrambled to the wreck with fire extinguishers as bystanders fled to safety. Tom followed the foot traffic off the dam. Ambulances, fire trucks, and all manner of police and rescue vehicles appeared and closed off the road. Tom stood in the back of a crowd of onlookers for a while and then started walking down the road. He hadn't gone far when an EMT in a four by four pulled along side him.

Hey.

Tom kept walking.

Hey.

The man said it again.

Tom stopped, his head down.

Let me look at that.

What.

Your arms man, they're bleeding.

Tom recognized the man as the first responder who'd pulled the woman from the car. The EMT cleaned and bandaged the cuts on his arms and wanted to take him to the hospital but Tom refused.

Let me at least give you a ride home then.

Tom looked at the parade of flashing lights and sirens on the dam and then looked down the road and at the surrounding desolate landscape and, appraising his chances of getting back to his campsite unnoticed as slim, he agreed.

It was cool inside the truck and when the doors shut all the ambient noise of the desert and the road suddenly stopped like muting a loud television. The truck felt high off the ground and otherworldly in its silence as it took the long arcs of Highway 93 through the canyons to Las Vegas.

I saw you, you know.

What.

Uh, with the rat.

Oh.

Tom shook his head and chuckled to himself. The man grinned and laughed a little and then the two men laughed together.

I won't ask.

Don't.

It was near dark by the time the truck pulled up in front of the Las Vegas Rescue Mission. They listened to the truck engine idle for a few moments before Tom started to leave.

You know, I've seen a lot of shit working this job, but that was some pretty fucking heroic shit you did up there.

Tom said nothing. As he shut the door and started toward the shelter the man called him over to the driver's side window. He pulled a hundred dollar bill out of his wallet.

Won this last night at blackjack. Take it, please.

Tom held it in his fingertips. He held it long after the truck had pulled away. It had been a long time since he'd last handled paper money. It felt different then he remembered it. The bill was crisper, sturdier, less like paper and more like some plastic fiber hybrid. He held it for a long time between his thumb and forefinger, trying to decide what to do. And then a gust of wind came and the bill fluttered loose and skipped down the sidewalk and across a vacant lot until it snagged on a chain link fence. Tom hesitated for a long moment and then went after it, but by the time he reached the fence it was no longer there. He returned to that spot many times over the coming days and weeks looking for the bill. But he never got it back.

Acknowledgements

Many thanks to Eric Knight, Mike Walsh, Adam Bernard, Mark Bailen, and Noah Edelstein. Special thanks to Jon Bassoff and his crew at New Pulp Press. All my love to Monica, my consummate editor and best friend.

CPSIA information can be obtained at www.ICGtesting.com
Printed in the USA
LVOW11s1556030614

388428LV00006B/847/P